THE BLACK SHEEP'S DAUGHTER

Also by Carola Dunn

THE BLACK SHEEP'S DAUGHTER

A Regency Romantic Adventure

Carola Dunn

Walker and Company
New York

First published in the United States of America in 1989
by Walker Publishing Company, Inc.

Published simultaneously in Canada by Thomas Allen & Son
Canada, Limited, Markham, Ontario.

Library of Congress Cataloging-in-Publication Data.
Dunn, Carola.
The black sheep's daughter : a Regency romantic adventure /Carola Dunn.
p.   cm.
ESBN 0-8027-1056-5
I. Title.
PR6054.U537B5 1989
823'.914—dc19
CIP

Printed in the United States of America
10 9 8 7 6 5 4 3 2 1

= 1 =

A RAUCOUS FLOCK of scarlet macaws rose screeching from the huge jacaranda, scattering lavender-blue petals beneath the horses' hooves as the riders entered the muddy stable yard. Sir Andrew Graylin looked about at the neat, white-washed adobe buildings,their red tiles aglow in the rosy light.

"Welcome to the Hacienda del Inglés," said his grey-haired host, drawing rein.

From one of the buildings emerged a tall, slender girl dressed in a white shirt and a calf-length skirt of brown homespun cotton over leather riding boots.

Andrew concentrated on dismounting gracefully from the ornate Spanish saddle. In the months of travel south from Mexico he had learned to appreciate it's comfort, but its high back made leaving it an awkward business.

As his foot touched the ground, a shot rang out.

His mount shied and he hopped after it, one foot caught in the stirrup. The echo of the shot was replaced by a trilling laugh.

Outrage warring with embarrassment, he disentangled himself and turned to see the girl holding a small pistol.

She hurried forward, hand outstretched. *"Perdóneme, señor!"*

"Sir Andrew is an Englishman, Teresa," interrupted the older man, grinning as he dismounted.

Andrew scowled at the cause of his discomfiture, who was attempting a curtsey, no mean feat in riding boots.

Annoyed as he was, he could not help but notice delicate features, golden complexion, huge dark eyes, and a delectable figure emphasized by a wide leather belt ornamented with silver. Her braided hair was raven black and glossy.

"Of course. Oscar said you were bringing home an Englishman, Papa. I beg your pardon, sir! I did not mean to startle you." She spoke English with no trace of an accent. "There was a snake, so close I had no time to warn you."

Following her gesture, Andrew glanced back. A four-foot snake, reddish brown with dark bands and bright red sides, lay there twitching, its head a bloody ruin.

"Good God!" he gasped, shaken. "Lord Edward, this is indeed a stimulating welcome."

An enchanting ripple of laughter greeted his feeble witticism as his host introduced, "My daughter, Teresa. *Querida,* this is Sir Andrew Graylin, an envoy of the British government."

"Miss Teresa." Andrew bowed his most elegant bow, trying to erase the unfortunate impression he had made on this disconcerting female. "Pray permit me to express my eternal gratitude for your rapidity in coming to my assistance."

Happy to find that though she was tall, he was taller, he looked down into brown eyes alight with mirth. Her lips twitched at the solemnity of his words, but she said gravely, "*Con mucho gusto,* Sir Andrew. I hope you will forgive me for discomposing you." Then she smiled. "It sounds very strange to hear you calling Papa 'Lord Edward.' Here he is known as Don Eduardo, you know."

"Enough of your teasing, minx," ordered her father. "Show Sir Andrew to his room, if you please. It has been a long day; I expect he will want to rest before he has to face the entire family at dinner."

"Dinner!" A bright green parrot swooped down from the roof, red and blue bars flashing on its wings, and landed on Teresa's shoulder. "Hello, hello, hello, dinner!"

She laughed. "He wants to meet you," she said. "Pray

allow me to present Gayo to you, sir. Will you shake hands?"

Andrew gingerly held out his hand. The parrot inspected it with care, then hopped to his finger and sidled up his sleeve. It rubbed its yellow-naped neck against his head, nibbling gently on his ear and crooning, "Hello, dinner."

"Gayo has a soft spot for a handsome stranger," Teresa said.

Andrew, far from comfortable with the bird clucking to him so intimately, flushed at her words and wondered what this extraordinary young woman would say next.

"If you will come through here, sir," she requested, leading him from the stables through an arch to another courtyard, where purple, crimson, and orange bougainvillea climbed riotously up the walls. Gayo flapped back to her.

"What did Don Eduardo mean when he mentioned facing your entire family?" Andrew asked, composure restored. "I take it there are more of you than just your brother Oscar and Lady Edward?"

"Lady Edward!" Again her infectious laugh rang out as they climbed wooden stairs to the open gallery that ran along the first floor. "I did not believe Papa when he said that was what Mama would be called in England. Here in Costa Rica she is Doña Esperanza, which is much prettier, you must agree. Here is your room. Your servant is already here as he came with Oscar from Cartago. If you need anything, send him to me. I shall return in time to take you to the dining room to face my multitudinous family."

"Thank you, Miss Teresa."

"Oh no," she said with that infuriating gravity belied by the mischief in her eyes, "you must address me as Miss Danville, for though I have ten brothers I am the only girl. You see, Papa has taught me the proper forms. *Hasta luego.*"

In the dusk, he watched her walk away along the gallery, admiring her graceful form. Lord Edward Danville had the strangest notions of bringing up a daughter, Andrew mused. The scion of an English duke, however long separated from his noble family, might be supposed to have more concern for propriety than to let the girl go about in short skirts with a pistol in her pocket and a parrot on her shoulder. And he knew that the Spanish bourgeoisie who had settled Costa Rica were still stricter in their notions.

Of course, he could only be glad that she had a gun and knew how to use it, however humiliating it was to owe his life to a female. It was the outside of enough that she had laughed at his discomfiture, but it was all of a piece with her teasing. She was outspoken to a fault, and he flushed again as he remembered her description of him.

The door to his room stood ajar; oil lamps burned within and he heard his servant moving about. The tropical night was falling fast and here in the mountains a pleasant coolness replaced the humid heat of the day. Andrew entered a chamber similar to those he had occupied during much of his mission to Central America: whitewashed walls with woven hangings in brilliant hues, heavy wooden furniture gleaming with beeswax, wood plank floor polished and meticulously swept. Lady Edward obviously ran an efficient household.

Rowson was laying out his evening clothes. Andrew regarded the wrinkled garments with distaste. He had grown used to living out of saddlebags, but this evening it was not good enough.

"See if you can press those, Rowson," he ordered.

"Right, sir, I'll see what I can do, and I'll fetch some hot water up." The manservant left, closing the door behind him.

Andrew checked that the curtains thoroughly covered the barred but unglazed window onto the courtyard, then began to undress. Recalling again Miss Danville's reference to him as a "handsome stranger," he paused to study his face in the mirror on the wall. It was the same face that had looked back at him any time these dozen years, unexceptionable but less than striking. His one good point, he had always thought, was his patrician nose, but that was now

4

decidedly pink from an excess of sun. The rest of his face was acceptably tanned; somehow his nose could never come to grips with the climates to which their lordships at the Foreign Office insisted on sending him.

Blond hair, bleached pale by that same sun, and blue eyes. Possibly Miss Danville had never seen such English colouring before, and therefore admired it. More likely she was quizzing him. Stripping off his riding breeches, he turned before the mirror. At twenty-nine he was leaner than he had been at twenty, muscles turned to whipcord by his travels through the wilds.

He frowned. The impertinent chit had him posing like a man-milliner!

Half an hour later, clean and refreshed, he was adjusting his cravat before the same mirror when Miss Danville knocked.

"Are you ready, Sir Andrew?" she called.

He turned as Rowson opened the door. Framed against the blackness outside, she was an eye-catching sight.

Like her earlier dress, her full skirt of scarlet cotton reached only to mid-calf; since she now wore sandals, this displayed an unseemly length of slender ankle. Her open-necked shirt was embroidered with crimson and green and blue curlicues; her hair, freed from its braids, fell loose to her narrow waist in a rippling ebony tide, adorned only by a scarlet hibiscus.

In the light of the oil lamps Andrew saw that she was older than he had supposed; in her early twenties, he guessed. The warm light, together with the vivid hues, made her amber skin glow.

She looked colourful, pretty, and thoroughly amused by his scrutiny.

"Ready, Sir Andrew?" she repeated, her tone dry.

He grinned, refusing to be taken aback by her teasing.

"I should like to see you in the latest London fashions, Miss Danville," he said.

To his surprise, her response was a sudden thoughtfulness, and she answered him absently as they went down.

When Andrew met the rest of Teresa's family, he began to realise why her nature was so far from retiring. Besides her mother, the only other female in the family was the timid wife of the second son, who spoke in a whisper that went unheard amid the clamour of male voices. Doña Esperanza was a quiet woman, severely crippled by arthritis, though still showing signs of the beauty that had attracted Lord Edward a quarter century ago.

It was obvious that Teresa ran the household whose efficiency he had admired. At her signal, a pair of maids carried in dishes of pork with *pejibaye* and beans, beefsteaks fried with onions and chiles, potatoes and *yuca* cakes and plantain fritters. It was the best meal Andrew had been served in Costa Rica, and he told her so.

"Thank you, sir." She was pleased. "Though it is really due to Papa and my brothers, since everything is grown on the hacienda, including the coffee. Have you been in Costa Rica long?"

"Some weeks. I am on an exploratory mission of diplomacy for the Foreign Office, which has taken me throughout Central America. I started in Mexico and my last meeting was today, with your leaders in Cartago. I shall go home from Puerto Limón, on your east coast, very soon. A frigate of the Royal Navy is to meet me there."

She cast him a speculative glance, but before she could comment one of her brothers asked Andrew about his mission. A lively political discussion ensued, in which she bore her part admirably. She was thoroughly in favour of the fight for independence from Spain and had no qualms about stating her opinions with vigour.

When the talk turned to hacienda business, Andrew told Teresa about his previous travels, in North Africa. She was fascinated by his descriptions of ancient walled cities, veiled women, whirling dervishes, and fierce, blue-faced Bedouin tribesmen ranging the deserts on their camels. Though not generally given to boasting, he was tempted to tell her that his work there had earned him a knighthood. He restrained himself with difficulty.

The maids returned with pots of fragrant coffee and bowls of bananas, mangos, pineapples, papayas, and melons.

"I should love to see the world," Teresa said wistfully, squeezing lemon juice on her papaya. "Don Eduardo wants to send Oscar to Jamaica to learn about growing coffee, to improve the yield."

"The flavour certainly needs no improvement," Andrew said, sipping appreciatively. "However, I shall be stopping in Jamaica on my way to London. Perhaps Oscar might travel with me."

"What an excellent idea, and how kind of you!" She paused, then went on hesitantly, "I hope you will not think I presume if I say that he has also spoken of sending Marco to England to study. He's seventeen and a bookworm, and the new university here is little more than a grammar school."

He laughed. "Two should be no more trouble than one."

"Truly? I shall tell Papa after dinner, privately so as not to raise the hopes of Oscar and Marco if he decides against it."

Andrew was about to suggest that he should be the one to approach Don Eduardo when that gentleman called to his daughter. "Teresa, I hope you will play your guitar and sing to us this evening!"

"Gladly, sir, only I must speak to you privately first."

He nodded his assent, and a few minutes later they went out. Don Eduardo had his arm about Teresa's shoulders, and Andrew was shocked to find himself envying that paternal privilege.

Father and daughter strolled in companionable silence to the book room. A full moon lit the courtyard, and the damp air was filled with the fragrance of some jungle flower. A vague melancholy swept over Teresa. It was a perfect night for a romantic tryst, for serenades and kisses. Impatient, she shrugged the feeling away. She had never met a man she wanted to kiss, but at last she was going to do something practical to remedy the lack.

"*Dear* Papa," she began as they settled on the leather sofa.

"Don't think you can wheedle me," he said with a smile.

She widened her eyes in feigned innocence, laughing, but said soberly, "Indeed, I mean to ask for a very great favour. However, I have some news to give you first that I trust will put you in a receptive mood. You know that Sir Andrew returns to England shortly? He has agreed to take Marco with him, and since he is going to Jamaica first, he will take Oscar there too."

"And how, miss, does he know my plans for Oscar and Marco?"

"I told him, Papa." She smoothed the frown from his brow. "I promise you I did not request his aid. He offered it freely. Nor did I tell him that I, too, wish to go to England."

"Teresa! *Querida!*"

"You used to tell me, when I was little, that one day I should go to London to learn to be a fine lady and find a fine gentleman to marry. Remember? I thought it a fairy tale. But I am three and twenty, and I have met no one here I care for. Now I have made Sir Andrew's acquaintance I know that indeed an English gentleman is very different from our local fellows. And even if I never marry, I should like to see something of the world."

"My darling, I have been selfish," Don Eduardo said with remorse.

She hugged him. "Oh no, Papa!"

"Hush, love. It is true. When you turned eighteen, I realised that none of the young men here were worthy of you and I seriously considered sending you to England. Somehow the right opportunity never came. I see now that the only real difficulty was that I could not bear to part with you. Besides, we have all grown to depend on you to keep us comfortable, when you ought to be busy with a family of your own."

"I had not thought . . . I cannot go. Mama is not well enough to manage the house."

"Nonsense," said Don Eduardo briskly, his mind made up. "She and your sister-in-law will deal between them, and I wager that when Oscar returns from Jamaica he will wed your cousin, the pretty one, what's her name?"

"You mean to send Oscar then? And Marco?"

"And you, *querida*. And there is a fourth bird we can kill with the same stone. You shall take some of our coffee beans to London and see whether you can interest anyone in buying. Now that Spain can no longer prevent us from trading with the rest of the world, it is time to develop an export market. Marco is too young and too dreamy to entrust with the business, but you are equal to anything, Teresa."

She laughed at his sudden enthusiasm. "I thank you for your confidence in me, sir. I shall at least feel that I am doing something for my family while I am gone."

"I have no doubts of your ability on that score, but I must warn you that you may not find it easy to conform to the dictates of English propriety. Where young ladies are concerned, they can be excessively restrictive and it may be that I have allowed you too much freedom. The Spanish idea of propriety is so straitlaced that perhaps I have gone too far the other way. When I left England, I vowed to be a very different sort of father from my own, and I have let you grown up as outspoken and strong-willed as your brothers."

"Then you do not like me the way I am?" she asked, hurt.

"I adore you the way you are, and would not change you in any particular, *querida*. But since you have chosen to go to England, I do want my daughter to take her rightful place in Society. You must learn to behave as Society expects of a proper young lady."

Teresa sighed. "I daresay I must, if I wish to meet proper young gentlemen. But who will teach me?"

"I shall send you to my brother, who is now Duke of

Stafford. His wife will be able to bring you out in style. And you need not suppose that you will be a poor relation. I have never taken a groat of my income in twenty-five years and more. Though it was but a pittance, by now it must amount to enough to give you a Season."

"You are very good to me, Papa. I only hope Sir Andrew is willing to escort me."

"Here is your first lesson. Leave *me* to approach Graylin."

"I like him. Do you think he likes me?"

"I cannot say, but I fear that you are unduly attracted by his sophistication because you are unused to it. Remember that you have known him only a few hours."

They talked for some time before Teresa retired to her chamber, the guitar concert forgotten. She sat by her window, looking out at the moonlit slopes of the volcano, Irazú, without seeing them. She imagined herself dancing the night away at a London ball, such as Don Eduardo had often described to her. Somehow her partner always had Sir Andrew's face.

That was perfectly natural, she told herself, since besides Papa he was the only English gentleman she knew.

The household retired early, for tomorrow was another day of hard work on the hacienda; but Andrew was not sleepy. He went up to the gallery outside his chamber and leaned on the railing overlooking the courtyard, pondering the completion of his mission. He must write the report of the Cartago meeting while the details were fresh in his mind.

The moon shone down through the scented air. It was difficult to think of business when the night breathed romance. As if in answer to his thoughts, footsteps approached along the gallery. For a moment he hoped it was the unconventional Miss Danville, then he recognised Lord Edward.

"Fine evening, eh, Graylin?" His host leaned beside him. "I hear you've offered to take my boys with you when you leave."

"I am delighted to be of service, sir."

"They're good lads, Oscar and Marco. Won't be any trouble to you." He humphed as if uncertain how to continue. "Well, demme me if I go in for roundaboutation. I'll give you the word with no bark on it, young man. M'daughter wants to go, too."

"Teresa? Miss Danville? To London?"

"It's a hard, dull life here for a woman. Not that she's ever complained, mind, but I don't care to see her wasting away on some lonely farm as she will if she marries here."

Andrew tried to imagine the lovely, vibrant Teresa as the overworked wife of a poor farmer. He knew Lord Edward's huge, flourishing hacienda was an exception in Costa Rica. To his dismay, he heard himself say, "I'll take her, sir."

Lord Edward clapped him on the back. "Very good of you, Graylin. I know you'll see her safely to m'brother's house. She deserves her Season and a chance at an eligible connection."

A vision rose before Andrew's eyes of Teresa at a formal dinner party expressing her views on the Corn Laws with the same enthusiasm she had displayed for independence.

He shuddered at the prospect.

= 2 =

A WEEK LATER, a cavalcade trotted down the slopes of Irazú towards Cartago. The volcano's summit was hidden in clouds but the sun shone on the riders—Oscar, Marco, Teresa with Gayo on her shoulder, Andrew, and his servant. With them rode a young Spanish maid and her brother, abigail and manservant to the Danvilles. Half a dozen pack mules carried all their belongings, and there were two peons to bring the animals back from Limón to the hacienda.

Teresa had often been to fiestas in Cartago and to visit her mother's relations, so this part of their journey was nothing new to her. The track was well travelled, the gently rolling hills mostly cleared of jungle. They passed several small farms, for the rich, black volcanic soil supported cattle pasture and a variety of crops.

When they reached the capital, Teresa regarded the town with a newly critical eye. She had seen woodcuts of the cities of Europe but they had always been so remote as to seem unreal. Now, she was on her way to London, greatest city of them all.

"How does Cartago compare with London?" she asked Andrew.

He roared with laughter, then apologised.

"Cartago would fit into one of London's parks," he explained. "In English terms, it is more of an overgrown village than a town."

"Tell me about London."

He shrugged. "You could live a lifetime in the city without knowing the half of it, Miss Danville. You must wait and see, for I cannot possibly describe it in terms you will understand."

Teresa turned away, resentful of the top-lofty young Englishman's scorn. It was easy for him to sneer, who had not had to build a nation from nothing in a land of volcanoes and tropical storms and ever-encroaching jungle.

Beyond Cartago the way grew steeper as they climbed out of the Meseta Central. The mountains were often wreathed in mist, and huge trees with buttressed trunks closed in until they rode through a gloomy green tunnel. Lianas hung in festoons like giant spiderwebs; tall ferns sprang from every nook and cranny; wherever sunlight lanced through the forest canopy, shrubs bloomed orange, purple, and scarlet. A family of peccaries wandered past, rooting in the undergrowth with their piglike snouts, and then an armadillo trotted across the track. The travellers forded frequent rocky streams, tumbling down the hillsides.

On the second day, they reached the bottom of a valley, full of stagnant pools. The constant whine of insects kept Andrew slapping at every inch of exposed skin. Mosquitoes seemed to recognise him as a thin-skinned foreigner and concentrated their efforts on him. Teresa thought it a very good revenge for his derision of her country, but she had no desire to see him come down with jungle fever.

"Here is an ointment," she said, holding out a small leather pouch. "It will keep them away."

He raised his eyebrows.

"At least try it," she said impatiently. "I was taught plant medicine by a Talamanca Indian *sukia*.'"

"*Sukia?*"

"*Curandero*—a witch doctor, or medicine man."

Though unconvinced, Andrew drew rein beside her and smoothed some of the pungent green ointment onto his face and hands. There was an instant diminution in the number of insects buzzing about him. Those that remained headed unerringly for the back of his neck.

Teresa watched his awkward efforts to cover that exposed spot, then took pity on him.

"Let me do that," she offered.

He stiffened at the gentle touch of her fingers on his nape.

She looked at him in surprise, then flushed. "I beg your pardon, sir," she murmured. "I had forgot you are not one of my brothers."

They had fallen behind the rest. Aware of her uneasiness, Andrew suggested they hurry to catch up.

She laughed at him. "Are you warning me to beware of you, Sir Andrew? You must know that I have brought a chaperone." She drew a pistol from her pocket, waved it at him, and declaimed, "Sirrah, if you do not immediately cease your unwanted attentions, I shall put a bullet through your blackguardly heart!"

Recalling her brilliant shooting of the deadly snake, Andrew suppressed his instinctive nervousness at the sight of the waving gun. Despite his disapproval, he was forced to smile.

"A potent argument," he said dryly. "I see your father had more in mind than the wildlife when he taught you to shoot. By the way, I still do not know how an English nobleman came to settle in such an out-of-the-way corner of the world."

"Then let me tell you the story. You know he is fourth son of the late Duke of Stafford? It was the duke who forced him to leave England. Papa says he was a cold, unnatural father, who cared for nothing but appearances. Papa fought a duel, you see, and killed a very important marquis, whose wife was his mistress."

"Miss Danville!"

"Oh dear, have I shocked you?" She sighed. "In general Papa does not like me to be mealymouthed, but he did say I am too outspoken for English notions of propriety. I can see that I must watch my tongue when I am with you." She cast him a sidelong glance and was pleased to see his face redden.

"I beg your pardon, ma'am," he said stiffly. "It is not my place to criticise your speech."

"I am glad you recognise that. Then I shall tell you the rest of Papa's story. When the duke told him to leave the country, he rode off to Bristol, where he found a ship called the *Jenny Belle*, about to set sail for Jamaica. He decided that this was a good omen, as Jenny was the name of his latest high-flyer."

Andrew bit his lip but held his tongue. Teresa decided to throw in one last provocation in an attempt to shake his resolve.

"As the ship sailed down the Bristol Channel, Papa made the acquaintance of a lightskirt, a maidservant attending a family on board." She did not dare look at Andrew's face lest she burst out laughing. "His enjoyment of her favours made the voyage pass rapidly, and not until they were a day or two out of Kingston did he begin to wonder what he should do when he arrived."

"I do believe you are teasing me," said Andrew in a long-suffering voice.

"It was irresistible," she confessed, grinning. "But since you have guessed it, there is no point in continuing. I shall omit the rest of Papa's amatory adventures and just tell you how he came to Costa Rica. I told you Papa had nearly reached Jamaica? Well, the *Jenny Belle* was taken by a Spanish privateer. He and his men plundered the ship, then let her continue to port unharmed. However, Papa decided to throw in his lot with the privateer."

"Lord Edward sailed with a Spanish privateer? You are gammoning me, Miss Danville!"

"Indeed I am not. When Papa was a boy, he wished he could be a pirate sailing the Spanish main, so when the opportunity came, he took it. He says it was mostly prodigious dull, uncomfortable, and unprofitable, not exciting at all. And then the ship was wrecked in a hurricane. Papa was washed ashore on the coast of Costa Rica and fell ill with jungle fever. Mama's family took him in, and Mama nursed him back to health, then he married her. Is it not a romantic story?"

"Undoubtedly, though I am sure that what came next was a great deal of very hard work," Andrew pointed out. "Lord Edward told me that he has never contacted his family in England since he left. Until I informed him of it, he did not even know that his father was dead and his brother succeeded to the dukedom."

"My uncle Gerald was the only one in the family he regretted leaving. Do you know him?"

"Only by sight and by reputation. I have heard him described as an affable gentleman, never too high in the instep."

"High in the instep?"

Andrew laughed. "An odd phrase, now I come to think on it. It means he does not stand upon the dignity of his rank. You speak English so well that I had forgot you can know only what you have heard from Lord Edward."

"I have read a great many English books," said Teresa, offended. Then her irrepressible sense of humour broke through. "And besides, Don Eduardo talks a great deal. He would say I am a featherbrained widgeon to quarrel over nothing."

"Not at all. You may be a mutton-headed wantwit, but I should never describe you as a featherbrained widgeon."

"And you must be touched in the upper works to cross swords with me," she riposted.

"I see your grasp of colloquial English is greater than I had supposed. Lord Edward must have frequent occasion to complain of his children's folly, to have taught you so many alternatives."

"Mooncalf," said Teresa, "nodcock, rattlepate, shatterbrain, knock in the cradle. He does have eleven children, remember."

Andrew laughed. Teresa thought how different, how much younger, he looked when he was amused. When he was not being disapproving, he could be kind and even charming.

At that moment Oscar rode back to urge them to catch up. "Don't let my peagoose sister hold you back," he said to Andrew.

"I was never in the least danger," responded Andrew. "Miss Danville has her pistol, and I know her to be a crack shot."

"Yes, bacon-brained but a crack shot," agreed Oscar.

Teresa was too pleased by Andrew's praise to rise to this bait. Instead she said, "Those are a couple I forgot."

Andrew laughed, but they did not explain the joke. Teresa smiled to herself as she kicked her horse into a canter. There was something pleasingly intimate about a private joke shared with a handsome young man.

After several days' travel they reached the hot, rainy coastal plain, where the jungle was more tangled and lush than ever. Occasionally the peons cleared encroaching growth with machetes, for without every traveller's help the track would soon disappear.

They crossed several rough log bridges over slow-moving greenish grey rivers. Once they disturbed a caiman sleeping in the sun, looking like a misplaced log until it opened its jagged-toothed mouth in a wide yawn. The sinister reptile slid off the bridge into the water with a splash, then surfaced to watch them with cold, unblinking eyes.

Teresa paused nearby to admire a cluster of pink and purple orchids. Entranced by a pair of giant blue butterflies, she fell behind the others. Andrew rode back and called to her.

A rustling in the treetops, far above, ceased momentarily at the sound of his voice. Then a clamour of barks and grunts broke out and a volley of twigs and nuts descended on Andrew. Teresa looked up cautiously. Attracted by his call, a troop of white-faced monkeys swung through the branches, chattering with glee as they threw anything that came to hand at the intruders.

Teresa gestured to Andrew to go on. Seeing that she was

following, he turned his horse to obey, and the shower of missiles grew less as the monkeys lost interest. Teresa rode after him along the narrow track.

They had nearly reached the others when she heard a coughing snarl above her, and a rank odour reached her nostrils. She glanced up and looked straight into the golden eyes of a jaguar.

Her mount had already smelled the jaguar's distinctive scent. With a frightened neigh the horse reared, then galloped off, leaving its rider prone on the ground. Dislodged from her shoulder, Gayo flew off, squawking his displeasure.

Startled, breathless, Teresa gaped up at the big cat as it lounged on a branch some fifteen feet above her. In that frozen instant before she began to think, she noted the rounded, white-furred ears, the sleek tawny coat stippled with black rosettes. The jaguar gazed at her with impassive eyes. Its black-tipped tail twitched and it yawned, long, sharp teeth gleaming ivory.

Teresa did not dare lose sight of the beast, but she needed to know if anyone had noticed her dangerous predicament. Very slowly she turned her head just a little. Andrew, his attention drawn by the horse's neigh, was grinning at her.

For a moment she was furious, then she realised that all he knew was that her mount had thrown her.

Andrew's amusement changed to concern when he saw that Teresa was not moving. He started towards her.

"Stop!" she hissed. "Jaguar!" She tried to roll her eyes upwards to indicate its position without startling it.

He stopped, looking puzzled and doubtful. She moved her hand just enough to point. Raising his gaze, he peered into the tangled greenery, then she saw his face pale beneath the tan.

He dismounted as Oscar and Marco came up. Pointing, he whispered, "A jaguar! Do you see it? In the tree above her."

Her eyes on the cat, Teresa heard Oscar say in a low

voice, "My rifle is with the mules. I'll get it."

"No." Andrew sounded aghast. "If you only wounded it, it would certainly attack. She is too close."

"What do you suggest then?" Oscar asked helplessly.

The three men looked at each other in despair. Oscar turned and rode off after the mules.

Out of the corner of her eye, Teresa caught sight of a movement in the branches above the jaguar. A pair of dark eyes peered down through the leaves. One of the monkeys had discovered the great predator. It screeched, and the rest of the troop swung down to pelt their enemy with sticks and fruit.

The cat turned its dispassionate golden gaze up to its tormenters. Ears twitching, it stirred restlessly. Suddenly Gayo swooped down, his wings brushing the animal's back.

"*Hijo de puta!*" he swore, and swooped again.

Teresa, her eyes never leaving the jaguar, sat up and began to inch backwards. Distracted, the cat ignored her at first, but then it turned its head and regarded her with calm unconcern. She jumped to her feet and ran, stumbling over roots and vines straight into Andrew's arms.

He hugged her to him. Catching her breath, she turned, his arms still about her and looked back.

The jaguar snarled. With majestic composure, it leaped to the ground and stalked away into the forest without so much as a backward glance. In moments, its speckled coat had merged with the pattern of light and shadow and the jaguar had vanished.

Limp with relief, Teresa slumped against Andrew's chest, suddenly very much aware of his comforting strength. His arms tightened about her waist, and she felt his lips brush her hair.

Marco was staring. Breathless again, Teresa pulled out of Andrew's clasp and willed her blush to subside. She must remember that Papa had said it was chiefly his unfamiliar sophistication that attracted her.

"Hold still a minute," said Marco, brushing leaf mould off

her back with a brotherly disregard of her narrow escape.

Oscar rode up, rifle in hand. "What happened?" he demanded.

"The jaguar jumped down and wandered off," Marco told him, laughing. "It decided she was not an appetising morsel."

"How wrong it was,"Andrew murmured in Teresa's ear.

She glared at him, not at all sure whether to regard his words as a compliment or an insult. Remembering the sensation of his strong arms holding her, she felt a hot flush rising to her cheeks again and she shivered. Never in her life had she felt so thoroughly confused.

The next day they met a train of ox wagons heading for the Meseta Central. Loaded with all the household goods of several immigrant families, the two-wheeled carts moved with painful slowness. Men and boys escorted them on horseback, but all the women and girls perched on top of their belongings on the wagons. They stared at Teresa as she rode past.

Oscar spoke to their guide, a local man he knew slightly. Teresa reined in until Andrew drew level with her.

"Had I insisted on travelling thus," she pointed out, "you'd not reach the coast for a month."

"In that case, I'd not have allowed myself to be persuaded to escort you," he retorted. "On a journey such as lies ahead of us, a missish female could be nothing but an encumbrance."

That, she decided uncertainly, could be taken as praise of sorts. And had there been an unexpected warmth behind his teasing smile?

They had to wait for two hot, humid, thoroughly uncom- fortable days in Puerto Limón before the Royal Navy frigate that had been sent to meet Andrew sailed into the little harbour. A rowboat came to ferry him aboard, and the Danvilles waited anxiously to hear whether the captain was willing to take on the extra passengers.

A long hour passed before Andrew returned.

"Captain Fitch was more than willing to convey Oscar and Marco," he reported. "He balked, however, at the thought of females on board the *Destiny*. I mentioned your close relationship to the Duke of Stafford, Miss Danville, but he was not persuaded. A sorry setback for a diplomat." He sighed.

Teresa gazed at him in dismay, then she caught the teasing light in his eyes.

"Wretch," she said. "What did you do next?"

"I then brought out the heavy guns. You may not know that your uncle Lord Cecil Danville is a Lord of the Admiralty. A reminder of that fact convinced the captain of the wisdom of offering transportation to all of you."

Oscar clapped Andrew on the back and Teresa beamed, until he added, "Of course, I may yet come to regret my success."

Sitting in the ship's boat, Teresa gazed across the harbour at *HMS Destiny*. Waves lapped gently at the wooden quay and fork-tailed frigate birds wheeled high above the blue swells of the Caribbean. Suddenly it was real to her, the fact that she was about to leave her native land and sail thousands of miles across the ocean to a world she could scarcely imagine.

She held tight to Marco's arm, very glad that he would be with her, for Sir Andrew Graylin's alternation between warmth, teasing, and disapproval bewildered her.

= 3 =

TERESA WAS TAKEN aback by the tiny cabin she was ushered to. It was little more than a closet—enough perhaps for the first mate who usually occupied it, but Teresa had to share it with her maid and Gayo. And Josefa was feeling ill.

There was a knock on the door. Teresa opened it and Andrew said, "We are about to sail. Do you care to come up on deck to watch? You will find it interesting, I believe."

"In a few minutes. My maid is unwell and I must try if I can find a remedy in my medicine chest."

He stepped in and looked at the pallid girl.

"Seasick already, and we are still at anchor! Not a common malady up in your mountains, Miss Danville, but I expect you will find something suitable. Your solicitude is admirable. I shall return shortly to show you the way." He bowed over her hand and kissed it warmly.

Already flustered by his closeness in the cramped space, Teresa pressed the back of her hand to her cheek as he left, then turned determinedly to search for an appropriate herb. She was annoyed with herself. Andrew was the most interesting and attractive man she had ever met, but she had no intention of throwing her cap over the windmill. The rare occasions when he looked at her with respect, even with admiration, were more than outweighed by the many times she had read disapproval in his face.

For all she knew, some well-bred young lady awaited him in England. He had never mentioned a wife or a sweetheart, but nor had he ever claimed to be an unattached bachelor.

It had been indiscreet of him to enter her cabin, and she was glad Josefa had been there. For the first time, Teresa realised that there was a good reason for Society's insistence on a chaperone for young ladies.

Andrew's manner was cool when he returned to escort her above deck, as if he realised his indiscretion. She responded in kind, trying to ignore his strong hand at her elbow as he helped her up the steep companionway. They joined her brothers on the poop deck, where she forgot her agitation as she watched, fascinated by the busy scene.

Sailors in striped trousers and short jackets scampered about in apparent confusion—climbing the rigging, coiling ropes, winding the windlass as the huge anchor rose dripping from the depths. The boatswain bawled commands and the three masts blossomed with white canvas. On the quarter deck, Captain Fitch directed orders to the helmsman; the breeze took the sails and the *Destiny* stood out to sea.

Teresa spent most of the day on deck, returning below occasionally to check on Josefa. Gayo made friends with the ship's carpenter's parrot and they spent hours exchanging curses in Spanish and English, much to the sailors' delight. However, the passengers did not meet the captain until the evening, when they were invited to dine in the wardroom with him and his officers.

Captain Fitch was a tall, very thin man with greying hair and the mournful, wrinkled countenance of an underfed bloodhound. His voice was equally thin and reedy. He greeted Teresa politely, but his distress at having a female aboard was apparent. From that evening on she did her best to stay out of his way. This was not difficult, since Oscar decided to spend the voyage teaching his sister all he knew about coffee, to enable her to discuss it knowledgeably with the London merchants.

The captain cheered visibly when, nine days later, Teresa announced at dinner that Josefa, still suffering from seasickness, adamantly insisted on going ashore in Jamaica with Don Oscar and his servant, her brother. Teresa, however, was anything but happy with this turn of events. She could not remain aboard without a female companion.

"The *Destiny* stays only to pick up supplies and despatches," the captain said delightedly. "We shall arrive tomorrow morning and leave in the afternoon. I fear you will not have time to find another maid. However, you may easily find passage on a merchant vessel, ma'am."

Teresa restrained herself from pointing out that once Andrew had sailed off aboard the *Destiny*, she might very well never see him again.

"I should prefer you to travel under Graylin's protection," said Oscar, frowning, "but you must agree that you cannot possibly continue without a maid."

Teresa noticed that Andrew's lean, tanned face was unwontedly flushed. "I must tell you something which will altogether change the situation," he said hesitantly. "Captain Fitch does not know it yet, but there is an order awaiting him from the governor of Jamaica. His Excellency's sister-in-law, Lady Parr, and her daughter are to sail to England on the *Destiny*."

The captain was appalled. His jaw dropped, and his long, weather-beaten face became a maze of furrows in which his horrified eyes nearly disappeared.

Oscar, on the other hand, was relieved. "It must be altogether unexceptionable for Teresa to travel in such company," he said.

Andrew's embarrassment was patent, and Teresa's happy smile faded as a disagreeable suspicion crossed her mind.

"How is it," she asked, "that you already knew what the captain did not?"

His flush deepened and he avoided her gaze. "I am betrothed to Miss Muriel Parr," he said.

There was a moment of shocked silence. Then pride came to Teresa's rescue. She could only be glad she had considered the possibility that he was married. It enabled her to keep her composure, though inwardly she seethed with anger and hurt.

After a scarcely noticeable pause, her voice was steady when she said, "I shall be happy to make Miss Parr's acquaintance."

She retired early that evening and avoided Andrew next morning, though she would have liked to question him about the bustling navy docks as they sailed into Port Royal harbour. He went ashore as soon as they dropped anchor.

Teresa and Marco sadly bade Oscar farewell, then she went below to move her belongings into the captain's cabin. To his great disgruntlement, he had to give up that bastion to the ladies—an imposition beside which the irritation of Miss Danville's presence aboard was insignificant. In fact, his regard for Teresa warmed steadily from the moment Lady Parr swept past him with a haughty nod, her majestic air unimpaired by the indignity of being lifted from the boat to the deck in a sling.

Despite the addition of two cots, along with the customary large bed, four chairs, and table, the captain's cabin seemed huge to Teresa after the first mate's cramped abode. Here she awaited the new arrivals with some trepidation. This was to be her first encounter with ladies of that polite world in which her father expected her to find a place.

For at least the fifth time she peered into the captain's little square of mirror. She had wound her long braid into a knot on the back of her head. She poked at escaping tendrils, tucked her shirt more firmly into the waistband, smoothed her full purple skirt.

There was a knock. The cabin boy opened the door, squeaked "Lady Parr, miss," and ducked out of sight.

Her ladyship, clad all in white cotton, reminded Teresa irresistibly of the *Destiny* under full sail, except that she altogether lacked the frigate's beauty. Miss Muriel Parr was a slight, silent figure in pale pink muslin, half-hidden by her mother.

Teresa curtseyed. "I am Teresa Danville, ma'am," she said.

Lady Parr, standing in the doorway, raised her quizzing

glass and examined her from head to toe.

"You are shockingly brown, Miss Danville," she stated disparagingly, "and quite the Long Meg, I declare."

"What a pity," commented Gayo. "*Buenos días*, hello, hello."

The full force of the quizzing glass was turned upon him and he quailed a little.

"A parrot," said Lady Parr. "I cannot share my cabin with a parrot. The bird must be removed at once. Sir Archibald would insist upon it."

"Yes, ma'am," Teresa murmured, determined to do her best to please the first English ladies she had ever met.

When Teresa returned from removing Gayo to the cabin shared by Marco and Andrew, the ladies' abigail, Kinsey, was scurrying about attempting to stow their possessions in the limited space. A short, round, rosy-cheeked woman, she smiled in a friendly way and bobbed a curtsey. Lady Parr sat in the captain's chair, a well-thumbed book of sermons open upon the table before her, while her daughter perched on the bed on the far side of the cabin, doing her best not to hinder the abigail's task.

Her hands were folded in her lap, her back as straight as if she found herself in the drawing room of one of the patronesses of Almack's. She had removed her bonnet, revealing blond ringlets, blue eyes, and a complexion pink and white as a china doll. No wonder Andrew had chosen Miss Muriel Parr as his bride! A wave of envy not far from jealousy swept over Teresa.

She fought it down and went to the girl's side. "How do you do," she said with a smile. "I beg your pardon for not greeting you before. I thought it best to remove Gayo immediately."

The answering smile was timid. "It is always best to heed Mama at once," agreed Miss Parr. Her voice was soft, apologetic, fading almost to nothing as she added, "I am so sorry she was rude to you. She always says just what she thinks regardless of other people's feelings."

"She was quite right, though," Teresa said ruefully. "When I see your face, I must agree that I *am* shockingly brown. However did you avoid getting sunburned in Jamaica? No, wait, we cannot talk comfortably here. Let us go up on deck."

Miss Parr's blue eyes grew large. "But there are sailors everywhere. Such rough men!"

"We shall go to the quarter deck. Only officers are allowed there."

"I must ask Mama."

Her ladyship was extremely doubtful of the propriety of two young ladies promenading on deck without an escort.

"I expect Sir Andrew and Marco will be there, ma'am," Teresa assured her, "watching the preparations for our departure."

"Marco?" The quizzing glass was brought into play.

"My brother, who goes with me to England."

"A foreign name, Miss Danville. Sir Archibald did not approve of foreigners."

"We were born and raised in Costa Rica, ma'am. It is a colony of Spain. Our father, Lord Edward Danville, is an Englishman, however."

"Lord Edward Danville," mused Lady Parr, sitting up straighter. "Is Lord Edward by any chance a connexion of His Grace of Stafford?"

"The duke is my uncle. Marco and I are going to live with him." Teresa crossed her fingers behind her back, remembering that her uncle was as yet unaware of her existence.

"I shall be happy to make Mr. Mark Danville's acquaintance. You may go up, Muriel. I believe Sir Archibald would have permitted it. Put on your bonnet and carry your parasol."

Though unhappily aware that nothing could make her complexion match Miss Parr's, Teresa donned her plain straw hat.

Neither Marco nor Andrew was on deck. Teresa was glad

to postpone her first sight of the betrothed couple together, glad also of the opportunity to talk privately with Miss Parr. Teresa had a thousand questions, about England and Society and fashion, and about Miss Parr's engagement to Andrew.

When they reached the quarter deck and began to stroll up and down, Teresa realised that the girl was somewhat shorter than herself, a dainty young lady whom Don Eduardo might have described as a Pocket Venus. Her gown was so different from Teresa's garments as to make comparison impossible. The high, round neckline was trimmed with lace, as were the tight cuffs of the long, full sleeves. The skirt fell straight in front from a waist bound with darker pink ribbon just below the bust, while a few gathers at the back gave it just enough fullness to enable its wearer to take tiny steps. The delicate colour of the fine mull muslin made Teresa's bright purple seem suddenly garish.

"I daresay your gown is in the latest London fashion?" she asked wistfully.

"Heavens no," answered Miss Parr with a refined titter. "I had it made up by a Kingston seamstress and all the pattern books in Jamaica are several months out of date at least."

"Months! Do fashions change so fast?"

"Only in details," conceded her companion. "Except during the London Season, one need not discard gowns even a year or two old. I expect things change more slowly in Costa Rica?"

"On the whole, we dress for practicality," Teresa admitted. "It would be difficult to work on the hacienda in a skirt as narrow as yours. How elegant you look, and cool!"

"It is impossible to look cool in Jamaica. I do not care for Jamaica. The people are so coarse and common that Mama did not let me leave the grounds of the King's House without two footmen to guard the carriage, and we never went into Kingston. I wonder that your papa permits you to travel without a chaperone or any servants."

Teresa assured her that she had left home with her elder

brother and a maid to take care of her. "I could not have gone farther had not you and your mama come aboard to lend me countenance. But what, pray, is the King's House?"

"That is the governor's mansion, in Spanish Town. It is by no means the equal of an English mansion. I quite long to be back in England."

"If you dislike Jamaica so, I wonder that you lived there."

Miss Parr explained that on the death of her father, Sir Archibald, fourteen months since, her aunt had invited them for a visit. Since her marriage must be postponed until after a year's mourning, and by chance Andrew had been able to escort them to Jamaica on his way to Mexico, the invitation was accepted.

"I wish we had stayed at home," she went on. "Everything is so strange here. Once we are wed, Andrew will not care to travel."

Teresa hoped for her sake that she was right. "How did you meet Sir Andrew?" she asked.

"He was presented to me as a partner at Lady Sefton's ball. Mama did not care for the match—he is only second son of a viscount, you know—but after all, Papa was only a baronet and my fortune is not large. It was my second Season and I had not had an offer from any gentleman I liked half as well."

Teresa had not known that Andrew's father was a nobleman, but she was prevented from discussing the fact, and from delving into the depth of Muriel's liking, by the appearance of the subject of their conversation.

On their arrival in Jamaica, Andrew had gone to Spanish Town to inform the governor of the results of his mission to Central America. There he met his Muriel for the first time in close to a year. He was struck anew by her gentle prettiness, the propriety of her manners, her deference to his wishes and opinions. She would make him an attractive, conformable wife, well suited to aid his advancement in his chosen profession. Already her connexion with the governor of Jamaica had stood him in good stead in the diplomatic service.

He had escorted his betrothed and her mother back to the naval base at Port Royal, then left them to board the *Destiny* while he completed some other business.

Now, mounting the steps to the quarter deck, he was struck by the contrast between the two young ladies who awaited him—Teresa, the exotic tropical bird, to Muriel's English dove. He had grown used to Teresa's dress, even enjoyed her forthright speech. Her unquenchable spirit was to be admired, but perhaps safest from a distance. She never hesitated to contradict and often teased him, whereas Muriel would always study to please.

Besides, he was betrothed to Muriel.

"Andrew," she welcomed him shyly as he bowed and kissed her hand. "I am glad you are come. I feared you might be too late."

"They are about to raise the anchor," said Teresa. "Where is Marco, I wonder? He will be sorry to miss the excitement."

Andrew was piqued that he did not have her full attention. "I picked up a couple of books for him in Port Royal, Miss Danville. He has had such a limited selection always that he is absurdly grateful for any addition to their number." He spoke lightly, but even to his own ears he sounded condescending.

"Don Eduardo has always bought every volume he could lay his hands on," said Teresa, resentment in her tone. "If you will excuse me, I shall go and see how my brother does."

He watched her go, sorry to have offended and hoping that she had not read his earlier thoughts in his face. He did not want her to think he ceased to value her friendship just because Muriel had reminded him of the ideal of decorous propriety.

"I hope you and Miss Danville will be friends," he said, turning abruptly to his betrothed.

"I hope so, if you wish it. She is . . . an unusual person."

"She has had no one to teach her how to go on. I begin to wonder whether her aunt, the duchess, will be willing to sponsor her if she does not learn to curb her tongue. Not that I mean to criticise her. But do you suppose that you might try to give her some notion of what is required of a young lady entering Society? She cannot do better than to model her behaviour upon yours."

Muriel blushed with gratification, but said anxiously, "I will do my best to give her a hint, only I should not like to offend her. Oh, I know the very thing! I shall give her some of my dresses. I daresay Kinsey will be able to alter them to fit. That will lead to talk of fashion, and I can always slip in a word of advice about how to go on in London."

"How good you are, Muriel." He took her hand and kissed it warmly, producing another blush. "You see, I cannot but feel somewhat responsible for Miss Danville's acceptance by her relatives, since her father entrusted her to my care."

"Of course, Andrew, I do understand. It will be good to have something to occupy me on the voyage. Jamaica was so very dull and I do dislike travelling above everything. How I long to be back in London, do not you?"

Andrew agreed, though not without a certain hesitancy. He would enjoy a few months back in civilisation, but so much of the world waited to be seen. Of course, everything would be different once they were married, he assured himself. Different in what way, he failed to ask.

Muriel's trunk was carried up from the hold by a grumbling sailor. Teresa held her breath as Kinsey set aside layer after layer of mourning clothes, grey and black. Underneath, the maid vowed, were several gowns she had packed "just in case." They were now two years old, out of date by London standards, but in the mid-Atlantic, who was to know?

There was a walking dress of pink jaconet, with white frills, and a rose spencer to go with it. Another, of the palest blue, had a matching blue-and-white-striped pelisse. Two morning gowns of white muslin, sprigged one with green and one with yellow, and a much beruffled white parasol completed the collection.

"Miss Muriel hardly wore these at all," Kinsey explained. "Seemed a right pity to leave 'em. After all, you never know."

"I remember, I had them made just before Papa died. Do you like them, Miss Danville?"

"Oh yes! They are beautiful. Only you will want to wear them, I am sure."

"I have enough new things for now, though I shall need a new wardrobe before I am married. You are welcome to them."

"Let's try 'em on you, miss, for I can see I'll have to do a spot of altering. Miss Muriel's shorter, but I've some white satin hid away somewheres. We'll put ruffles round the bottom."

Lady Parr, who had raised no material objection to the expropriation of her daughter's clothes but was watching suspiciously, broke in. "Muriel's figure is excellent. Gentlemen do not care for tall females, Miss Danville. Sir Archibald always admired a petite woman."

"Yes, ma'am," said Teresa, biting her lip in an effort not to laugh aloud. Her ladyship was short enough, certainly, but it was impossible to imagine that her figure had ever been admired.

"Most gentlemen are taller than you," Muriel whispered indignantly, "and it is fashionable to be tall and slender."

"How kind you are," murmured Teresa, squeezing her hand.

That evening, for dinner in the wardroom, Teresa was still clad in one of her homemade cotton skirts, and for the first time in her life, she was utterly dissatisfied with her attire.

Captain Fitch, having finally resigned himself to losing his cabin to a bevy of females, was in a chatty mood. He held forth at length on the history of the buccaneers in Jamaica. Teresa once more had to bite her lip when she realised that he regarded Henry Morgan, scourge of the seas, as quite a hero. Unfortunately she caught Andrew's eye and he had clearly been struck by the same thought. The giggle which sprang to her lips was irrepressible.

"You are amused, Miss Danville?" asked the captain, regarding her with his mournful, doggy eyes.

"I beg your pardon, sir. I was just thinking how odd it was that Sir Henry was made lieutenant governor of the island after his undeniably unorthodox career."

"I am amazed, Miss Danville," pronounced Lady Parr, "that you should find such iniquity amusing. Sir Archibald considered the buccaneers to be barbarians."

Captain Fitch cast a look of profound dislike at her ladyship and changed the subject. "In these modern times," he said, "since we are not at present at war, the most barbarous sailors in these waters are the slave traders."

"The Greek philosophers had no moral objection to slavery," said Marco. A quiet boy, he crimsoned when everyone looked at him in surprise, and hurriedly filled his mouth with food.

Captain Fitch decided to ignore his comment. "The slave trade has been outlawed by the British government," he continued doggedly. "The Royal Navy is dedicated to stamping it out. I was informed in Port Royal that a suspected slave ship, the *Snipe*, is known to be heading for Cuba. If we sight her we are duty bound to engage her." He ended with a triumphant nod at Lady Parr.

"Engage, Captain? You will do no such thing whilst I and my daughter are aboard. Sir Archibald would most certainly complain to the Admiralty at the very suggestion."

"Sir Archibald is not here, ma'am. And if he were, he could not stop an officer of His Majesty's navy in the course of his duties. We shall engage the *Snipe*, I say."

"Surely only by the merest chance will we cross its path," Andrew said hurriedly, seeing his future mama-in-law turn purple.

"Our course lies through the Windward Passage, between Cuba and Hispaniola. The *Snipe* must needs pass one end or t'other. And she's one o' these new-fangled Baltimore brigs with the raked masts, easy to recognise." The captain's scowl silenced even Lady Parr, and no more was said of the slave ship that evening.

= 4 =

TERESA WAS AWAKENED at dawn by shouts and the clatter of running feet. The Parrs and their abigail were still sound asleep, her ladyship with her open mouth issuing a ladylike snore, but Teresa was wide awake and full of energy. She decided to dress and investigate. She was putting on her shoes when a crashing roar shook the air and the ship's timbers vibrated. The others all sat bolt upright, sleepy eyes filled with alarm.

"Lawks, what was that?" cried the abigail.

Teresa shrugged. "I've not the slightest notion," she admitted, "but I mean to go up at once and find out."

To their amazed horror, she took her pistol from under her pillow, checked that it was loaded, and thrust it into her pocket.

"Muriel, I absolutely forbid you to leave the cabin," squawked Lady Parr.

"Yes, Mama," whispered her daughter, looking as if it were the last order she would be likely to disobey.

"I shall come back to tell you what is happening," said Teresa, "but I suspect we have caught up with the slavers the captain mentioned."

The *Destiny*'s lower deck was cleared for action. The starboard gunports were open, and the cannons manned by watchful seamen. One gun, in the bows, was being reloaded. Everyone was too busy to notice Teresa. After a moment's consideration, she decided it was probably no more dangerous on deck than below. If she found she was in the way, she could always go back down to the cabin.

Marco and Andrew were already on the quarter deck with Captain Fitch and his officers. Teresa followed the direction of their gaze and saw a two-masted ship, smaller than the frigate, a couple of hundred yards away. Its sails were being hastily lowered and a white flag waved from amidships.

"Looks like they're surrendering," grunted the captain with satisfaction.

As the *Snipe* lost speed, a boat was lowered over her side. Four men climbed down a rope ladder to it and began rowing towards the *Destiny*. The white flag went with them. They were climbing aboard the *Destiny* when a hollow boom rang out. The *Snipe* shuddered visibly, though no damage could be seen.

"What was that?" asked Teresa. "Did we shoot at them again?"

The third mate turned to her, pale-faced.

"They've blown a hole in their own ship, ma'am. They're scuttling the evidence."

Shouts and screams could be heard across the water, and they saw men jumping overboard.

"That'll be the rest of the crew," said Captain Fitch. "The officers abandoned them. Lower the gig, we'll go and pick 'em up. Maybe they'll turn king's evidence."

"But what about the slaves?" demanded Teresa. "Why are they not jumping?"

"They'll have battened down the hatches, Miss Danville," explained Captain Fitch grimly. "No use scuttling the ship if the cargo escapes to tell tales."

"But we must rescue them!" she cried in agony, oblivious of the glares of the four slavers. "Send a boat to release them, quickly!"

"I can't order my men onto a sinking ship, ma'am."

"Call for volunteers," urged Andrew. "I shall lead them. Miss Danville is right, we cannot leave the slaves to drown, Captain."

"I will go with you," said Teresa. "There is no time to waste searching for volunteers."

"I shall go, too!" cried Marco, his face alight with excitement.

"The *Snipe*'s boat is ready and waiting." After one dismayed glance at Teresa's set face, Andrew decided not to argue with her. "Captain, give us a couple of men to row us across. They need not board the ship."

The *Snipe* was drifting closer to the *Destiny* and they reached her in no time. They climbed up to the deck. Teresa was glad she was still wearing her own skirt. The rope ladder would have been impossible in one of Muriel's gowns.

The ship was listing slightly, though it seemed steady beneath their feet. They heard cries and groans from below, thumps and thuds as the terrified wretches tried desperately to break out of their deadly prison.

"Teresa, Marco, to the aft hatch," ordered Andrew, taking in the situation at a glance. "I'll tackle this one."

It was the work of a moment to undo the fastenings. Teresa and Marco struggled to lift the heavy hatch but it was beyond their strength. Andrew rushed to help as a swarm of dark-skinned, half-naked women and children burst up from the forward hold and milled about on the deck.

The aft hatch swung open and another dozen women staggered out. No one else appeared. Teresa peered down into the gloom, hearing yells in deeper male voices.

"Break loose the railings, the spars, any timber you can find," Andrew shouted to Marco. "Make them jump with it. It's their only hope."

"Andrew, there are people down there still!" A foul stench rose from the hold and Teresa gagged.

He rejoined her at the hatch. "I wager they are shackled," he said grimly. "Give me your pistol. I hope you have powder and ball. I shall have to shoot their irons off. You help Marco to persuade the rest over the side."

He thrust into his pocket the leather pouches she handed him and went below, gun in hand.

Teresa hesitated, torn between fear for his safety and Marco's pressing need of assistance. She was proud of her quiet, studious brother as she saw him swinging a crowbar at a broken crate. She ran to him and passed out pieces of wood to the African women, urging them with gestures to jump.

Shots echoed from below and soon the men were straggling up one by one to join them.

The ship shuddered and listed a little further.

"She's going!" cried Marco, scared. "Where's Andrew?"

Teresa turned back towards the hatch just as Andrew emerged, his face black with powder smoke.

"That's the last of them," he said cheerfully. "Time to go, I think."

All the Africans had gone overboard, so the three rescuers hurried down the ladder. The sailors had already taken several children into the boat. They pulled away from the doomed ship. They were halfway back to the *Destiny* when Teresa saw the *Snipe* tilt over on its side and slide smoothly beneath the placid blue swells.

Floating wood and bobbing heads dotted the sea's surface, as the *Destiny*'s boats crawled among them.

Numb with exhaustion, Teresa had to be lifted to the deck in a sling. Willing hands helped her aboard. She stood in a daze until Andrew appeared over the side, picked her up, and carried her down to the cabin.

Before she fell asleep in her cot, she was aware of Muriel bending over her, tucking her in, her blue eyes wondering.

"You are a heroine," she breathed.

It was long past noon when Teresa woke, ravenous. Sitting up, she announced, "I'm so hungry I could eat an ox!"

"A lady ought to have a delicate appetite and never to mention it," Lady Parr informed her. "I eat like a bird and so, I am happy to say, does Muriel. It is quite otherwise with gentlemen. Sir Archibald had an excellent appetite. I have decided, Miss Danville, to take you in hand. I fear it will never do for you to present yourself to Her Grace of Stafford until you have overcome certain odd notions of behaviour. I flatter myself that I am as able as anyone to teach you how to go on unexceptionably, though I daresay you will never be as pretty behaved as Muriel. Muriel is exceptional."

"Yes, ma'am, and I thank you, but I missed both breakfast and luncheon."

"Kinsey, fetch some nourishment for Miss Danville. And you may tell Miss Muriel to come down. She has spent quite enough time with young Graylin for this afternoon."

The maid curtseyed and left, and the cabin boy soon arrived with a tray.

"Cap'n's compliments, miss," he said, "and there's seventy-eight Africans been saved. I seen 'em, miss. They's up on deck wi' a bit o' canvas rigged to keep the sun off. I seen them slavers, too, in irons in the brig. They knows as it was you saved them blacks and they was cussing something awful. Just like your parrot, miss."

"That will do," said Lady Parr severely, and the lad departed in haste.

Muriel came in just as Teresa finished eating. "Captain Fitch wants to see you on the quarter deck," she said, "if you are quite recovered. Oh, Miss Danville, you were splendid! I cannot imagine how you could be so brave. Why, it frightens me only to see their black faces at a distance."

Teresa looked at her in surprise. "They are people," she said gently. "I could not stand by and let them drown. Pray excuse me, ma'am. I must go up to see the captain."

Andrew was leaning on the rail. He grinned at her disconcerted expression when Captain Fitch asked what she expected him to do with her protégés.

"I'll impress a score or so of the men," the captain went on. "We've lost that many of the crew to yellow fever and such, and there's enough of 'em healthy. The rest, there's the women and children, and a lot of 'em sick."

"Then the first thing is to attempt to cure them," said Teresa. "After seeing the conditions they were kept in, I should say fresh air and decent food will be enough for most of them. However, I shall fetch my herbs and see whether I can help any of the rest. Perhaps the doctor could meet me there?"

As Teresa joined the ship's doctor amidships, she looked round at the rescued slaves. Some of the children were sufficiently recovered from their ordeal to run and play, and a number of the men were standing and stretching or walking about. Others sat huddled or lay sprawling. She imagined they must enjoy simply having space to breathe.

When they saw her, many of them called out in strange words. A young girl, perhaps fifteen or sixteen, came toward her. She was clad only in a piece of white cloth tied above her breasts and hanging to mid-thigh.

"They are blessing you, miss," she said in excellent English. "They know that without you they would be dead. I am Annie, miss, and I, too, bless you and thank you."

Teresa felt her cheeks grow hot and quickly asked, "How is it that you speak English?"

Annie explained that since she was a small child her mother had lived with a white man, who had treated her as a daughter. Her mother and her adoptive father had died of some nameless tropical disease, and she had been sold to the slavers by the local chief.

She made herself useful interpreting, as Teresa and the doctor moved among the others, cleaning and binding wounds, dosing fevers, washing inflamed eyes with herbs. When they had seen all the sick, Teresa went to report to Captain Fitch.

As she climbed the steps to the quarter deck, she looked up to see Andrew watching her and gave him a weary smile.

"I think they will all survive," she said. "How glad I am that we went to the *Snipe*. You risked your life to save the men."

"You risked yours, too, Miss Danville. At times a disregard for convention is estimable."

His voice was serious, and when Teresa looked for a teasing light in his eye, she read only admiration. She turned away to hide her flushed face.

Captain Fitch had decided to set his unwanted passengers ashore at Grand Turk, in the Caicos Islands, which they would pass close to in a few days. He assured Teresa that it had a healthful climate and that the men would certainly find work in the salt industry which flourished there. She had to agree that it would probably suit them better than England, had it been possible to convey them thither.

She went down to the cabin to dress for dinner. After the day's adventures, she was ruefully aware of a ridiculous feeling of excitement at the thought that she was to wear her new gown.

She watched Kinsey help Lady Parr and Muriel into their finery and arrange their hair. The first thing she must do when she arrived in London, Teresa decided, was to find a competent abigail. There was clearly an art to it, far beyond the services her Spanish maid had rendered her, which had amounted to little more than mending and laundry. Muriel, whose blond ringlets had been sadly disarranged by the breeze during her visit on deck, emerged from Kinsey's clever hands fit to grace a ballroom.

Then it was Teresa's turn. She held her breath as the muslin slipped down over her shoulders. It fit perfectly.

Kinsey took the captain's tiny mirror off its hook and held it tilted while Teresa twisted and turned, trying to see herself in her new finery. At last she gave up, laughing.

"I must take it on trust," she said, then added with unwonted shyness, "Do you think you can do anything with my hair?"

Kinsey sat her down at the table. Muriel obligingly sat opposite, holding the mirror while the silky black tresses were loosed from their bounds and brushed vigorously.

"It's beautiful," Muriel assured her, "but you will have to cut it shorter to be *à la mode.*"

" 'Twould be easier," Kinsey agreed. "I'll plait it again,

but different like. Lots of little braids and wind them into knots at the sides. Then this here'll make a sort of coronet on top. Isn't that fine as fivepence now, Miss Muriel?"

"Charming!"

Lady Parr raised her quizzing glass. "Astonishing! I'd not have thought Miss Danville could look half so well. In my youth we all wore our hair long. It was quite the fashion then to pile it up high. Sir Archibald admired it exceedingly. Of course, my hair was golden." She studied Teresa's raven locks, sighed, and rose to lead the way to the wardroom.

Even dressed in puce, rather than white, her ladyship bore a startling resemblance to a ship in full sail. Muriel was, as usual, a figure of quiet elegance in pale blue. Teresa followed her into the room, her eyes seeking out Andrew's.

She knew at once that he was not impressed by her appearance.

He could find no fault with the new gown, so the anticipated transformation had not taken place. Perhaps it was only that white muslin did not suit her. She knew very well that bright colours became her best. However, Lady Parr insisted that unmarried girls must wear pastels.

If she could not win Andrew's admiration with her looks, then she must learn from Lady Parr how to behave just like Muriel. She did not hope for his love, but she vowed to make every effort to gain his approval.

"You look every inch a lady," he said kindly.

Since this implied that she had not looked like a lady before, Teresa's eyes flashed with indignation at his intended compliment. Marco was more successful.

"You're complete to a shade!" he exclaimed, having learned any amount of useful slang from Andrew.

Captain Fitch had never noticed anything amiss with Miss Danville's appearance and was at a loss to understand the present interest therein. He had matters of more moment to discuss. He proceeded to congratulate himself upon the successful pursuit and capture of the *Snipe*, much to Lady Parr's irritation, since she would have preferred to ignore the unpleasant subject. He had talked to the slaver captain, Harrison, a very nasty sort of fellow, who flew into a passion when he learned that his slaves had been rescued. He would surely be transported for his part in the infamous trade. Indeed, he might even be hanged for murder since a number of the unfortunate Africans had drowned.

"He would not tell me who financed the voyage," the captain continued. "Certainly it was not his own ship, or he'd never have scuttled her. There are gentlemen in England still who put up funds for scoundrels like Harrison, and it is generally impossible to prove their complicity."

"It is still a profitable trade then," observed Andrew.

"Aye, and will be until the Americans and the French cooperate with us," growled the captain. "We cannot stop American ships, and the French never punish their citizens when we catch them."

Lady Parr managed to turn the conversation to the infamous behaviour of the French and the Americans in general, both of them given to revolutions that quite cut up everyone's peace. Teresa and Andrew between them managed to silence Marco when he attempted to inform her that Costa Rica, and indeed all of Central America, was on the verge of its own revolution. Teresa did not care to give her ladyship any more ammunition to use against her. She already had plenty.

Teresa's lessons in deportment began on the morrow. Lady Parr commandeered the wardroom between the hours of nine and one, pointing out to the unfortunate officers that they might very well go to their cabins or on deck.

Here Teresa paraded in front of her ladyship's eagle eye until her carefree stride was reduced to a dainty step. Soon she could walk arm in arm with Muriel without pulling her along.

She learned to curtsey gracefully and to adjust the depth of her curtsey to the rank, called out by Lady Parr, of the person to whom she was supposedly being presented. She had some difficulty in distinguishing between the deference due to the King or Queen and that due the Prince Regent.

"Not that you will meet the King, of course, for he is quite mad by now. Duke!" Her ladyship frowned in thought as Teresa produced a creditable ducal curtsey. "I daresay you will not go so low to the Duke of Stafford as he is your uncle—at least once he has acknowledged you. Viscount! No, no, girl, that is deep enough for an earl, or even a marquis."

Muriel helped her practise conversing in a soft voice upon unexceptionable topics such as the weather. Lady Parr had nothing but praise for her low, musical voice. Her laugh, however, was sadly deprecated and proved impossible to remedy. The only alternative Teresa managed to produce was a horrid titter, which she herself refused to consider acceptable.

"We cannot expect perfection," Lady Parr sighed. "You will have to confine yourself to smiling, Miss Danville. Sir Archibald did not approve of laughing females, so that will do very well. Your teeth are good, I am glad to see."

Another failure was the art of fluttering fan and eyelashes: Teresa could not take it seriously enough to concentrate. In fact, the effort invariably called forth that unfortunate laugh.

Despite Lady Parr's objections, the lessons were interrupted twice a day when Teresa made her rounds of the ex-slaves, attending to their ills. Andrew was openly admiring of both her compassion and her medical skills. On the second day Muriel asked permission to help, and though she was ill at ease, continued to join her thereafter. Teresa respected her efforts to overcome her timidity, and she found herself growing fond of Andrew's future wife.

She also felt a growing attachment to Annie. The girl was always cheerful and ready to help. When the *Destiny* anchored off Grand Turk and the boats started ferrying the Africans ashore, Teresa decided to ask Annie to stay with her as her abigail.

Annie accepted joyfully. Despite Lady Parr's protests at sharing the cabin with a savage when it was overfull already, a pallet was made up for Annie on the floor. Kinsey took the girl under her wing at once, and Muriel donated a couple of her mourning dresses to make her some decent clothes. Clad demurely in grey, Annie was miraculously transformed from savage to maidservant, and under Kinsey's kindly tutelage she began to learn an abigail's skills.

Marco was taking lessons of his own. His intellectual curiosity was unbounded, and he had persuaded Captain Fitch to teach him the science of navigation. At all hours of the day and night, he could be seen wielding sextant, astrolabe, and chronometer, consulting the *Nautical Almanac*, or bending over Admiralty charts with dividers in hand.

Teresa's course of instruction continued meanwhile with the rules of behaviour in Polite Society.

"A young lady never dances more than twice with any gentleman at the same ball and must not waltz until given permission by one of the patronesses of Almack's."

"I am not likely to break that rule, ma'am"—Teresa laughed—"'for I have no notion how to waltz."

Nor, shockingly, did she know how to dance the cotillion or the quadrille or any English country dances. Andrew and Muriel were enlisted, and Marco reluctantly joined in the lessons to make up the numbers. With the wardroom table cleared to one side there was just space enough to learn the steps as long as the dancers moved with great care. Since their only music was Lady Parr's tuneless hum, it would in any case have been impossible to infuse any spirit into the exercise.

As for conversational training, there was a list of possible subjects of polite discourse, and a list of the unmentionables, which included religion, politics, prizefighting, and most parts of the body. Certain works of literature, such as poetry and the latest novels, were acceptable topics, in moderation.

"Do you read, Miss Danville?" enquired her ladyship.

"Why yes, ma'am. I have read most of my father's library."

"Do not on any account mention it. Nothing is so fatal to a young lady's chances as being known as a bluestocking. Sir Archibald never permitted Muriel to enter his library. Do you sketch? Play the piano? The harp, perhaps?"

"Only the guitar, ma'am. And I sing."

Not having her guitar, she sang a Spanish song *a capella*. Muriel thought it charming, but Lady Parr was not impressed.

"Quite unsuitable," she declared. "French and Italian are acceptable, even German perhaps. Spanish is beyond the pale."

Teresa began to feel thoroughly inadequate yet again. "It is a lowering reflection," she confided to Marco later, "that my one talent, shooting straight, is not on the list of ladylike accomplishments."

However, by the time the Scillies were sighted, Lady Parr pronounced herself satisfied. "You are vastly improved, I vow, Miss Danville," she said. "I daresay it is not too much to hope you will not disgrace yourself in your uncle's house. I should be excessively mortified were the duchess to lay any fault in your conduct at my door."

"Indeed I must thank you for your efforts in my behalf," said Teresa. "I shall endeavour to behave with utmost decorum." She sank in the precise curtsey proper to a baronet's widow.

Teresa's resolve was very soon put to the test, when the *Destiny* sailed into Spithead.

"A lady preserves her composure under all conditions," she remembered. "Only yokels gape."

Nonetheless, she wanted to gape at the spectacle of hundreds of vessels sailing to and fro in the narrow waterway between Portsmouth and the Isle of Wight. With great effort she managed to preserve her countenance, though she did say to Andrew, "I never dreamed there were so many ships in the whole world!"

It was dusk when they tied up to the quay at the naval dockyards. Captain Fitch had come to bid them farewell with so obvious an air of relief that, as had become her habit, Teresa sought Andrew's eyes to confirm her amusement.

With a sudden pang, she realised that even if she saw him in London, they could never again be on such intimate terms. He would soon be married to Muriel, and she herself, Teresa decided, would collect dozens of beaux, among whom she was bound to find someone else who shared her sense of humour.

While they waited for Rowson to bring carriages to take them into Portsmouth, the slavers were marched off the frigate in chains. As they passed, their captain, Harrison, spotted Teresa at the rail.

"You wait, Miss High-and-Mighty Danville," he snarled, lips twisted in a vicious grin. "I'll get you for this!"

"Don't you mind him, miss," Captain Fitch reassured her. "The fellow will soon be stowed away where he can't get to anyone."

Teresa had seen the hatred in Harrison's eyes. She prayed that the captain was right.

= 5 =

A HIRED CARRIAGE pulled into the well-lit courtyard of the Star and Garter. From it descended a tall, fair young gentleman. The landlord, who had just stepped out to take the air on this mild September evening, bustled forward. Yes, he had several excellent rooms available. A private parlour? Of course. Two post chaises and three riding horses to start for London in the morning? Certainly, certainly. He rubbed his hands together and bowed to the imposing matron who followed the gentleman from the carriage. A youth and two young ladies emerged next. As mine host ushered the party towards the door, he heard another carriage drive up and glanced backwards.

"That will be our servants," the fair gentleman informed him.

From the second carriage stepped a respectable-looking manservant. Behind him came a perfectly normal lady's maid, then a female African, dressed as if she, too, were a perfectly normal abigail, with a parrot on her shoulder.

"Y-your servants, sir?" stammered the innkeeper.

The gentleman's lips twitched, but before he could answer, the elder of the two young ladies, the dark one, spoke up.

"Yes, and please see that the parrot comes into the parlour. It is by far too cold to leave him in the stables." As if it were a point of contention between them, she threw an indignant look at the gentleman, who shrugged resignedly.

"Hello, hello," said the parrot. "Hello, dinner."

As the heads of several ostlers, an idling tapster, and a passing sailor all turned towards the bird, the landlord swallowed his instinctive protest.

"Hungry is 'e?" he asked ingratiatingly. "What's 'e like to eat?"

The young lady smiled in triumph at the gentleman.

"You see," she said, "there's no objection to Gayo's presence." Walking into the inn beside the landlord, she told him, "He is always hungry. He likes fruit and nuts and seeds, but he will eat almost anything."

"Messy eaters, parrots," said the landlord with a judicious air. "I seen 'em afore. Might be better if your man feeds 'im in the taproom."

"That will do very well," agreed the young lady, a sunny smile curving her pretty lips.

As the landlord had anticipated, the news that there was a talking parrot in the taproom of the Star and Garter spread like wildfire. The crowd that gathered to hear Gayo swear at them in English and Spanish drank more ale in an hour than the regulars drank in a week. What was more, many of them stayed on even after Rowson took the bird upstairs, and in the morning a new crowd waited in hope of his reappearance. Many of the latter were lucky enough also to catch a glimpse of the African abigail.

"I feel as if I'm in charge of a travelling circus," Andrew muttered to Rowson as he mounted his hired hack.

" 'E's got some vocabulary, that bird," said Rowson with a grin. "Annie's a good girl though, sir."

Teresa, who had been impressed by the amenities of the coaching inn, was silenced by the bustling streets of Portsmouth when she saw them in daylight. She understood at last why Andrew had referred to Cartago as a mere village. The coach, in itself a wonder to one used to ox carts, rolled smoothly along on the paved surface, past row after row of neat brick buildings. There were people everywhere, on horseback, in carriages, walking or running, dressed in finery or rags, talking, shouting, whistling, enjoying the rare sunny day.

Since Lady Parr did not admonish her for gaping, Teresa guessed that she had succeeded in schooling her expression to hide her awe.

They reached the end of the town and continued along the open highway. Nothing could have been more different from the jungle trail to Limón. The road was wide enough for two vehicles to pass each other. In fact, their chaise frequently overtook slow-moving wagons, and was itself overtaken by a mail coach and a curricle or two.

Teresa was fascinated by the countryside. The rolling hills were patchworked with ochre fields, already harvested, and pasture of a brilliant green hue quite unlike that of the tropical forests. Autumn was already tinting the woodlands with russet and gold. In the hedgerows, crimson haws and scarlet hips vied with silky white tangles of old man's beard. Humpbacked stone bridges crossed gentle, gurgling streams that sparkled in the sun, so very different from the rushing mountain torrents and slow, smooth lowland rivers of Costa Rica.

Every few miles they passed through villages where thatched cottages clustered round a stone church. The cottage gardens blazed with tall pink hollyhocks, honey-scented alyssum, and blue-mauve Michaelmas daisies.

To Teresa, everything looked peaceful and prosperous, and somehow smugly self-satisfied.

"Is it not delightful to be back in England, Mama?" Muriel sighed happily. "How I have missed it! I shall never go away again, I vow."

They stopped in the small town of Petersfield to change horses and drink tea in one of the many coaching inns. The main street was lined with modern houses of red brick, with regular facades of rectangular windows, giving an impression of restrained elegance.

Teresa fetched Gayo from the servants' coach and carried him into the inn's coffee room, where a fire blazed in the wide hearth. For the first time in weeks she was glad to throw off Muriel's heavy cloak.

"Do you really think I shall grow accustomed to a northern climate?" she asked Andrew. "This is the first time I have been warm enough since we left the tropics."

He held out his hands to the flames.

"If I could grow so accustomed to your heat in the course of a few months that I am now shivering in an English September, then I wager you will adjust in time. At this moment, I am ready to set sail immediately for warmer climes."

They both looked at Muriel, standing by the open window in her delicate muslin, and shook their heads in amused amazement at her hardiness.

Gayo was on his best behaviour. He nibbled delicately at a biscuit supplied by the fascinated waiter. Even when the inevitable crowd gathered, he confined his swearing to Spanish, incomprehensible to all but one old Peninsula soldier, who sat in a corner cackling.

Annie had her own group of admirers. In Portsmouth, where black sailors were not uncommon, a black abigail was a momentary wonder. In rural Petersfield she was a sensation. It was all Rowson could do to stop the yokels feeling her fuzzy hair to see if it was real.

"Travelling circus it is, sir," he said to Andrew as they set off again.

Marco chose to join the ladies in the carriage for a stage. He found riding with an English saddle prodigious tiring. By the time they stopped in Godalming for lunch, his thighs—one of those unmentionable parts of the body—had stiffened, so that he staggered into the King's Arms and collapsed into a chair with a groan.

The King's Arms gained as much custom from their presence as had the last two inns. In fact, the innkeeper confided that Gayo and Annie drew a bigger crowd between them than had turned out when Tsar Alexander stopped at his hostelry a few months since.

The triumphal procession continued through Guildford without halting, and paused for tea and a change of horses in Esher, to the delight of yet another landlord. They crossed sinister Wimbledon Common in the twilight without Teresa having to draw her pistol against a highwayman, then rumbled across the wooden bridge at Putney.

It was dark when they drove through Fulham and Chelsea and Kensington, but Teresa could tell by the twinkling lights of a thousand villas that the open country was behind them. She could not repress a gasp as at last they entered the gaslit streets of Mayfair.

Lady Parr nodded indulgently and patted her knee. " 'Tis amazing bright, is it not?"

"Indeed, ma'am, I can scarce believe it is night. And the houses! There are so many houses, and so tall!"

"London is a monstrous fine city," said Muriel with a delighted smile. "Kingston and Spanish Town are nothing to it. I am prodigious glad to be back."

A few minutes later the chaise came to a halt and Andrew appeared at the door.

"Here we are in Hill Street," he announced, opening it. "The house is all lit up, my lady, so I believe your brother is at home. We shall leave you here and go on to Stafford House. May I have your permission to call tomorrow morning to see how you go on?"

One of the postilions had run up the steps and banged on the door, which opened to reveal a glimpse of the elegant interior. A couple of footmen came down and, directed by Kinsey, began unloading the Parrs' mountain of luggage from the second carriage.

Lady Parr and Muriel both kissed Teresa's cheek before descending to the pavement.

"I am grown excessively fond of you, child, I declare," said her ladyship in a surprised voice, then sailed up the steps and into the house.

"You will visit us, will you not?" asked Muriel wistfully, and disappeared in her mother's wake.

Andrew and Marco joined Teresa in the chaise and they set off again.

"Not far now," said Andrew reassuringly. "'Stafford House is on Park Lane. I hope the duke and duchess are in residence at present."

"Where else would they be?" asked Marco. "Is that not their home?"

"I had not thought," said Teresa, "but I recall that Papa spent most of his childhood in the country. I expect the duke has a country house as well?"

"Several."

Teresa was silent, trying to imagine what it would be like to have more than one home. Her father's family clearly lived on a lavish scale she found hard to believe. How could she ever make a place for herself in such a world? She was not merely a yokel, but a barbarian. She reached for Marco's hand.

Judging by his anxious clasp, he was equally dismayed.

All too soon the carriage pulled up. Rowson appeared, opened the door, and lowered the step. Andrew jumped out and turned to help Teresa down.

"Be brave," he whispered.

Wide stone steps between elaborate wrought-iron railings led up to a pedimented front door; above, a row of pilasters added to the air of impressive elegance. Teresa looked up, counting row upon row of windows, but the top of the facade was lost in darkness.

Marco stepped down beside her.

"Ionic columns," he said matter-of-factly, pointing to the pilasters. "I've seen them in pictures of the old Greek temples. Narrower and more elaborate than Doric, but less ornate than Corinthian."

Teresa laughed. If her little brother accepted this enormous mansion with such apparent nonchalance, she could certainly do no less.

"Very decorative," she said, and went up the steps.

Rowson had already knocked and the door was swinging open. A wrinkled old man in green livery with crimson piping bowed to Teresa.

"Can I help you, ma'am?" he enquired in a reedy voice.

"The hall porter," Andrew hissed in Teresa's ear as he stepped forward. "His Grace's niece and nephew, Miss Danville and Mr. Marco Danville, to see His Grace," he announced with cool formality.

The porter looked flustered. He beckoned to a liveried footman who stood motionless against the wall, and whispered to him. The footman departed in haste. A few moments later a portly butler in black appeared. He was completely bald, and as he advanced with stately tread across the hall, the light of several dozen wax candles reflected from his shiny pate.

"Miss Danville?" His voice managed to be at once imperious and suspicious. "His Grace is not at home. I believe His Grace is not expecting you?"

"No, he does not even know of our existence," said Teresa candidly. "We could not advise him of our arrival since we only reached England yesterday."

"Indeed, miss." The butler's nostrils quivered in an inaudible sniff. "I am given to understand that you claim to be His Grace's niece."

Teresa's chin rose. A light rain was beginning to fall and she had no intention of standing on the doorstep getting wet while this haughty man interrogated her. He was, she reminded herself, no more than a servant.

"I *am* the duke's niece, Lord Edward Danville's daughter. We shall wait here until he or my aunt returns."

As she spoke she advanced into the hall, followed by Marco, Andrew, Annie, and Rowson.

In the face of this concerted front, the butler stepped back. Then he saw the parrot on Annie's shoulder. His spine stiffened visibly.

"The bird can wait in the stables," he said coldly, and

54

beckoned the footman, whose eyes were popping in his still otherwise expressionless face. "James, take the bird round to the mews."

James's jaw dropped and he stepped forward with every indication of alarm.

"Me, Mr. Boggs?" he faltered.

"*Hijo de puta!*" said Gayo indignantly. "Misbegotten sea scum!" Squawking, he flew to Teresa.

"The parrot will stay with me," she told the butler. "It is far too cold for him in this abominable climate." She noticed that Andrew's shoulders were shaking and glared at him. Then she turned back to her adversary and asked, with all the hauteur of an aristocrat born and bred, "Where do you wish us to await my uncle?"

Routed, Mr. Boggs looked around the hall as if he wondered whether he dared keep them standing there indefinitely.

For the first time Teresa noticed her surroundings. The circular, domed entrance was floored with pink-veined marble, and marble pillars flanked each doorway that opened onto it. At some point Rowson, with quiet efficiency, had carried in their bags and the pathetic little pile looked hideously out of place.

Opposite the front door, a double stair with ornately carved banisters, gleaming from much polishing, curved up to a wide landing. Marco, oblivious to the altercation behind him, was examining a glossy red vase displayed in a niche between the staircases.

"Samian ware," he announced.

Andrew joined him. "I believe that must be the original Greek pottery, not a Roman imitation," he proposed. "The late duke was reputed to be something of a connoisseur."

"*If* you will come this way, miss, gentlemen," Boggs interrupted the discussion of classical pottery.

Leaving Annie and Rowson perched on the edge of a pair of straight chairs in the hall, the butler ushered Teresa, Marco, and Andrew into a small, chilly, back parlour. To

Teresa's annoyance and Andrew's amusement, he stationed James outside the door.

"For all the world as if we were burglars," she fumed.

"I trust he does not mean to call in the watch," Andrew said with a smile.

By the time they had waited three quarters of an hour, Teresa's annoyance had grown to wrath and Andrew was no longer amused. They had not eaten since luncheon in Godalming, which now seemed part of another life. Not only was the room to which they were confined cold but its furniture was sparse and uncomfortable.

"I believe this chair was designed to discourage sitting," observed Marco after twisting and turning for some minutes. He was stiffer than ever from his introduction to the English saddle.

"I believe this room was designed to discourage importunate visitors," Andrew snorted. "I am going to send James to discover at what hour the duke is expected to come home." He started towards the door.

"I cannot imagine why we did not enquire before," agreed Teresa. "Do you think we might with propriety request a tea tray at least?"

Andrew grimaced. "I'm afraid not, as you are not yet resident here." He opened the door, conferred with the footman, and returned to announce, "The duke is dining with Lord Liverpool. He is not expected back before eleven."

Teresa glanced at the clock on the mantel of the empty fireplace. It was half past eight. She shivered. Gayo, bored, flapped over to the window and began to climb the curtains, muttering imprecations.

"Perhaps we had best go to an inn for the night and return in the morning," suggested Teresa. "Only we already owe you, Sir Andrew, for last night's accommodation and for the hire of the carriage, and I cannot pay you until I have seen Don Eduardo's banker."

"I can stand the nonsense, but I think you will do better

to wait here, tiresome though it is. By the time we have summoned a hackney, found an hotel, and settled you in it, the duke will have returned home, and then the battle is to be fought again tomorrow."

"It was a battle royal, was it not?" She laughed. "I fear it is yet to be won. Surely my uncle cannot be half so formidable as his butler. Perhaps you are right and we ought to stay, but we must not keep you from your own fireside, not to mention your dinner."

An expression of yearning crossed Andrew's face but he said staunchly, "I shall not desert you after these thousands of miles we have crossed together."

At that moment a loud, cheerful voice was heard outside and the door was flung open. A tall, broad-shouldered young man stood there grinning. His face was so much like Don Eduardo's that Teresa gasped as she rose to her feet.

"I'm John Danville," he announced. "That rascal Boggs tells me you're my cousins. Damned—beg pardon, dashed— if I knew I had any I hadn't met, but welcome to London."

"Thank you," said Teresa, curtseying with a joyful smile. "I am Teresa Danville, and this is my brother Marco. How very like Papa you look, Lord Danville."

He strode forward to take both her hands in his and kiss her cheek.

"Lord Danville's my elder brother, Tom," he corrected, shaking Marco's hand vigourously. "Starchy sort of fellow, make a first-rate duke one of these days. I'm just Lord John. Cousin John to you, of course."

He looked enquiringly at Andrew, but before Teresa could introduce them Gayo took an exuberant hand, or claw, in the proceedings.

"Hello, hello, hello," he cried, swooping down from the top of the curtains where he had been quietly shredding a fringe. He landed on Lord John's shoulder, flapped wildly till he found his balance, then leaned toward his lordship's ear and said in a confidential tone, "Son of a sea snake."

To Teresa's relief, though her big cousin looked startled, he laughed.

"Boggs did mumble something disgruntled about a bird," he said.

Teresa glanced at Andrew, remembering his introduction to Gayo. When she recalled that she had described him to his face as a handsome stranger, she cringed. Lady Parr had taught her that it was vulgar to make personal remarks, though that was a caveat more honoured in the breach than the observance by her ladyship.

"This is Gayo. He appears to have fallen in love with you at first sight," she said.

"As do all the girls," Lord John boasted, but with such a engaging twinkle in his eyes that it was impossible to be offended.

He turned again to Andrew and held out his hand.

Andrew shook hands and introduced himself. "I had the honour of escorting Miss Danville and Marco from Costa Rica," he explained. "Now that they are safely in the hands of a relative, I shall be on my way."

"I was going out to dine with friends," said Lord John, "but dashed if I don't stay home to improve my acquaintance with my pretty new cousin. Boggs! Boggs, I say! Ha, knew you were listening at the door, you rascal. We'll have something to eat in the breakfast room in half an hour. Tell Jacques a cold collation will do, but make it substantial. You'll join us, won't you, Graylin?"

The diplomat declined, standing firm against their urging. Teresa thought he looked somewhat miffed. She wished she could think that he was the least bit jealous to see her welcomed with such enthusiasm by a handsome young gentleman. But no, he was affianced to Muriel.

Her cousin's lively volubility prevented any speech with Andrew beyond the brief expression of her deepest gratitude and a promise to repay very soon the blunt he had laid out in their behalf. He departed with a curt nod of acknowledgement.

A few minutes later, Teresa ventured to interrupt Lord John's amiable chatter to ask if it was possible to change her travel-stained gown before eating. The housekeeper was summoned and took her upstairs, scarcely blinking at the parrot that accompanied them.

"You'll be Lord Edward's daughter, miss?" asked Mrs. Davies. "A prime favourite he was with the staff. I was still a tweeny when he went off so sudden. There's not many left as knew him. That Boggs, now, only been here ten year, he has."

Warned by the butler that Lord John had taken his alleged cousins under his wing and that they would likely stay the night, Mrs. Davies had already ordered a suite prepared. Annie was in the dressing room, unpacking Teresa's minimal wardrobe, while a pair of maids bustled about making up the bed, lighting a fire, fetching hot water.

"This was Lady Pamela's chamber before she married Lord Jordan," said the housekeeper.

"It looks very comfortable," said Teresa, trying not to appear impressed by the primrose silk-hung bed, the matching Hepplewhite chairs, the patterned Axminster carpet.

The dressing room had two huge armoires with mirrored doors, a dressing table with another mirror, a chest of drawers, and a marble-topped washstand. It could be used as a private sitting room also, as there were a chaise longue and two comfortable-looking armchairs by the fireplace.

"I had best leave Gayo here," she went on hesitantly. "Annie will stay with him until he is settled."

Mrs. Davis, who still had a fondness for the dashing Lord Edward, willingly agreed to send up a tray for the abigail and a selection of fruit and nuts for the parrot. Teresa wished Andrew could see how the housekeeper welcomed Gayo, contrary to his dire predictions. The woman was enjoying herself hugely, and Teresa soon found out why.

"My cousin's always boasting about her mistress's black page boy," she confided in a whisper as she left. "Just wait till I tell her we've a black abigail in the house, and a parrot to boot."

Teresa washed and changed quickly, and hurried down to the entrance hall. The footman, James, directed her to the breakfast room and she went in to find her brother and her cousin already seated, with Boggs about to serve them.

"Thought you wouldn't mind if we didn't stand on ceremony," said Lord John jovially. "All family, after all, and young Marco and I are deuced sharp-set."

"If by that you mean that you are excessively hungry, then I must forgive you, for so am I," Teresa said with a smile, taking the chair the butler held for her.

Without a second thought she ignored Lady Parr's instructions about delicate appetites and did justice to every one of the French chef's delicious concoctions.

At last even Lord John, a notable trencherman, was satisfied. He pushed his chair back from the table and called for port. Teresa knew that ladies always retired before the gentlemen started on the port, but he persuaded her to stay and take a glass of canary.

"We're all family," he repeated, "and I rely on you, cousin, to tell me about my uncle Edward and your home and your journey, for young Marco's a silent sort of fellow. Told me just enough to whet my appetite."

Marco grinned at his teasing tone, unoffended. He was quite accustomed to such treatment from his brothers, so it made him feel at home. He told his sister later that their cousin was a great gun and had promised to show him around London. She hoped Lord John would prove as admirable a patterncard as had Andrew.

Boggs provided port, canary wine, and bowls of nuts and dried fruit, then took himself off. They sat round the table, sipping the wine and nibbling at raisins and apricots and figs, while Teresa described the Hacienda del Inglés and began the tale of their journey to England.

Lord John was commenting that the jaguar must have been a deuced flat to miss snapping up so delectable a morsel as his cousin when they heard the sound of new arrivals in the front hall.

"That'll be m'father," he said, jumping up. "Come on, I'll make you known to him. I'd wager a monkey he'll be pleased as Punch. Good sort of chap, m'father."

Despite these encouraging words, Teresa and Marco followed him with some trepidation.

= 6 =

LORD JOHN AND his cousins reached the hall just as Boggs took hat, gloves, and cane from the duke and passed them to James, while Mrs. Davies helped the short, plump duchess out of her damp pelisse. Both the upper servants were talking at once. Though Teresa could not distinguish their words, she was sure that the butler was telling his master that they were impostors, and the housekeeper telling her mistress that they were not.

Lord John broke into the chatter.

"Here's m'cousins come all the way from the Americas, sir," he announced. "'Mama, let me present Cousin Teresa, and this is young Marco."

Teresa sank in a ducal curtsey and Marco performed his best bow.

"You've both a look of Edward," said the duke, and swept them into his jovial embrace. "I trust you have come to stay for a good long visit?"

"Stafford, you cannot mean it," wailed the duchess. "I feel quite faint. Davies, my smelling salts!" She collapsed onto the nearest chair and moaned weakly, "They are certainly frauds. How can you let yourself be deceived, Stafford. Only look at their clothing, they cannot possibly be relatives of yours."

Mrs. Davies patted her hands while Boggs sent James scurrying for Her Grace's dresser.

Neither her husband nor her son took much notice of this performance.

"There, there," the duke said soothingly, then turned to Marco to ask eagerly for news of his brother.

"M'mother's given to the vapours," Lord John explained to Teresa. "No use letting it cast you into the dismals."

Teresa gathered that her genial uncle was not influenced by his wife's distempers. As far as he was concerned, she and Marco could stay, for the rest of their lives if they chose.

The duchess's dresser, Miss Howell, swept into the hall, a tall, angular woman with a frosty grey eye. Her intimidating expression clearly showed that she had no good opinion of poor, foreign relations come to batten on her mistress. She held a glass of hartshorn to her mistress's lips, then supported her faltering steps up the stairs.

However warm the duke's welcome, it seemed improbable that his wife would agree to sponsor Teresa in Society. Don Eduardo wanted her to join the haut ton, not merely to live as a poor relation in his brother's house.

Teresa lay in bed the next morning, pondering the situation, which was as uncomfortable as her feather mattress was comfortable. Her pride rebelled at staying in a house against the will of its mistress. Yet it would be shockingly rude to leave at once when her uncle was so pleased to receive them. Therefore, the duchess must be persuaded to change her mind.

Then she remembered that Don Eduardo had given her a letter to his brother. At least she could prove that she and Marco were indeed his niece and nephew. That must convince Her Grace of their right to be there. For the rest, Teresa would follow Lady Parr's directions with the greatest precision and prove to her aunt that she was worthy of a Season.

She would also show Andrew she was perfectly capable of taking her place in the highest Society.

The china clock on the mantel, with its idealised shepherd and shepherdess, showed a little after eight. Lady Parr had said that a lady never appeared belowstairs before ten in the morning. Teresa was wide awake and wondering how to fill her time until she could go in search of breakfast. Her room was warm—a maid must have slipped in earlier to light the fire without waking her—so she got up and went barefooted in her cotton nightgown into the dressing room.

"*Buenos días!*" Gayo greeted her. He was perched on a bare towel horse, to which Annie had leashed him. Excited to see her, he flew to meet her and the wooden towel horse toppled over with a crash. "What a pity," he mourned as his flight came to an abrupt halt.

"*Estúpido,*" she said as she unhooked the tether and smoothed his ruffled plumage. "You know you cannot fly when you are tied."

Annie slipped into the room, bearing a tray.

"I brought your chocolate, miss. What was that great crash?" She saw the towel horse. "Oh, Gayo, you naughty creature."

"It made an excellent perch, but he had best be tied to something else in future. It is such a help to me that he likes you, Annie, and equally important that you like him. Tell me, how are the other servants treating you?"

"Fine, miss, though some of them do stare. Mrs. Davies and Mr. Boggs keep them polite. Did you know an abigail sits above all other maids? Only Her Grace's dresser, Miss Howell, is higher than me, except Mrs. Davies, of course. Oh miss, I'm so glad you didn't leave me on that island."

"So am I," Teresa assured her.

In a house full of strangers, the girl was more an old friend than a servant, though they had met little more than a month ago. She wished she knew when she would see Andrew again or Muriel or even Lady Parr.

Teresa found her father's letter to the duke tied together with others to his lawyer and his banker. Donning once again Muriel's green-sprigged muslin, she went down to the breakfast room at ten. Marco and the duke were there, Marco unusually loquacious in response to his uncle's friendly curiosity about life in Costa Rica. John, as his father informed her, had gone out last night and would doubtless not be seen before noon. The duchess invariably break-fasted in her room.

The butler poured Teresa a cup of coffee and she chose two rashers of bacon and a toasted muffin from the long list of dishes he offered her. His manner was austere. She guessed that he had not entirely given up his suspicion of their credentials.

The duke seemed to have not the least doubt that Teresa and Marco were his brother's children, but Teresa was glad to have Don Eduardo's letter to give him. He set aside his newspaper and read it, guffawing now and then.

"Edward always could make me laugh, the scapegrace," he said. "It sounds as if he's done very well for himself, after all. So it's a tutor you want, Marco. Won't be any problem with that. There are always a dozen bright and deserving young men looking to me for a position. And a London Season for you, missy. Now that's for your aunt to see to."

Teresa sipped her coffee, suddenly losing her appetite as she reflected on her aunt's reaction to their arrival.

The coffee was good, but not in any way comparable with what she was used to at home. She remembered her father's commission. If she failed at being a lady, at least she would take him back a satisfactory coffee contract, she promised herself.

"Her Grace requests Miss Danville's presence in her dressing room directly after breakfast," Boggs told her as she left the room a short while later. His commiserating tone told her that Lord Edward's letter had at last convinced him of her authenticity.

She hurried upstairs, going as fast as possible without actually running, which was forbidden by Lady Parr. In her own dressing room she anxiously studied her image in the looking glass while Annie assured her that her hair was neatness itself, her morning dress spotless, her entire ap-pearance unexceptionable. Teresa suppressed the thought that her maid knew as little as she did, and proceeded at a decorous pace to the duchess's suite.

Even her encounter with the jaguar in the jungle had not been near so frightening as the prospect of meeting her excitable aunt again. And this time Teresa would not be able to run to the comfort of Andrew's strong arms.

A green-liveried footman stood in the hallway, waiting lest he be needed to run errands for Her Grace. When she stopped to ascertain that she had come to the right place, he scratched on the door for her.

The dresser looked at her askance as she admitted her into a luxurious dressing room. Teresa, after her *contretemps* with the butler the night before, had no intention of letting herself be intimidated by a servant, however toplofty. She might be unused to the luxury of Stafford House but she was no peasant girl. She had dealt with servants all her life.

She looked squarely and coldly into the woman's resentful eyes and said, "My aunt asked for me. Kindly inform her that I am here."

Howell pursed her thin lips but dropped her eyes and curtseyed. "Yes, miss. Please come this way. Her Grace is expecting you."

Heartened by this minor victory, Teresa followed into a pink bedchamber. The bed and window draperies were pink silk, the counterpane was pink, the carpet was beige with pink roses, the chairs covered with pink satin, the walls papered with more roses. On the hearth a huge fire blazed, and the room was suffocatingly hot. Teresa repressed a nervous giggle at the notion that she had been swallowed alive.

The duchess, dressed in a pink wrap that matched her face to perfection, lay back against a pile of pillows. Since the pillow slips were also pink, she might have vanished entirely were it not for her white lace nightcap.

Teresa curtseyed her ducal curtsey.

"Good morning . . . " Aunt? Ma'am? Duchess? Your

Grace? she wondered desperately. Lady Parr's words floated through her mind: It is always better to be too formal than too familiar. "Good morning, Your Grace."

"Come here, miss," commanded the duchess in a fading voice belied by her bright eyes and pink cheeks.

Teresa approached the bed and curtseyed again, not quite so low this time. The bright eyes looked her up and down, then closed, with an air of acute suffering.

"*Where* did you come by that gown? Howell, my vinaigrette, quickly."

Teresa glanced down at the sprigged muslin. Admittedly it was somewhat shabby after having been worn constantly on the journey, but it was positively modish compared to the clothes she used to wear at home.

"It was given to me by a young lady I met on the voyage, ma'am."

"Castoffs! I believe I shall have a spasm. A Danville in castoffs!" She waved away the glass of hartshorn quickly presented by Howell and sat up straighter, adjusting her cap. "I suppose you *are* a Danville, miss?"

"My uncle is satisfied," said Teresa with considerable indignation. She was growing excessively tired of having her identity doubted. "This morning he read the letter my father wrote him."

"Then you must purchase some new gowns, Miss Danville. I cannot permit even a poor relation to be seen about the house in rags."

"Papa wishes me to have a Season, ma'am, and I believe my uncle concurs."

"A Season! This is aiming high indeed. You are shockingly brown, Miss Danville, and I daresay it is your natural complexion, so that crushed strawberries cannot be expected to help. You are past your first youth, and I have not heard that you possess a portion worth mentioning. Besides, you were brought up in the jungle, I collect, and cannot possibly know how to go on in English Society. As the Duchess of Stafford I have high standards to uphold.

Your inevitable failure would be utterly mortifying."

"I do not expect to be presented as a debutante, ma'am. I do not expect to be acclaimed as an Incomparable, nor to make a brilliant match. I am twenty-three years old and have no dowry, unless there is something left in Papa's bank account when Marco's and my expenses have been paid. But I have had lessons in correct behaviour from Lady Parr and I am very willing to accept any further instruction you think necessary. Don Eduardo—Lord Edward— says I am to have a Season. I am accustomed to obeying my father, ma'am."

"Hmm, I am glad to hear it, miss. And who is Lady Parr? The name is unknown to me."

"She is the widow of a baronet, who travelled with us from Jamaica."

"A baronet's relict. Shabby genteel, I make no doubt. I daresay I shall have to correct the half of what you have learned, for I've no desire to foist yet another simpering miss upon the ton."

Teresa smiled, her dark eyes lighting. "Then you will sponsor me, ma'am?"

"Well, I do believe you are quite passably pretty when you smile. And at least this Parr woman has not succeeded in crushing your spirit. You may call me aunt. Howell, send for Miss Carter. This promises to be quite exhausting." Her Grace leaned back against her pillows and closed her eyes.

Teresa was about to tiptoe from the room, but Howell put her finger to her lips and indicated a chair, so she sat down. The abigail hurried out.

Teresa studied her newly acknowledged aunt. The duchess did not look in the least as if she suffered from nervous debility. Her round face with its rosy cheeks was the picture of health. Recalling Lord John's words, she decided that Her Grace, being of unimposing stature, used the threat of imminent collapse as a weapon to uphold her dignity. Her family had learned to ignore it, but that it intimidated strangers she herself could readily attest.

Howell returned. The duchess sat up with renewed vigour, swung her legs—limbs, Teresa reminded herself— out of bed, and headed for the dressing room.

"I shall dress," she announced. "The Little Season is beginning and we shall have a great deal to do to make Miss Danville—Teresa, is it not?—presentable. Is Stafford still in the house? Send to ask him if he will be so good as to spare me a moment. And while you are about it, send for the *modiste*, that Frenchwoman who is all the crack, I forget her name, and for Monsieur Henri. He went back to France? We shall have to make do with his assistant then, that nasty little man from Birmingham. That hair must come off, and he knows his business in spite of that dreadful accent. Let me see your teeth, girl. They are quite as important in a female as in a horse. Excellent, and though you are tall, your figure is acceptable. Now walk about, pray, while I dress so that I may see how you move."

Teresa walked with carefully mincing steps towards the window, a false smile pinned to her lips in the hope that it was making her look "passably pretty." For a nostalgic moment she wished she was back on board the *Destiny*, parading before Lady Parr, Muriel, and Andrew. Her aunt's voice brought her abruptly back to the present.

"As I feared, shabby genteel. My dear, you look as if you were hobbled like a horse. Let me see how you move naturally, if you please."

Teresa strode towards her and nearly fell flat on her face as the narrow skirt tangled round her ankles.

"I *am* hobbled, Aunt," she said, laughing.

"Far too mannish." The duchess gazed at her speculatively. "But that laugh is superb. I'll tell you what, Teresa, if you stick with gentlemen who consider themselves amusing, you may yet do me credit. Now walk again, something between the fop and the Corinthian, if you please."

Teresa set off for the window again. No disparaging comments halting her, she reached it and looked out. On the other side of a wide, paved street, she saw lawns and trees.

"Oh, you are quite in the country!" she exclaimed. "I had thought Stafford House to be in the middle of London."

"That is Hyde Park. The fashionable world drives or rides or walks there to see and be seen."

"How delightful! I quite long to go."

"You will not leave this house until you have decent clothes on your back. Now walk this way. You are improving already, I am glad to see."

At that moment the door opened and Miss Carter came in. An impoverished cousin who acted as the duchess's companion, she looked amazingly like her patroness—small and round with a pink face. She was placid and agreeable. Teresa thought Her Grace might share her temperament as well as her looks if it were not for the necessity of preserving her rank.

"You wanted to see me, Aurelia?" enquired Miss Carter, looking rather like an inquisitive sparrow in her brown silk gown.

"Yes, Amelia. This is Stafford's niece, Teresa Danville. I am to bring her out and we shall need your invaluable assistance."

Teresa curtseyed, a nicely calculated bob suitable for an older female of unquestioned gentility but no status.

Then she wondered whether Lady Parr's carefully graded curtseys were as shabby genteel as some of her other notions were turning out to be. It was a relief not to have to walk as if her ankles were tied together, and a still greater relief not to have to avoid laughing. However, she decided it would be best to comply with her ladyship's advice until her aunt told her otherwise. It was bound to be more appropriate than her natural, unaffected manners.

Before the duchess could reveal Miss Carter's role in the transformation, there was another knock and the duke put his head round the door.

"Come in, Stafford, do," invited his wife. "I gather you

intend Teresa to have a Season, and I must know what you mean to do for her."

"Buy the gal whatever she needs, Aurelia. You will know best."

"My father said I am to use whatever money is in his account, sir," Teresa objected firmly. "He expected it to be enough for both Marco and me."

"Fustian, missy! If a man cannot buy a few dresses for a pretty niece, what can he spend his blunt on? Use Edward's account for your pin money, by all means. I'm off to White's, Aurelia. I look to see Edward's girl dressed to the nines, mind."

The "nasty little man from Birmingham" arrived shortly thereafter, delighted to be called to the ducal mansion. He was actually tall and lanky, and when he told Teresa that her hair was beautiful, she could not think him nasty. He did have the most peculiar accent, a combination of Midlands English with a patina of French acquired from his mentor, Monsieur Henri, who had returned to his native land after Waterloo.

Teresa took a seat before Her Grace's dressing table and the *coiffeur* unpinned her hair, which Annie had braided and wound into a knot on top of her head. His nimble fingers unplaited it and brushed the dusky cloud.

"Merveller," he said in his approximation of French, "and it'll take a curl, I'll be bound, once it's cut. Not too much off, though. Miss is tall enough to carry off long ringlets as 'ud look silly on a shorter female. Just enough so's it's easy to put up and don't overweigh the face. Miss's visage is tray delicah."

"Speak English, man!" snapped the duchess.

"Delicate features, Your Grace. Don't want to hide 'em under a bushel, do we?"

He started snipping away.

Teresa sat with her eyes shut. Her head grew lighter and lighter as the scissors clicked on. He had said he would not take off too much, she told herself.

"Vwahlah," said the hairdresser at last. "I mean, there we are. Now let's see what we can do with it."

Teresa opened her eyes and was relieved to see that there was still plenty left.

"Should not my abigail be here?" she asked. "She will need to know how to dress it."

"Howell, send for Miss Teresa's abigail," the duchess ordered.

A few minutes later Annie trotted in. Howell had seen her in the servants' hall and told the duchess, but Miss Carter was taken by surprise.

"Ooh," she squealed, "an African!"

"Do try not to be such a ninnyhammer, Amelia," scolded her cousin. "Remember Teresa comes from the Americas, where everyone has black servants."

Teresa did not think it was the moment to explain that there were practically no blacks in Costa Rica and that she had rescued Annie from a sinking slave ship. She had a lowering feeling that the duchess would not approve of that particular exploit. The fewer people who learned of it the better.

By the time the man from Birmingham had demonstrated several possible styles, her head was aching and she almost wished he *had* cut all her hair off. He departed, promising to return in person to dress it before her first ball. She was too exhausted to feel the slightest spark of enthusiasm at the prospect of that great event.

Miss Carter took one look at her drawn face and said, "Aurelia, Miss Teresa needs a cup of tea. I do believe she has the headache, poor child."

"A little," acknowledged Teresa, "but I shall do very well if I lie down for half an hour."

"Howell, tea in my sitting room and something to eat. Something light, for the dressmaker will be here shortly."

Teresa groaned inwardly at the thought of spending the afternoon being measured and draped and pinned. However, lying for a few minutes on the sofa in the duchess's sitting room restored her usual energy. After consuming several cups of tea and a couple of Jacques's divine chicken *vol-au-vent*, she was eager to discover the duchess's views on suitable apparel for a young lady.

Madame Roquier, who had no intention of going back to France while business in London was so good, arrived with an assistant bearing pattern books. They were followed by three of the duke's footmen loaded with bolts of cloth.

She took one look at Teresa and began picking out all the rolls of white and pastel fabrics. "Zese you may take back down to *mon équipage*," she said, to Teresa's astonishment. Those were just the colours that, according to Lady Parr, should be worn by an unmarried girl.

The *modiste* turned to the duchess and explained, "Your Grace, I know nozzing of zis young lady I am to dress, so I bring everysing. White she cannot wear. It makes to look sallow zis golden skin. Ze pale colours—pah! Miss must wear ze jewel tones, vibrant, alive. *Regardez-moi ça.*"

She seized a length of amethyst silk and draped it around Teresa's shoulders.

There was a murmur of approval.

"I cannot see," wailed Teresa.

"Put those down," the duchess directed the two footmen who still stood holding the rest of the fabrics, "and fetch the cheval glass from the dressing room."

Teresa looked at her reflection and gasped. Her face was no longer shockingly brown, but warm amber. The rich sheen of the silk made her complexion glow, and her dark eyes shone with excitement.

She turned to her aunt and smiled.

"*Not* merely pretty," said the duchess. "Not an Incomparable, perhaps, but do you know, my dear Teresa, I'd wager we shall do very well!"

$$=== 7 ===$$

MADAME ROQUIER DID not mean to risk losing such a lucrative and influential customer as the Duchess of Stafford. Early the very next afternoon her young assistant delivered two gowns. Annie took her up to Miss Danville's dressing room so that she could make any necessary adjustments.

"*Buenos días,*" said Gayo. The girl screeched and dropped the pile of boxes. "What a pity," he said sadly.

From one of the boxes spilled a promenade dress of bronze *gros de Naples*, with a cashemire shawl patterned in bronze and cream and a huge muff of cream-coloured fur.

Teresa admired it briefly, but she was captivated by the walking dress. It was sapphire blue, a figured silk patterned with tiny rosettes of darker blue. The neckline was trimmed with cream Brussels lace; otherwise the bodice was very plain. The skirt fell straight from the high waist, ornamented just above the hem by a wide band of the same lace, which also finished the long sleeves.

Teresa hurried out of Muriel's old morning gown, for the last time, she hoped. Madame Roquier's assistant helped her don the new walking dress, then stood back and clasped her hands.

"Well I never," she marvelled.

"Oh, Miss Teresa, you look quite beautiful," cried Annie. "I see now that Miss Muriel's gowns were all wrong for you." She darted forward and rearranged the long, glossy ringlets that caressed Teresa's shoulders. "Now look at yourself in the mirrors."

Teresa stared. Why, she looked positively elegant. The simple bodice, high waist, and long straight lines of the skirt displayed her slender figure to advantage. The rich colour flattered her complexion, and the new hairstyle added the finishing touch.

Surely if Andrew saw her now, he would find something better to say than that she looked "every inch a lady"!

As the dressmaker unwrapped a dark blue pelerine the duchess bustled in, with Miss Carter in tow. Teresa turned before her, hope and anxiety warring in her breast.

"You look very well, child. Now that you are decently clad, Amelia shall take you shopping."

"That will be delightful, Aunt. I do thank you, Miss Carter. Only there are one or two people I ought to call on first."

"Nonsense. Before you pay any calls you must have gloves and stockings and slippers and boots, and reticules and handkerchiefs and, oh, a hundred other odds and ends. Not to mention hats and bonnets."

Teresa would gladly have foregone such fripperies. All she wanted was to see Andrew's expression when she appeared in her new finery. But doubtless he would agree that the finery was incomplete without gloves and a bonnet.

She sighed.

"Very well, Aunt. I have not yet tried on the promenade dress. If it fits as well as this, I shall wear it, if Miss Carter will not mind waiting a few minutes."

Miss Carter, beaming, pronounced herself perfectly satisfied. It was half an hour later that the two ladies, accompanied by Annie, set out for the milliner's in the duchess's barouche. Green with red trim to match the servants' liveries, this smart vehicle displayed the Stafford crest on the door panels, which ensured due deference wherever they went.

Every day for a week, boxes arrived from Madame Roquier's workshops, until both Teresa's wardrobes were full. Every day Miss Carter took her shopping, until not another embroidered handkerchief could be stuffed into the chest of drawers and Annie begged her not to buy any more hats.

Every day, the duchess took her visiting. She met her uncle Cecil, a very large and finicky bachelor who was one of the Lords of the Admiralty. She met a variety of second and third cousins, and more distant connexions. Bearing Lady Parr's instructions in mind, she managed to behave with perfect propriety, though her aunt now and then chided her for being missish. She learned to strike a balance between the shabby genteel and her own natural outspokenness.

Her Grace declared her ready to meet some of those hostesses upon whose invitations her social success must depend.

That evening, the duke and duchess were dining out. Lord John, for the first time all week, was not. He had not seen his cousin since the fashionmongers of London had transformed her. His eyes widened as she entered the drawing room wearing an evening gown of emerald satin.

"Cousin Teresa?" he said, incredulous. He advanced across the room and lifted her hand to his lips. "My compliments, cousin. You are ravishing."

She blushed a little, smiling. She had learned a great deal from Miss Carter, and now, studying his dress, she recognised his style as Corinthian. His dark blue coat and fawn pantaloons fitted superbly over his muscular form, but not so tightly that those muscles were unusable. His waistcoat was of blue and gold brocade, his shirt points of moderate height, his cravat neat yet not so elaborate that it must have taken hours to tie. He looked like a gentleman fond of sport, and she was ready to wager he spent a good many afternoons at fisticuffs in Gentleman Jackson's Saloon or shooting at Manton's Gallery.

She had to admit that he was handsomer than Andrew. On the other hand, his way of life was much less to be admired. Miss Carter had whispered that many Corinthians, after those unexceptionable afternoons, indulged in other sports less acceptable, such as boxing the watch and consorting with fallen females.

Dismissing Andrew from her mind, Teresa concentrated with sparkling eyes on John's extravagant compliments.

Marco came into the room.

"Teresa, I must talk to you," he said urgently. "You are always out, or at least I can never find you alone."

"Speak, halfling," said John. "I shall take myself into a far corner and close my ears."

"Oh, I don't mind you hearing . . . though maybe Teresa would. It is all these curst females I want to avoid, and perhaps it is best if my uncle does not know."

"What is it, Marco?" asked his sister, concerned. "Are you not happy with your tutor? Give the poor man a chance. You have had him only three days."

"No, no, I like Mr. Netherdale very well. It's something I read in the newspaper. Oh, bother!"

This last exclamation was riven from him by the arrival of Miss Carter, closely followed by Boggs with the announcement that dinner was served.

Teresa was on tenterhooks throughout the meal. She scarcely noticed what she ate, failing to do justice to Chef Jacques's always superb dishes. She could not imagine what her brother might have read in the paper that was so important, and that her aunt and uncle were not to know.

In spite of her preoccupation, she conversed politely with Miss Carter and exchanged witty repartee with Cousin John. He asked after Gayo, to whom he had taken a great liking, and promised to visit the parrot soon.

He was only a year or two older than Teresa, and she found him easy to talk to, charming even, though she doubted his sense of propriety. It was unlikely that a gentleman ought to tell a young, unmarried lady, even his cousin, that the children of Jane Harley, Countess of Oxford, were known as the Harleian Miscellany because of their variety of fathers.

It rather spoiled the story that she had never heard of the Harleian Manuscripts. Lord John explained with his usual affability that these were a valuable collection made by an earlier earl, later bought by the government for the British Museum. Since this was the only part of the conversation overheard by Miss Carter, she concluded that their discussion was decorous, if excessively learned.

"Will you ride with me in the park tomorrow, Teresa?" John asked some time later. "I should like to show off my beautiful cousin to my friends."

"I have no riding habit," said Teresa, her voice filled with disappointment and longing. It seemed for ever since she had ridden, whereas at home she spent as much time on horseback as off it.

"You do ride, don't you? Order a habit and we shall go when it arrives."

"Uncle Stafford has already bought me so many clothes. I cannot ask for more. And Annie will be quite overset if she has to find room in the wardrobe."

He laughed. "I shall ask for you. I daresay m'mother never thought to suggest it, for she does not ride. And we'll find you a mount in the stables, never fear. Half of them just stand around eating their heads off. One for you, too, sprout," he added to Marco, noting his hopeful face.

At last dinner ended. Teresa and Miss Carter retired to the drawing room, whither both gentlemen soon followed them. Marco had not yet developed a taste for port, and John preferred carousing with his bosom bows to drinking sedately in his parents' dining room.

In no time Miss Carter, as was her custom, was nodding off in her chair by the fire.

"*What* did you read in the newspaper?" demanded Teresa. "No, wait a minute. Whisper, so that I can tell if I want our cousin to know."

"It was about Harrison, the captain of the *Snipe*," whispered Marco.

"Harrison! I am glad you did not blurt it out before the

duke and duchess, for I do not in the least want them to learn that story. I daresay it will not hurt for Cousin John to know, if he promises not to breathe a word to a soul."

"Cross my heart and hope to die," said John, "or if you prefer it, upon my word as a gentleman. I am like to die of curiosity."

"It was in the *Times*. He has been arraigned, and a date set for the trial."

"Whoa! You go too fast, young Marco. Who is Harrison and what is our interest in his misdeeds?"

Teresa and Marco told the tale of the hunting of the *Snipe*, how the slavers had scuttled her with all the slaves aboard, and how they had been saved. Teresa was inclined to belittle her part in the affair, but her brother insisted on the rescue having been her idea in the first place.

"And though only Andrew went below, you and I both helped him open the hatches and we persuaded them to jump, and you were the one who nursed them back to health, Teresa."

"The devil you were!"

"Sir Andrew could not have rescued them without our assistance," Marco pointed out again.

"Who is this Sir Andrew you keep mentioning?"

Teresa felt her cheeks redden and was furious with herself. "You met him," she reminded, "when we arrived here."

"Oh, that fellow," said his lordship dismissively. "So what is it has you in the boughs, halfling? Not just the notice of Harrison's trial, I'll wager."

It was Marco's turn to redden. "I daresay it is nothing of importance. The paper said he accused a gentleman of high rank of financing his voyage."

"They did not mention his name?" asked Teresa

"Hah, afraid of a suit for libel," explained John. "Anything else?"

"He uttered fearsome threats against those who incriminated him."

"Well, I do not like it, but we did hear him before, remember."

"I do wish you will stop interrupting, Teresa. I thought you ought to know that the *Destiny* has already sailed again with all her crew, so the prosecutor will be calling the passengers as witnesses."

"Heavens above!" Teresa paled. "The whole story will be published to the world. I dare not think what the duchess will say."

"Half the world will call you a heroine," said Lord John, frowning. "Unfortunately, the half that matters to Mama is more like to damn you for your lack of decorum."

"I'll tell you what I think," offered Marco. "You ought to go and consult Andrew. He will know what's best to do."

Teresa was so pleased with this advice that she flung her arms round her brother and kissed his cheek, much to his embarrassment.

Later, snuggling into the cosy warmth of her feather bed, she was overcome with guilt. It was ten days since her arrival in London and she had called on neither Lady Parr and Muriel nor Andrew. To all of them she owed her gratitude, and to the latter money as well. She hoped they did not think her so puffed up with pride in her aristocratic relations that she considered them beneath her touch.

The next day Teresa begged the duchess to postpone briefly their visits to the hostesses of the ton. Her Grace was not best pleased to hear that her niece intended to call upon Lady Parr, that shabby-genteel relict of a mere baronet. However, Teresa managed to persuade her that it would be the height of incivility to fail to acknowledge the lady who had chaperoned her across the Atlantic Ocean.

"Very well." Her aunt sighed. "But you must not expect me to go with you, and pray do not invite them to Stafford House. Stafford abhors mushrooms."

Teresa was too pleased that the duchess was not to go with her to wonder what her uncle's taste in vegetables had to do with the matter. Somehow she had not mentioned that she intended also to call on Sir Andrew Graylin. If Her

Grace disapproved of Lady Parr, a young diplomat, who worked for his living, might well be considered quite beyond the pale.

She knew better than to go alone. She and Annie set out at eleven in the morning, the proper hour for paying visits, in the landaulet the duke had put at her disposal.

Teresa had dressed with unusual care. She desired neither to offend Lady Parr, however shabby genteel, nor to outshine Muriel. On the other hand, she wanted to stun Andrew.

She wore an amethyst walking dress, cut with the exquisite simplicity that was the hallmark of London's premiere *modiste*. Her kid gloves and half-boots were of the same shade, her pelisse of darker violet cloth, and her bonnet trimmed with a jaunty bunch of violets. She felt every inch a lady of fashion as the carriage rattled down Park Lane.

If Andrew merely told her again that she looked every inch a lady, she would take a leaf from her aunt's book and succumb to the vapours, she vowed. Then she was ashamed of herself for the thought. He was affianced to Muriel, her friend, and though Teresa hoped he was her friend, too, she had no business caring what he thought of her appearance.

The groom drew up the horses outside the Parrs' house in Hill Street. Teresa told him she would send a message if she decided to stay more than half an hour, and she and Annie trod up the steps. The brass knocker summoned an elderly butler, who said he would see if her ladyship was at home and then creaked away up the stairs.

Teresa gazed curiously around the entrance hall. She remembered her brief glimpse of it from the carriage on her arrival in London. It had impressed her as palatial then. Now, accustomed as she'd become to the magnificence of Stafford House, she found it unremarkable. The duchess's comment about mushrooms returned to her, and she recalled what Miss Carter had said on the subject. Miss Carter's information was imparted in an endless stream of gentle chatter that seemed to flow in one ear and out the other; but much of it stuck all the same, to reappear unexpectedly at the moment it was needed.

"Mushrooms," she had explained, "pop up overnight in fields, though there was no sign of them the day before. In Society, a mushroom, though without known family background, pops up among people of the highest rank."

At the thought of Lady Parr's shocked expression if she found out that the duchess considered her a mushroom, Teresa laughed aloud.

Then, she saw Andrew running down the stairs to greet her. A smile crossed his face when he heard her laugh. A look of astonishment followed as he caught sight of a modish young lady he scarcely recognised.

"Teresa! Miss Danville!" Words failed him.

She read wonder in his face and was satisfied. She held out both hands to him. He took them and pressed a kiss on each, warm enough to be felt through the thin kid, then he flushed and released her.

"Andrew, what a happy chance to meet you here." Her own colour was heightened but she smiled with careful composure, imagining how his kiss would feel on her cheek, on her lips. "I was going to call on you next."

"Then thank heaven I am here." He blanched at this candid avowal. "Under no circumstances does a young lady visit a gentleman's lodging."

"I have brought Annie. I know better than to go about alone."

"In this case a maid is insufficient," he said sternly. "No escort less than the duke or duchess could make such a visit respectable. You must promise me that you will never call on me."

Teresa was flushed with annoyance now. Nearly two weeks without seeing him, an altogether gratifying greeting, and here they were already come to cuffs.

"I beg your pardon." His smile was rueful. "We agreed long since that I had no right to guide your conduct, and now you are under the duke's protection I am sure I have no need."

"I did not tell anyone I meant to visit you," she confessed, disarmed. "I had a notion it might be frowned on, though I did not guess it was unforgivable."

"Nothing you do could be unforgivable, Teresa. I am amazed at how quickly you are learning the rules of Society, but they are many and your mentors cannot be expected to foresee every eventuality. For your own sake, I hope you will consult the duchess when in doubt. I should not care to see you in the briars."

"How can I resist such an appeal? I shall not call on you, I promise, unless I can persuade my uncle to bring me. I suppose my cousin John would not be an eligible escort in such a situation?"

He frowned. "No," he said abruptly. "Shall we go up? Muriel and Lady Parr will be wondering what has become of you, for it is some minutes since you were announced."

As they went up, Teresa asked him how much she and Marco owed him. "A round sum," she added. "I do not expect a detailed account."

"I can stand the nonsense," he growled. "I am sure you have better things to spend the ready on." He glanced at the stylish violet pelisse.

"Uncle Stafford has been more than generous. I have had no expenses so far. I am certain that Papa did not expect that you should frank us, sir, and I do not care to be beholden. Pray tell me the amount."

He muttered a figure.

"I shall bring it to your lodging as soon as I have seen Don Eduardo's banker."

"Teresa!" He caught the twinkle in her eye. "Oh, you are roasting me. Dashed if I hadn't forgot what a tease you are. I have missed it, I vow." He ushered her into a small saloon decorated in the Egyptian style. "Ma'am, Muriel, here is Miss Danville."

With a soft cry of pleasure, Muriel rose from an uncomfortable-looking chair with lions' feet and started towards Teresa, her languid movements belied by her expression of eager welcome. Then she took in the apparition of fashionable splendour and her gliding steps faltered.

"Oh Muriel, you cannot be shy of me." Teresa hugged her and kissed her cheek. "Fine feathers do not make fine birds, you know." Despite her new elegance, she found she still envied her friend's blond prettiness. After all, that was what Andrew admired.

Muriel was wearing a new morning gown of pink mull muslin. Teresa knew now that it would not have suited her in the least, yet it became Muriel's dainty fairness very well. If perhaps some of Lady Parr's notions were shabby genteel, her daughter was perfectly presentable. Teresa resolved not to give up the acquaintance only because her aunt was excessively high in the instep.

She turned to Lady Parr, who was inspecting her through her quizzing glass, and curtseyed a trifle lower than her ladyship's own rules provided for a baronet's widow.

"I hope I see you well, ma'am?"

My lady was amazingly subdued by her ex-protégée's blossoming into a lady of fashion. In the conversation that followed, she only once quoted the late Sir Archibald's opinion and that in a complimentary manner. When Teresa begged her to allow Muriel to drive with her in the park, she agreed with every evidence of delight. At once she rang for a maid to fetch her daughter's spencer.

Teresa suddenly recollected that she had to consult Andrew about the trial of the slaver captain. She did not want to alarm the ladies should they not have heard the news, though as they had stayed below during the entire incident, they were not likely to be called as witnesses.

"There is something I must discuss with you privately," she told him in a low, worried voice. "Will you come to Stafford House, as soon as may be?"

Puzzled but intrigued, he assented.

"Tomorrow afternoon at three?" he asked.

"Thank you, that will do very well."

No sooner were the words uttered than she recalled the

duchess's adamant rejection of mushrooms. Her aunt had told her not to invite the Parrs, but she had not specifically named Andrew. Of course she had not known that her niece meant to call on him.

She looked at him, trying to judge whether he looked like a mushroom. He, too, had purchased new clothes since returning to England. Though his brown coat and knit pantaloons had none of the flair of Lord John's apparel, he was dressed with the utmost propriety. In her opinion, the riding clothes he had worn when they first met suited him better. However, she could see nothing in his present appearance which might give the duchess a disgust of him.

His father was a viscount, she remembered. Surely the invitation would not land her in a scrape.

= 8 =

ANDREW WAS IN a quandary. The Foreign Secretary wanted
to see him at half past three, and he was promised to Teresa
for three o'clock.

According to his immediate superior, the great man
wanted to thank him for the sterling service he had done
in Central America. It was not the sort of meeting an
ambitious young man could afford to miss. Had his conflicting appointment been with any other person of his acquaintance, he would simply have sent a note postponing
it. But this was Teresa. And what was more, she had
sounded worried. The idea of Teresa worrying caused an
inexplicable sinking feeling in his middle.

He had been overwhelmed by her appearance at their last
meeting. Not only was she stunningly lovely in that fashionable gown, so much better suited to her dark beauty
than Muriel's pastels. More important, all the life and fire
Lady Parr had tried so hard to subdue had been restored by
her new mentor. Teresa was no longer a poor copy of
Muriel. Teresa was a vision from his dreams.

And she needed him.

He decided to present himself at Stafford House at ten in
the morning. It was an unconscionable hour to pay a visit,
but she was therefore unlikely to have already gone out.

He dressed with his usual plain neatness, then, just as
Rowson was about to help him don his dark brown cutaway
coat, he was overcome with dissatisfaction. Before his eyes
rose a vision of Lord John's careless elegance.

"Wait," he said. "I believe I shall try something more elaborate with my neckcloth. Do you know how to tie a Waterfall?"

"Nay, sir," said Rowson, shaking his head mournfully. "I've tended ye through desert and jungle without ever learning to tie a fancy knot. If that's what you want, 'tis a proper gentleman's gentleman you'll need."

Andrew frowned at the offending cravat. He had been quite happy with the same simple style for years. Now it seemed inadequate.

"Let me try. Is there another cloth ready?"

He struggled for several minutes. First the knot was off centre, then the creases were all crooked, then it was so tight he could not breathe.

"The devil with it!" he said at last, ripping it off and retying a fresh one the usual way. "It will have to do. Is this the best waistcoat I possess?" He regarded the amber satin with distaste.

" 'Tis your favourite, sir," said Rowson, his voice reproachful.

"I shall buy some more waistcoats." Andrew put on his coat, took up his gloves and top hat, and turned before the mirror, peering at himself. "Damned if I haven't done this before," he muttered. "Posing like a man-milliner." Then he remembered that last time he had been naked, and he grinned. "Find me a hackney, Rowson, I'm running late."

At this early hour there were more pedestrians in the streets than carriages. However, the hackney was pulled by an aged and infirm nag and moved at scarcely more than a walking pace. Andrew had all too much time to think. He was overcome by a wave of guilt.

It was all very well to decide to refurbish his staid image, but he ought to be doing it for Muriel, not for Teresa.

What a beauty she had turned out to be with a little town bronze to give her polish. She was not at all his style, of course. He had always admired blondes with fair complexions, and had won the hand of the prettiest of them all. And

Teresa was far too lively for comfort. A man wanted a quiet, conformable wife who would make him a peaceful home and not contradict him at every turn.

He could not deny that his heart beat faster at the thought of seeing Teresa again. It was worry, of course, at what sort of bumblebath she had fallen into this time. For all her new town bronze she was not yet up to snuff, and he had an obligation to Lord Edward to keep an eye on her.

His guilt rationalised away, he reached Stafford House at half past ten and bounded up the steps. Boggs, being an excellent butler, recognised him and admitted him without delay.

"Miss Danville?"

"Miss Danville is not at home, sir."

"She asked me to call on a matter of business. If you tell her I am come, I expect she will see me."

"I beg your pardon, sir, but I did not intend to convey that Miss Danville is not receiving. She is gone out. If you would care to see young Mr. Marco, sir, I believe he is yet at breakfast."

"Yes, I had best see Marco." Andrew frowned. "Perhaps he knows what this is all about. Tell him I am here, if you please."

Boggs returned a moment later. "His Grace requests the pleasure of your company in the breakfast room, sir. Mr. Marco is with him."

Ushered into a room redolent of grilled ham, kippers, and toasted muffins, Andrew made his bow to the duke. He nodded to Marco, who looked anxious, and a gentleman of about his own age whom he vaguely recognised.

His Grace of Stafford stood up and shook his hand, then waved him to a seat.

"Coffee," he offered, "or something more substantial? So you are the young man who brought my niece and my nephew. My thanks to you, sir. A most welcome addition to my family, and of course I was more than happy to have news of my brother after all these years. You know my son, Danville?"

"How do you do, Graylin," said Viscount Danville, a solidly built gentleman as good-looking as his younger brother but for his haughty expression. "We have met, I believe."

"Yes, my lord, some years since." After a few minutes of conversation, the duke affable, his heir stiff, Andrew said, "If you will excuse us, Your Grace, I should like a few words in private with Marco."

Marco breathed a sigh of relief, bowed to his uncle and cousin, and led his visitor to the library.

"This is where I have my lessons," he explained as they sat down. "No one else uses it at this hour, and Mr. Netherdale does not arrive until eleven. Have you come about the trial? Teresa said she had no chance to consult you yesterday, but I thought you were coming this afternoon."

"The trial?"

"Did you not read about it? The *Times* reported that the *Destiny*'s passengers are to be called as witnesses in the trial of the crew of the *Snipe*. You know my sister, she is pluck to the backbone, but the thought of all London knowing of her exploit has her in a quake."

"Do the duke and duchess know?"

"No, only Cousin John. He thinks it is a famous adventure and calls her a heroine, but even he says it will ruin her if it becomes generally known. He is up to every rig and row in town, you know, and Teresa was quite distressed when he said that."

"I daresay it will not do to tell the duchess, but it may be necessary to confide in the duke. He has the influence to quash a subpoena, and he is fond of you both already, judging by his manner just now. I doubt he will turn you out into the street. Where is Teresa, by the way? I thought I was early enough to catch her."

"She went to see Don Eduardo's banker. She is always too busy later in the day. We both need a spot of the ready in our pockets, besides what we owe you."

"She went to the City? Alone?"

"Of course not, she took Annie. She is not stupid, you know."

Andrew groaned. "No, but she is green. Ladies of quality do not go to the City without a male escort. Indeed, it is not *comme il faut* for a young lady to visit a man of business at all."

"Then I had best go after her at once to lend her countenance. Pray excuse me, sir, I must leave a message for my tutor. Thank you for warning me. I shall pass on your advice to my sister regarding Harrison's trial."

"I shall go with you. My intention is to help, not to criticise, but I cannot help wondering what will be her next start."

By the time they set out, the streets were bustling with traffic. The barouches, phaetons, and chaises of Mayfair gave way to the stagecoaches and carters' wagons of less exalted quarters. Their hackney threaded its way through the narrow streets and alleys of the City, past St. Paul's, and turned into Lombard Street. Fortunately Marco remembered the name of the bank. The carriage drew up before it and they climbed out.

"It's a good thing you did come with me," admitted Marco as Andrew paid the driver. "I haven't even sixpence for the hackney. You can see how necessary it was for Teresa to come here."

"Teresa said that your uncle franks you. I am surprised that he has not offered you an allowance."

"Teresa would not accept it," said the youth proudly as they were ushered into the bank. "Uncle Stafford insists on paying all our expenses but she says our pin money must come from Papa's account." He turned to a bowing, black-clad clerk. "We are looking for my sister, Miss Danville. Do you know whether she is still here?"

The clerk led them through a counting house full of more black-clad clerks, bent over huge ledgers, and up some stairs to a small office at the back. As he opened the door they saw a plump, middle-aged man sitting behind a desk, his face wreathed in smiles, then Annie, in the corner, and Teresa, with her back to them.

"Sir Andrew Graylin and Mr. Danville, sir," announced the clerk.

Teresa jumped up, ran to Marco, then flung her arms around him. "We're rich!" she crowed.

Andrew watched with amusement as Marco disentangled himself from his sister's embrace. In this place, in her sapphire outfit, she looked like a peacock among crows. She turned her laughing eyes to him and curtseyed, half mocking.

"I beg your pardon, sir, but it is monstrous exciting when you think you are a poor relation to discover suddenly that you are rich. Papa thought there would be enough for Marco's education and my come-out. It seems his little pittance has multiplied with such vigour that we have enough for that even if the money is divided equally with all my brothers."

"Which I cannot advise," put in the banker. "To split up such a fortune among so many is almost as bad as simply squandering it."

"I must consult Don Eduardo, of course. But even if he agrees with me that it must be shared, I shall have a proper dowry."

"You are already considering marriage?" asked Andrew, scowling. His thoughts flew to Lord John, then he wondered whether Lord Danville, heir to the dukedom, might be a greater attraction.

Teresa laughed. "Is not marriage the first business of young ladies?" she teased, though there was an edge to her voice. "No, not yet. However, I expect to meet a great many charming young men shortly, for my aunt is planning a party to introduce me to the ton. But we are wasting your time, sir." She turned back to the banker. "For the present, I should like one hundred pounds each for myself and for my brother, in notes and coins, and the draft you prepared is for this gentleman. You will notify me when you have arranged the meeting?"

"Certainly, Miss Danville." The stout banker rang a bell, then bowed and shook her hand. "It has been a pleasure doing business with you, ma'am, though I must hope that you will reconsider splitting such an admirable fortune. Sirs, your servant."

The clerk arrived to show them out.

"Just how rich are we?" demanded Marco as they went down the stairs. He whistled as she named the figure. "Each? I shall be able to devote my life to my studies, and with that for a marriage portion, you can look to the highest in the land for a husband."

Andrew objected strongly to all this talk of marriage. He could not voice his objection as he had no justification for such an attitude, so he said severely, "We came after you, Teresa, to provide a respectable escort. Ladies do not visit the City unaccompanied by a gentleman."

Teresa sighed heavily as he helped her into the landaulet. "I made sure it was all right. I mentioned to my uncle last night that I must see Papa's banker and he raised no objection, I assure you."

"Nonetheless, it is so. Perhaps he expected you to summon the man to Stafford House, which is what he would do. But in fact, young ladies are supposed to be entirely ignorant of business."

"You know very well that Don Eduardo entrusted me with his business. Indeed, I have arranged to meet with a number of coffee brokers to discuss a contract. I suppose Marco will have to go with me."

"It cannot be necessary for you to meet them in person."

"I intend to. I must prepare the coffee for them to sample so that I know it is properly done."

"Marco is too young to be an adequate escort." Andrew ignored Marco's insulted snort. "If you insist on doing this, then I shall go with you."

"That will be delightful." Teresa beamed. "I could ask Cousin John if it is inconvenient for you, though."

"Certainly not! I mean, Lord John knows nothing of Costa Rican coffee, whereas I may perhaps be of assistance."

"It is most kind of you, Sir Andrew. Now tell me, has Marco explained about the trial?"

As the groom drove them back through the crowded streets, Andrew tried to persuade her that her only recourse was to confess all to the duke. Though reluctant, she was at last convinced.

"I daresay he will be proud of you," Andrew reassured her when they dropped him off in Whitehall, convenient to the Foreign Office. "I am, you know."

She flushed with pleasure. "And Cousin John said some would think me a heroine," she said hopefully.

Damn Cousin John, thought Andrew as he waved farewell.

When Teresa reached Stafford House, she found that her new riding habit had been delivered. Since she had ordered it so as to be able to ride with Lord John, she went to look for her younger cousin.

Boggs directed her to the back of the house, where he was playing billiards with his brother. He declared himself happy to squire her to Hyde Park at the hour of the fashionable promenade. To her surprise Lord Danville requested permission to join them, and even begged her to call him Cousin Tom.

The duke's heir had been in the country, supervising some business at one of the family estates. He had only returned to London the previous night, so she was not well acquainted with him. She remembered John describing him as starchy, and his manner was certainly stiff compared with both brother and father. Yet he had not looked askance at the unexpected presence of herself and Marco. He had greeted them with kindly aloofness, and she was prepared to like him, if given a chance to know him better.

After changing into the habit, she met John on the

landing. She had never worn a dress with a train before and it felt strange to have all that extra fabric dragging behind her. She was about to start down the stairs when he put his hand on her arm and held her back. She looked up at him enquiringly.

"You must drape the train over your arm," he explained, "or you will go down headfirst. You claimed to be an accomplished horsewoman, cousin."

"So I am," she assured him. "Only I have never had a proper habit before."

He grinned down at her. "I should have liked to see you ride without a train to cover your . . . limbs," he said with regret. "Ah, Tom, there you are. Let us be on our way."

"Ought I to take my maid with me?" asked Teresa uncertainly as they descended. "She does not ride. Oh no, I expect a groom should accompany me."

"Fustian," Lord John scoffed. "You will come to no harm with us."

Teresa had definite reservations about his sense of propriety after his previous remark. She looked at the viscount, whose opinion must surely be trusted.

"I think in this case, since we are your cousins, a servant may be dispensed with. You are residing in the same household, after all. If ever you ride with only one of us, you had best take a groom."

"Thank you, cousin. I will abide by your advice."

She dimpled at him and he smiled. He was excessively handsome when he smiled, she noted.

Their mounts awaited them in the street. Teresa, used to the rough working horses of the hacienda, fell in love at first sight with the Thoroughbred bay mare the duke had provided for her. She longed to try her paces, but Lady Parr had forbidden galloping in the park. Teresa wondered if that particular prohibition was one of the shabby-genteel notions she might ignore with impunity. When Andrew scolded her for offending the proprieties, he did not realise how difficult it was to steer a course between conflicting codes.

They had only to cross Park Lane to enter Hyde Park by the Grosvenor Gate, and she knew at once that this time Lady Parr's rule was simply common sense. As far as she could see, lines of elegant phaetons and barouches moved at a walking pace, their still more elegant occupants bowing, waving, or stopping to talk to each other and the strollers and riders.

"Half the population of London must be here!" she exclaimed in surprise.

"This is only the Little Season," John reminded her. "You should see it on a fine day in May. Drove my curricle once and dashed if I didn't get stuck in the crush for half an hour. Since then, I always ride."

As they merged into the stream, a plump, dowdy lady waved an imperious summons from a carriage coming towards them.

"Come, cousin," said Lord Danville, "I shall introduce you to Lady Castlereagh." He led the way.

John leaned towards Teresa and whispered, "One of Almack's patronesses. If they approve you, you'll get vouchers next Season. Deuced flat place, but it's all the rage among the females and you won't want to be excluded. The Marriage Mart, they call it. Of course they won't care to offend m'mother, unless you do something truly outrageous, and Lord Castlereagh is one of m'father's bosom bows."

Lady Parr had stressed the importance of being seen at Almack's. No female banned from those august premises could be considered a social success. Thanking providence that her aunt was a duchess, Teresa followed her cousins.

The viscount introduced Teresa as Lord Edward's daughter. Lady Castlereagh asked kindly after her father, whom she had met in his rakish youth. As they parted after a few moments of conversation, she promised to invite Teresa to a small *soirée* she was holding in a few days.

Teresa breathed a sigh of relief. That was one patroness, at least, who seemed to approve of her.

Making sure she was out of earshot, she said, "I realise I am newly acquainted with London fashions, but is not Lady Castlereagh dressed oddly?"

"She is noted for it," John laughed. "It is said that at the Congress of Vienna she attended a party with his lordship's Order of the Garter decorating her hair."

The viscount frowned. "Do not make fun of her, John. She is a respectable and benevolent lady, and her husband was greatly instrumental in Bonaparte's defeat."

His brother hastily disclaimed any intended disparagement, but began to mutter that riding in the park was deuced flat entertainment.

Teresa had noticed a pair of riders cantering in the distance, and she suggested that they leave the crowd and stretch their mounts' legs at a faster gait than a sedate walk. "Their limbs, I mean," she corrected hastily.

Lord Danville shook his head. "You will note that both riders are gentlemen," he pointed out. "It will not do for a young lady at this hour. If you wish to rise early, a gallop even is unexceptionable before nine or so." He smiled at the idea of a female rising early for such a reason.

"A capital notion, Tom." John was enthusiastic. "Eight o'clock tomorrow, coz?"

Teresa accepted with alacrity.

As they rode on at a snail's pace, her cousins introduced her to so many people that she was sure she would never remember them all. It amused her to note that the viscount's acquaintance consisted of sober gentlemen of middle years and respectable matrons with marriageable daughters, while his brother's friends were all bucks of the first stare. She was equally grateful to both. When she began to go about in Society, it would be comfortable to know both young ladies with whom to chat and young gentlemen with whom to dance.

One middle-aged gentleman on horseback caught her eye. His horse was a magnificent black stallion. He was richly dressed, with a large ruby in his neckcloth and several gold fobs, but his face had a cynical, dissipated look. Her cousins both nodded to him as they passed, but did not offer to introduce him.

"I see Carruthers is in funds at present," said John.

"Who is he?" Teresa asked.

"Loose fish," he said briefly.

Lord Danville elaborated. "Baron Carruthers is a game-ster who lives by his wits. He is rumoured to be involved in various unsavory dealings. Unfortunately he lives near us in Sussex, so we are bound to acknowledge him, but I should not dream of making him acquainted with you."

"In Sussex? Is that Five Oaks, where my father grew up? I hope I shall see it one day."

"We generally spend Christmas there," John told her. "Now there's the place for a good gallop."

At that moment, Teresa saw Lady Parr and Muriel driving towards them, with Andrew riding beside their antiquated carriage.

For a moment she despaired. The duchess did not want Lady Parr to visit. Did that mean it would be wrong to introduce the Parrs to her cousins? Yet she could not cut them, for they had done nothing to deserve such an insult. Was it possible to talk to them while pretending her cousins were not there? That seemed even less possible.

Nothing Teresa had been taught covered this situation. How she wished she had been brought up knowing the correct way to deal with every circumstance.

Lord John took the decision out of her hands. "Isn't that your friend Graylin?" he asked. "And who's the charmer in the carriage with the dragon? I must ask him for an introduction."

=== 9 ===

Muriel was dressed in a pale blue gown which enhanced the celestial colour of her eyes. Beneath a chipstraw hat decorated with blue bows, her golden ringlets shone in the autumnal sunlight. Teresa was not in the least surprised that her cousin John was eager to meet her.

It pleased her to be, for once, the one performing the introductions. Lady Parr was clearly delighted to make the acquaintance of her noble relatives, though Teresa noted with relief that neither her character nor her sense of decorum led her to toad-eat them. Muriel blushed and smiled with a pretty shyness which Teresa wished she could emulate.

Andrew, on the other hand, greeted their lordships with what she could only view as suspicion. She realised that no mention had been made of his engagement to Muriel, so she hastened to remedy the omission. For some inexplicable reason, this made Andrew look still more resentful, while her cousins redoubled their attentions to the enchanting Miss Parr.

Teresa found herself riding behind the carriage with Andrew beside her.

"I'm sorry," she said, "should I not have revealed that you and Muriel are affianced?"

"It was perfectly proper to tell them," he said noncommittally.

"I thought you were annoyed that they admired her, but when they learned that she is betrothed, it only seemed to increase their admiration. I do not understand. I expected the reverse."

He laughed. "That is because you are a very straight-forward person, without a devious notion in your head. Gentlemen of rank and fortune like your cousins are the natural prey of the matchmaking mamas with marriageable daughters. When they are also young and handsome, like your cousins, even the most milk-and-water misses grow predatory. Since Muriel is already spoken for, however, they are safe in making her the object of their attentions."

Heads turned as Teresa's peal of laughter rang out.

"You are not roasting me?" she said, still grinning. "No, it does make a twisted sort of sense. Oh dear, everyone is staring. Lady Parr warned me that my laugh is not suffi-ciently restrained."

"Fustian! If you raise your eyes, you will see that you have brought smiles to a dozen sour faces. Your laugh is a tonic and you must not subdue it for any consideration. I fear my next question will do just that, however. Have you yet spoken to the duke about the trial?"

"No, he was away from home this afternoon, but I expect I shall have an opportunity this evening to speak with him privately. I trust that your appointment with the Foreign Secretary proved satisfactory?"

"Lord Castlereagh was most complimentary."

"Lord Castlereagh? I had not realised that he is the Foreign Secretary. I met his wife just now. It seems that she is just as important in her way, for she is one of those who controls access to Almack's. I will not say that she was complimentary, but she did promise me an invitation. Andrew, Castlereagh is one of my uncle's particular friends. I must make quite certain that he understands how indebted we are to you, and that you are a diplomat. With his patronage, I daresay you will be made ambassador in no time."

"Perhaps." He smiled at her enthusiasm. "In the mean-time, I have been offered a mission to China."

"To China! What an adventure!" Teresa fell silent for a moment, remembering how his betrothed dreaded travelling abroad. "What does Muriel think of it?" she asked cautiously.

"I have not told her yet. I escaped from the Foreign Office only just in time to accompany her hither."

He tried to sound unconcerned, but Teresa knew him well enough to detect apprehension in his voice. He must suspect that his future wife would not be best pleased at the news. In fact it might well be the only subject on which she would ever cut up stiff.

In an effort to cheer him up, she told him, "My aunt is giving a party next week to introduce me to the ton. I hope you will come? I shall need a few friendly faces to lend me countenance."

Before he could answer her, Lord Danville rode up beside them.

"Lady Parr has agreed to bring Miss Parr to my mother's party next week. I hope we may count on your acceptance also, Graylin?"

As Andrew pronounced himself happy to attend, Teresa burst into laughter again. She refused to explain the source of her amusement. She could hardly tell either gentleman that the duchess had explicitly warned her against inviting the Parrs to Stafford House.

She dropped back to ride beside the carriage, chatting with Muriel. Before parting, they arranged to meet the following afternoon for a walk.

Her cousins escorted her home through the twilit streets and she went abovestairs to change. In her dressing room, she found the duchess reclining on the sofa while Annie and Howell displayed Teresa's evening gowns before her. She jumped up and swept her niece into a scented embrace.

"My dear, your first dinner party. I happened to mention to Lady Kaye that you are residing with us and she immediately extended the invitation to include you. The écru crêpe, I believe, Howell, the one with the coquelicot ribbons. Yes, that will do very well. We shall leave at half past seven, Teresa, so I shall send Howell to you at a quarter past the hour to make sure all is in order."

The duchess and her abigail left, and Teresa hugged her maid. "Oh, Annie, my first London party. I hope I shall know how to go on. Of course, it may be my last London party if I have to appear as witness at that dreadful man's trial. I must arrange to see my uncle in the morning."

She was glad to find, when she went downstairs, that Lord Danville was to accompany them. She did not expect Lord John. He had once told her that most of his parents' friends were a bunch of slow-tops and it was his habit to plead a previous engagement when included in their invitations. She knew John better than his brother, and liked him very well, but on this occasion she felt cousin Tom's more staid demeanor might offer firmer support.

He complimented her gravely on her looks and handed her into the carriage after the duchess, placing rugs around the ladies' knees to guard against the late September chill.

It was but a few minutes' drive to Lord and Lady Kaye's town house. On her cousin's arm, Teresa followed her uncle and aunt up the steps.

"You will do very well," he reassured her, patting her hand as the door opened. She smiled at him gratefully, surprised by his understanding. "I remember how nervous my sister Pamela was at her first formal dinner," he added in explanation.

He stayed close beside her as they entered the drawing room, and presented her to their host and hostess. Lady Kaye professed herself delighted, while studying Teresa with undisguised curiosity.

As more guests came up, they moved away and were accosted by a dark-haired young beauty Teresa thought she recognised.

"Danville! I did not expect to see you here. Now it will not be such a horrid bore after all." Her voice was somewhat shrill, but her appearance could not be faulted. She had green eyes with long, dark lashes which fluttered provocatively. Her gown of primrose sarcenet set of her milk-white skin to perfection, though Teresa suspected that the delicate pink of her cheeks owed more to rouge than to nature.

Lord Danville bowed. "Cousin Teresa, you remember Lady Mary Hargreave. We met in the park this afternoon."

The two young ladies nodded to each other, then Lady Mary leaned closer to his lordship.

"So dull for you, having to escort your country cousin," she whispered, quite loud enough for Teresa to hear, then began to chat about people Teresa could not possibly know.

For two or three minutes Teresa felt more and more uncomfortable as Lady Mary, with practised skill, edged Lord Danville away from her. Cousin Tom, however, was equally adept at avoiding such manoeuvres.

Bowing, he took Teresa's arm and said, "Pray excuse us, Lady Mary. I must make my cousin known to Miss Kaye."

The daughter of the house was a pert blonde, short and a trifle plump, but nonetheless pretty. She had a deplorable tendency to giggle at all remarks addressed to her, all very well if they happened to be amusing, otherwise somewhat disconcerting. Though she fluttered her blackened eyelashes at the viscount with as much abandon as had Lady Mary, she was friendly towards Teresa.

"We shall have a comfortable cose after dinner," she promised, giggling, "while the gentlemen are dawdling over their port."

Dinner was announced. The duke, as highest in rank, led their hostess into the dining room, while Lord Kaye gave the duchess his arm. The rest of the guests were left to sort themselves out.

Lady Mary materialised beside Lord Danville with an expectant look. His lordship offered Teresa his arm, and Lady Mary shot her a venomous glance. Even amicable Miss Kaye pouted a little, and Teresa began to understand why her cousin was attracted to Muriel Parr, who was already betrothed.

Yet another hopeful debutante sat on the viscount's other side at dinner. He conversed with her politely, but when the courses changed, he turned to Teresa with such obvious relief that she nearly laughed aloud.

Meanwhile, she had noticed, sitting at the far end of the table, the man her cousins had declined to introduce to her when they rode in Hyde Park.

"I am surprised to see Lord Carruthers here," she said in a low voice.

"He has *entrée* everywhere, I fear, for his manners are impeccable and his family long established. Nothing definite is known to his discredit, save his excessive gambling, and who does not gamble? I hope you will heed my advice though, cousin, and avoid him when possible."

"I do not like his face," said Teresa decisively.

"I daresay he will be at Mama's ball next week."

"Ball! I had thought it was to be a small *soirée*."

He grinned, and once again she thought him quite the most handsome man she had ever met.

"Her Grace is quite incapable of giving a small *soirée*," he explained. "Her guest list starts with forty names, and then she keeps adding those to whom she owes an invitation, those who will be bitterly offended not to receive one, those who happen to cross her mind. That is why I did not hesitate to invite Miss Parr—and Lady Parr, of course, and Graylin. I can guarantee you a full-scale ball, and I doubt there will be fewer than four hundred in attendance."

"I shall never remember all their names."

"No, but they will remember you, cousin, and not only because the ball is in your honour."

Though aware that he intended a compliment, she said with a laugh, "Yes, for I shall probably commit some dreadful *faux pas* before half the ton. I should have preferred a small party for my debut."

When the ladies withdrew, the duchess summoned Teresa to be introduced to two or three matrons. All seemed disposed to be amiable, and Teresa pondered again the benefits attached to her relationship with a peer of the highest rank. She could not deny that it was excessively pleasant, yet she thought the situation she had been brought up with more equitable. In Costa Rica a man's worth was judged by what he had managed to create out of raw jungle. A wave of homesickness swept over her as she glanced around the elegant drawing room with its beautifully dressed, perfectly mannered ladies making polite, meaningless conversation.

Just then, Miss Kaye trotted up. "Teresa . . . May I call you Teresa? And you must call me Jenny, for I vow we are going to be friends. . . .Pray come and meet Daphne Pringle; she is the sweetest creature and quite longs to know you."

She bore Teresa off willy-nilly to join in a discussion of the best place to buy French lace and silk flowers.

Lady Mary was not a member of this cosy group. She sat at the pianoforte, idly turning over the music with an uninterested air, picking out a tune here and there. She brightened as soon as the gentlemen arrived. Somehow, without appearing to hurry, she reached Teresa's side before Lord Danville, who came straight towards them when he entered the room. He brought with him a couple of young gentlemen, who, he claimed, had begged to be introduced to his cousin.

After a few minutes of general conversation, Lady Mary turned to Teresa. "Will you favour us with a tune upon the pianoforte, Miss Danville?" she enquired.

"You must excuse me, I do not play," Teresa said warily.

"Ah, the harp is your instrument. I will beg Lady Kaye to have the harp brought out. No? Then you sing. I shall be happy to accompany you."

"My voice is nothing out of the ordinary, Lady Mary, and I know only Spanish songs, but if you will support me with an accompaniment upon the guitar, I shall do my poor best to entertain the company."

Lady Mary flushed, but made a quick recovery.

"The guitar is a peasant instrument," she declared. "I am certain Lady Kaye has no such thing in her house."

"Oh, but she does," Jenny broke in with a giggle. "My brother was in Spain with Wellington, Teresa, and he brought back a guitar. He plays it, too, and quite well. What a pity he is not here tonight."

"Nor is it a peasant instrument," added one of Lord Danville's friends indignantly. "I, too, was in Spain, and the gentlemen serenade their ladies with guitar music. Quite delightful, though it does grow a little tiresome around two in the morning."

"Rolled up, horse, foot, and artillery," the other gentleman murmured in Teresa's ear as Lady Mary flounced off. "I'll tell you, Miss Danville, she only wanted to be asked to play herself. Her performance upon the pianoforte is generally judged superior, but I believe you have spared us that tedium for this evening at least."

"Thank you, Sir Toby," Teresa said, laughing, glad that she had not offered to play her own accompaniment on Jenny's brother's guitar. "And thank you, Jenny, Mr. Wishart, for coming to my defence. But I hope one of you will ask Lady Mary to play, for I quite long to hear it. As far as I know, there is not a single pianoforte in all Costa Rica. Indeed, the transportation would be impossible on our rough tracks and I daresay the climate would ruin it."

Instead of asking Lady Mary to play, they all besieged Teresa with questions about her native land. By the time the party broke up, she realised happily that she had several new friends. In the carriage she asked her aunt whether any of them had been invited to their *soirée*.

"The Kayes will be coming, of course," said Her Grace. "As for the others, I cannot possibly remember who is on the list, but I shall show it to you tomorrow and you may add whom you will."

"Thank you, Aunt," said Teresa, exchanging a glance of amusement with her cousin.

The next morning Teresa rose early, as she'd promised to go riding in the park with Lord John. Well aware of his usual habits, she took the precaution of sending a message via Annie and his valet before she dressed. Leaning out of the window to check the air, she felt the nip of frost and put on a warm pelerine over her new habit.

Her cousin stumbled downstairs, rubbing his eyes, a mere five minutes late. "I did remember to send a message to the stables yesterday," he said sheepishly. "Devil of a night last night, begging your pardon, cousin."

"You can go back to bed when we return," she suggested, smiling. "However, this is by far too beautiful a day for me to excuse you. It may rain tomorrow."

"The horses are waiting, miss, my lord," announced Boggs.

The butler shook his bald head in wonder as they went down the front steps. It was years since Lord John had risen at such an unconscionable hour, except in direct response to a command from his father. Boggs closed the door and went back to his preparations for the ball, for he knew, as well as did Lord Danville, that Her Grace's small *soirée* was to be the great event of the Little Season. Miss Teresa's arrival was turning the household upside down, Boggs thought indulgently, and he for one was thoroughly enjoying it.

Teresa and John warmed their horses with a short trot, then galloped wildly along the edge of the Serpentine, sending ducks and swans flapping for the safety of the water. At last Teresa drew rein, laughing with exhilaration.

"It has been too long since I had a good ride!" she exclaimed. "And poor Gayo has been cooped up inside as well. Do you think I could safely bring him to the park, if we came early, when there is no one about?"

"I cannot see the harm in it." John had taken to visiting the parrot in Teresa's dressing room, and had even coaxed him into accepting tidbits from his hand. "Dashed if I'm getting up at this ungodly hour again just to exercise your parrot, though."

"Of course not. I shall bring Annie. Oh look, is that not Sir Andrew?"

Her cousin waved and hallooed. "Graylin! Well met. Don't tell me you make a habit of rising so devilish early." Andrew rode up on a superb chestnut gelding. "Good morning, Miss Danville, Lord John. Yes, I usually ride at this hour."

"There you are then, Teresa. No need to spoil my beauty sleep, Graylin will be delighted to escort you in future. Better bring a groom, though."

"You brought no groom?" Andrew looked around with a frown.

"John is my cousin," pointed out Teresa, feeling slightly guilty as she recalled that Lord Danville had said she ought to take a groom. "And besides, I have my protector in my pocket." She touched her hip.

"In Hyde Park! Teresa, if anyone saw it—"

"Your protector?" interrupted John. "Some fierce jungle creature I have not yet met?"

"My pistol," Teresa explained, laughing. "Just in case we are set upon by footpads."

"Females don't shoot."

"This one does," said Andrew, "and better than most men. However, I beg you will not demonstrate in Hyde Park, Teresa," he added hastily. "It really will not do."

"I'm accounted something of a crack shot," John announced, a glint in his eye. "We'll have a match sometime, cousin." He caught Andrew's minatory glance and added hastily, "Not in Hyde Park, of course. Somewhere private."

Andrew decided it was time to change the subject. "Do you care to ride with me tomorrow morning, Miss Danville?" he asked.

"Oh yes," she accepted with a joyful smile. "That will be delightful. And I promise to bring a groom."

On the way home, Teresa remembered that she had intended to take Gayo to the park the next day. She mentioned it to John, and he suggested that she should take him instead to the small garden behind Stafford House. As it was private, they could go at any time of day.

"Deuced if that ain't the place to have our shooting contest, too!" he exclaimed.

"But not at the same time, John! Gayo is all too likely to decide to sit on the target."

Teresa ate a hearty breakfast, then collected Marco from the library and went with him to her uncle's study, where she had arranged to see him at eleven. Sitting behind his huge oak desk, he dismissed his secretary, waved them to seats, and enquired as to how he might help them.

Teresa told him the whole story of the capture of the *Snipe* and the rescue of the slaves.

"And my sister is a true heroine, sir," Marco insisted when she finished her tale, "whatever the tattlemongers may make of it."

"She is indeed, lad," agreed the duke, "but you are right to fear the rumour mill. Is there any reason why it should become the latest *on-dit*? Are the, ah, the Parrs likely to spread the tale, or your abigail?"

"Annie will not say a word, Uncle, nor, I believe, will the Parrs. The only problem is the trial."

Marco explained what he had read in the newspaper.

"I shall not permit my niece to be called as witness," the duke said, a hint of steel visible beneath his usual affability. "You need have no fear of that. I shall have to consider whether it will be wise to allow Marco to testify. Indeed it will be better if your abigail does not, my dear. I should prefer to keep the family name out of it altogether."

"But I wish to testify," cried Marco. "Harrison deserves hanging, or at least transportation. Besides, if he goes free we may be in danger, for he made the most dreadful threats. We heard him, on the *Destiny* and then again on the quay when we landed in England."

"Graylin's testimony may well be enough," His Grace reassured him, "and the captain of your ship probably left a deposition when he sailed."

"There's Rowson, too," Teresa reminded her brother. "Sir Andrew's servant," she explained to her uncle.

The duke sat back, satisfied. "Very well. I shall consult Graylin and, I believe, the prosecutor, to make sure he has enough evidence to convict the villain without you. I cannot think that it will be necessary for any of my household to appear. I am gratified, my dear, that you came to me with this problem."

"Thank you, Uncle, I am very glad we told you." Teresa curtseyed, then gave way to impulse and rounded the desk to drop a kiss on his cheek. "Papa always said you were the best of brothers."

Marco bowed and said hopefully, "If you please, sir, may I at least attend the trial, if I am not to be a witness?"

"Certainly, my boy. Ought to be a part of any gentleman's education. Take your tutor—what's his name?—Netherdale, with you."

As soon as the study door closed behind them, Teresa said, "Since you have escaped from Mr. Netherdale for the nonce, will you join me with Gayo? Cousin John says there is a garden behind the house where he can go free for a while, and I have a couple of hours before I meet Muriel."

Marco agreed with alacrity. A footman showed them the way through the ballroom. The garden was surrounded by the house on two sides and a ten-foot brick wall on the other two.There was a flagstone terrace off the ballroom, with steps down to a lawn crossed by brick paths. In the centre grew a spreading chestnut, now losing its golden leaves and prickly fruit, with benches about its trunk. Chrysanthemums and a few late roses bloomed in the flower beds round the edge of the lawn.

"Perfect," said Teresa, and they went to fetch Gayo.

Miss Carter caught her as she stepped out of her chamber with the parrot on her shoulder. It was absolutely necessary to hold a consultation on what she was to wear this evening. Sighing, Teresa handed Gayo to Marco and turned back.

Marco took the parrot out, and he flew wildly up and down the garden, shouting "hello!" at the top of his voice. Tiring of this, he then perched in the tree and settled down to find out whether there was anything edible within the prickly brown covering of the chestnuts.

Marco's mind wandered to the abstruse theories of probability mathematics, which he had been studying avidly with the erudite Mr. Netherdale.

A pink rose caught Gayo's eye and he swooped down on it, picked it, and shredded it methodically.

"Sea scum," he said, and reached for another.

Marco suddenly noticed what he was up to and dived for him. All he caught was a single green tail feather as Gayo fled, disappearing into the house through an open window with a mournful "*ay de mí!*"

"Oh no," groaned Marco. "I should have made sure all the windows were closed."

Through the window came a series of crashes accompanied by a stream of multilingual vituperation.

"*Sacré nom d'un chien!*"

"*Hijo de puta!*"

"*Canaille! Cochon!*"

"Slimy son of a sea snake!"

"I catch, I cook *cet oiseau du diable!*"

"I think Gayo found the kitchens," said Marco despondently.

== 10 ==

JACQUES WAS PACKING to return to France, where good cooks were properly appreciated. Her Grace the Duchess of Stafford was laid down upon a sofa, calling for sal volatile and burnt feathers, while Amelia Carter fluttered about her helplessly. Gayo was back on his perch in the dressing room, scolding himself in a sad, soft voice.

Marco went up to the cook's chamber in the attic and humbly apologized, blaming the whole fracas on himself. He should not have snatched at the parrot, frightening it. Better a whole gardenful of roses be destroyed, for what was a mere gardener's anger compared to the righteous wrath of a French chef? Such an insult must never happen again.

It was difficult adjusting oneself to the customs of a foreign land, did not Jacques agree? Everything was so different. The parrot was homesick. He, Marco, was homesick. Was it possible that Jacques was also homesick? One heard that France was a beautiful country.

Jacques broke down and wept. Of course he was homesick, all exiles must be homesick. *Le pauvre petit perroquet*, in a cold country far from his jungle, must also suffer from *la nostalgie*. Did Monsieur Marco suppose the unhappy bird would enjoy an apricot tart?

Monsieur Marco did, and went off congratulating himself heartily on having paid attention to Andrew's discourses on diplomacy

He found Teresa on her knees in the drawing room. She was bathing her aunt's temples with one of her herbal concoctions and swearing that tonight's guests would be served a good dinner even if she had to cook it herself. Miss Carter clucked with dismay, scandalised at the idea of the duchess's niece in the kitchen.

"No need," said Marco. "Jacques is on his way back to the scene of the crime. I am very sorry, ma'am, it was all my fault. I was supposed to be watching Gayo."

"I ought to have know it was not safe to let him fly free," Teresa said.

"If we are all beating our breasts," said Lord John, coming in with an ill-concealed grin on his face, "I am to blame for suggesting the garden in the first place."

"Burnt feathers," murmured his mother weakly, unwilling to give up her vapours.

John's grin broadened. "No, no, Mama, you cannot expect to make a burnt sacrifice of the poor parrot. Doing it much too brown!" Overcome with helpless laughter at his double pun, he sank into a chair.

"Perhaps this will be sufficient?" enquired Marco with mock anxiety, drawing a single green tail feather from his pocket before he, too, collapsed.

"Oh, do go away, you odious wretches, and leave my aunt in peace," said Teresa, shooing them out, careful to keep her back to the duchess until she had mastered her own mirth.

"I only hope this has not given John ideas." Her Grace sighed. "He was always a mischievous little boy and I do not for a moment believe he has grown out of it. Perhaps the conservatory next time, my dear, with all the doors and windows shut?"

Teresa hugged her. "You and my uncle could not be kinder if you were my own parents," she said with a catch in her voice. "Now, if you are feeling more the thing, I must go and change. I am going walking with Muriel Parr at two."

The duchess sat up and straightened her cap. "Thomas asked me to add Miss Parr to my guest list. I should be sorry to think he has conceived a *tendre* for such an unsuitable female. He is, after all, heir to a dukedom."

"Muriel is betrothed already, Aunt. I am sure Cousin Tom was only being kind to me by inviting my friend."

This reassurance would have borne less weight had the duchess known that not twenty minutes later, her eldest son was offering to escort the two young ladies on their walk. Teresa had hoped to talk to Muriel privately about Andrew's China mission, but in the face of her friend's obvious pleasure she had not the heart to fob him off. Trailed by Annie and Kinsey, they crossed the road and entered the park.

Though Lord Danville took pains to include her, Teresa was soon unutterably bored. Her companions covered every topic of conversation approved by Lady Parr, from the weather to the preferred shade of upholstery for his lordship's new curricle. Teresa was relieved when he asked anxiously whether Miss Parr was not growing tired and turned their steps homeward.

As they parted, Muriel whispered to her, "How lucky you are to have so charming a cousin, Teresa. And he is so very considerate."

The viscount gazed after her carriage as it drove off. "As pretty behaved as she is beautiful," he said. "I shall tell Mama that she need not doubt the wisdom of your friendship with Miss Parr. On the contrary, from what I have heard of a certain parrot's domestic exploits, a certain young lady might even benefit from her acquaintance with such an admirably well-bred female."

He smiled at Teresa, but for once she did not notice how very handsome he was. Furious, she escaped upstairs before she said something she might later regret. It was too bad, when she had been doing so well, that her own cousin should join Andrew in preferring Muriel's manners to hers.

Despite Gayo's depredations, the duchess's dinner party went well. Teresa was brought to the attention of yet more prospective hostesses and received promises of several invitations. She was in good spirits when Andrew called for her to ride in the park next morning, though it was a grey, mizzling day.

He complimented her on the delightful picture she presented on her bay mare.

"In a proper riding habit, too," he added with a teasing grin. "It suits you admirably. Though I admit there was a great deal to be said for your Costa Rican costume, and for those hardworking little horses, too."

"These beauties would have a hard time of it in the jungle," she agreed as they crossed Park Lane, followed by the duke's groom. "Your chestnut is superb."

"Not mine." He shook his head regretfully. "I spend too much time abroad to set up my stables. He is my father's, but I have the use of him whenever I am at home."

"Tell me about your father, and the rest of your family. You have met almost all my swarms of relatives and I know nothing of yours."

As they rode on through the grey morning she learned all about his widowed father, his older brother, whose tyrannical wife had much to do with his liking for travel, his three married sisters. They were all in the country at present, though they would come up to town in the spring. Andrew spoke of the small estate in Warwickshire, inherited from a great-uncle, to which he hoped to retire one day.

"But not until I have seen the rest of the world," he said, laughing. "It's days like this that make me long for North Africa," he added as it began to rain. "We must go back before you are soaked."

"I am not afraid of this sprinkling. Have you already forgot the downpours we call rain at home? I have not yet had my gallop."

"Then I shall race you to the gate, for this may be no more than drizzle, but you must admit the temperature is quite different from your tropical storms."

They were damp, if not soaked, when they reached Stafford House. Teresa invited Andrew in to dry off and have some breakfast.

"I am glad you asked," he said, "or I might have gone so far as to invite myself. I have an appointment with the duke later this morning to discuss the trial."

"My uncle has everything well in hand, I believe. Boggs, have Sir Andrew's coat dried, if you please, and show him into the breakfast room. I shall be down shortly."

She returned to find Andrew already busy with a dish of ham and eggs and muffins. Boggs seated her and then presented her with a silver salver.

"Your post, miss."

"Mine? All those? Who can possibly be writing to me?"

"Invitations, I'd venture to guess, miss." He poured her coffee. "Bacon, miss?"

"How can I think of food! Look Andrew—*soirées*, routs, musicales, dinners." The table was littered with papers.

"It seems you are well on the way to social success already, just as Lord Edward wished."

"What is this?" She picked up the last of the pile and broke open the seal. "From my banker. He as arranged for me to meet with half a dozen coffee brokers at the Gloster Coffee House in Piccadilly."

Andrew frowned. "A respectable coaching house, I believe, but I shall make enquiries. I shall go with you, of course, and you will take Annie. Marco had best go, too. Which day is it to be?"

"Next week, Friday morning. I am sure I shall be safe with Marco and Annie." Why did he have to spoil such a delightful morning with his disapproving assumption of authority? "If Don Eduardo ever expected you to take responsibility for me, it ended when my uncle took me under his protection."

"Then you will request your uncle's escort, or your aunt's perhaps? No, I shall support you in this because Don Eduardo expected it of you, but you know the duke and duchess will be the happier for knowing nothing of your foray into the world of commerce."

A sound at the door alerted Andrew and he noticed that

an uneasy fascination had altered the butler's usually impassive expression.

"Not a word of this to anyone, Boggs," Andrew hissed as Lord Danville came in.

Blank-faced again, Boggs bowed, murmured, "Certainly, sir," and went to seat the viscount.

With Andrew exerting himself to avoid all mention of coffee and the law courts, and Lord Danville determined not to speak of either Gayo's misdeed or Andrew's betrothed, conversation faltered. Neither seemed able to think of anything else to talk about. With some idea of what was on their minds, Teresa took pity on them and introduced the subject of horseflesh. To her surprise, for she thought they had little in common, they had soon arranged to visit Tattersall's together in search of a pair for his lordship's new curricle.

Then the duke came in, the talk turned to politics, and she left them to it.

The next few days sped by, full of morning callers, afternoon callers, shopping, drives in the park when it was fine, and small parties of one sort or another in the evenings. The duchess assured her that after her own *soirée* the invitations would flood in.

"Dear aunt"—Teresa laughed—"I have never known such a round of gaiety in my life. I cannot imagine how it can increase, for already I have scarce a moment to call my own."

She called on the Parrs again. She thought Muriel looked unhappy and guessed the reason, but it was impossible to talk intimately in Lady Parr's presence. Teresa invited her friend to drive in the park the next afternoon.

The next morning, riding with Andrew, she discovered as she expected that he had told his betrothed about his mission to China.

"She dislikes the idea excessively," he said in a gloomy voice. "Of course I do not insist that she go with me. I shall not leave until the end of February, so we might be married at once and have several months together. Then she can reside with my father, or with her mother, if she prefers it, until my return. That is not unreasonable, is it? I know it is far from ideal, but many diplomats' wives must live with long separations. And think of navy wives."

"Poor Muriel," Teresa murmured, disturbed by his lack of sympathy for his beloved. She found herself unable to summon up any words of consolation and they cut short their ride, feeling out of charity with each other.

That afternoon, disobeying her mother's every precept, Muriel burst into tears in the middle of Hyde Park. Teresa shielded her from curious eyes as best she could with her parasol, and they hurried homeward through the side streets.

"Why cannot he be satisfied with a position in the Foreign Office?" wailed Muriel.

"If you love him," said Teresa with exasperated sternness, "you should be glad that he has been offered a job so in tune with his tastes."

"But he wants me to live with his father, and his sister-in-law is perfectly horrid to me."

"Then you must live with your mother." Teresa could not imagine a more dire fate, but after all she was not Lady Parr's daughter.

"I could not bear to go on living with Mama when I am a married lady."

"Well, Andrew will not be gone forever, but if you cannot bear his absence, you must needs go with him."

Teresa returned home in a stormy mood, unable to understand how two people in love could make each other so miserable. Summoned to the drawing room to take tea with her aunt and several visitors, she sent a message that she had the headache.

In her distress, she had forgotten that this was the night of the ball.

The duchess appeared in her chamber, calling for hartshorn and followed by Miss Carter, Howell, and Annie, all offering conflicting advice. Somehow the news spread. Mrs. Davies, the housekeeper, arrived with her sovereign remedy. Chef Jacques sent up a French tisane. Boggs enquired whether a footman should be sent for the doctor.

At the height of the clamour, guaranteed to produce a headache where none existed, Marco stalked in with a brotherly disregard for propriety. "Stop fussing, Teresa, everyone is busy with preparations for your blasted ball and you're setting them at sixes and sevens," he said callously. "Take some of your own herbs. You've been treating other people for years, have you no faith in yourself?"

"I'm *not* fussing," she said, with justifiable indignation, since she had not been able to get a word in edgewise for some time. "My head is much better already. It was no great thing and I believe has been cured by everyone's good wishes. Thank you, dear aunt, all of you, for your solicitude."

"A nervous megrim, I daresay," the duchess diagnosed, being an expert on the subject. "Lie down for an hour on your bed before you dress, child, and do not worry. You are certain to cast all the insipid misses in the shade tonight."

Marco lingered behind after all but Annie had left. "Nervous megrim, is it?" he said with a grin. "Now that's cutting a wheedle for I don't believe you know the meaning of the word."

"Go away, you horrid boy." His sister pulled a face at him. "Of course it was no such thing, but I am tired and I intend to follow Aunt Stafford's advice."

"She's right, you know, you will be the prettiest girl there, so cheer up and do not worry." He leaned down and kissed her cheek. "Papa would be proud of you."

"And of you," she said softly as he left. "You are growing up, little brother."

Annie drew the curtains and helped Teresa undress. To her surprise she fell asleep. When she woke, the maid was lighting candles.

"It's time to dress, Miss Teresa. Just come see what's waiting for you."

"Waiting for me?" Feeling refreshed, Teresa stretched and slid out of bed. Annie draped her robe about her and she went into the dressing room. "Flowers! How pretty! Did you look at the cards? Who sent the crimson rosebuds?"

"They're from Lord Danville. He had an unfair advantage, knowing what you're wearing, for he asked me. Shall you carry them?"

"Mmm, they smell sweet. Do you think you can pin one or two in my hair?" She looked at the other four posies, all from various gentlemen she had met in the past week. There was nothing from Andrew, and she told herself firmly that of course he could not send flowers to anyone but his affianced wife. "How kind everyone is. What is this?"

She picked up a small box of gold-embossed leather.

"I didn't open it, miss. It's from His Grace."

"Oh, look, Annie! A ruby necklace, and eardrops. Oh, Annie, I think I am going to cry."

"You mustn't do that," said her abigail bracingly. "Don't want your eyes to match your gown, too, do you?"

Teresa's first ball gown was of ruby satin with an over-skirt of ivory lace, open down the front, and more lace trimming the low-cut bodice and puffed sleeves. By the time she had washed and put it on, Howell had arrived to supervise her toilette, and the coiffeur from Birmingham came to help with her hair. Under his expert hands the glossy black mass was caught up behind, with one heavy lock falling forward over her shoulder and tiny ringlets framing her face. With instructions from Howell, Annie's nimble fingers wove a wreath of the red rosebuds, and they fixed it in a coronet about her dark head.

Annie knelt to help her put on her ivory satin dancing slippers.

"Her Grace sent this," said Howell, producing a fan of pierced ivory and slipping its ribbon over her wrist. She stepped back. "Well, I have to say, miss, as how Her Grace is right. You'll take the shine right out of all those pink and white misses. Looks almost royal, don't she, Annie?"

Annie nodded, eyes shining. "Like a princess. You'll dance every dance, Miss Teresa," she prophesied, "and they'll be fighting to take you in to supper."

There was evident admiration on the faces of her cousins when she descended to the drawing room. As she curtseyed to the duke and duchess, Lord John stepped forward and swept a bow that would have done credit to a cavalier.

"Madam, may I have the honour of the first dance?" he requested. "I wager half the fellows in the room will be ready to call me out for forestalling them."

"I hope you will not call out your papa, then," she said, twinkling up at him. "He asked me yesterday."

John turned to the duke.

"Sir, name your seconds!" he cried melodramatically.

His Grace shook his head reprovingly and murmured, "I daresay you will grow up one day. You look magnificent, Teresa."

"Thanks to your gift, Uncle." She touched the ruby pendant, her face glowing as bright as the jewels. "How very kind you are, sir. And Cousin Tom, thank you for the roses. You see I am wearing them."

"Thus greatly enhancing their beauty," said Lord Danville gracefully, if a trifle ponderously.

"Dash it all, Tom, you've stolen a march on me, too," his brother accused. "I ain't in the petticoat line in general," he apologised to Teresa. "Should have thought of flowers. The muslin company don't expect such graces," he added wickedly in a whispered aside.

"How lucky you did not send any," she teased, pretending she had not heard his last remark. "I could never have chosen between my cousins' offerings and must have declined to wear either."

Marco stepped forward, proud and handsome in his first evening breeches and black velvet coat. With a bow as graceful as John's, if less elaborate, he handed his sister a small package.

"I hope it is right," he said anxiously. "I asked Aunt Stafford what would be suitable."

It was an ivory bracelet, intricately carved, that matched Teresa's fan to perfection. She put it on at once and turned to Marco. He hurriedly backed away.

"No hugs! You will crease my coat."

"Never say my little brother is become a dandy." She laughed. "Thank you. The bracelet is perfect."

"It is from China. Cousin John took me to Limehouse, down by the docks. There are hundreds of Chinamen there."

From China. Teresa studied the entwined dragons with interest, trying to suppress a wish that it was she, not Muriel, who had the opportunity of going to that mysterious land with Andrew.

The guests arrived, forty for dinner followed by another two or three hundred for the ball. The duchess excused Teresa early from the receiving line so that she should not be too tired to dance. She went into the ballroom, dazzling with mirrors, the diamonds of the ladies, the gilt chandeliers with their hundreds of beeswax candles. Her dance card was filled, all but the waltzes, long before the duke came to lead her onto the floor to open the ball.

The first dance was a quadrille. Concentrating on the complicated figures, Teresa forgot to be nervous and laughed with delight. The duke beamed at her.

"I wish Edward were here to see you," he said. "And your mama, of course. You quite take the shine out of all the young ladies."

Teresa agreed wistfully that it would be beyond anything great to have her parents present, but she could not really imagine them mingling with the haut ton. The hacienda on the volcano's slope was in another world.

Lord Danville was waiting to claim her for the next dance. As she stood with him at the side of the room, Baron Carruthers approached them. She had seen him several times since her original glimpse in the park, but had never been formally introduced.

He bowed to her partner, his cold eyes appraising her. They reminded her of the jaguar.

"Servant, Danville. I am come to beg a favour. Pray present me to your beautiful cousin."

Lord Danville looked uneasy but found it impossible to refuse a direct request. Though Teresa curtseyed politely to the baron, she did not hold out her hand. He bowed low and asked permission to sign her card.

"I am sorry, all the dances are taken," she said in relief. There was something about him that repelled her, quite apart from her cousins' warnings and the rumours she had since heard about his dissipated way of life. He bowed again, his words of regret accompanied by an expression close to a sneer. He did not press her, and headed for the card room as Cousin Tom took her arm to escort her onto the floor.

When it was time for the first waltz, Teresa went to sit beside the duchess. Most of her friends had already made their debuts the previous spring, so the patronesses of Almack's had graciously granted them permission to waltz.

Teresa watched a little sadly as the floor began to fill. She was enjoying her first ball more than she had dreamed possible, and it was a shocking waste of time to have to be a wallflower, however briefly. Then she saw Andrew making his way toward her. She had missed his arrival in the crush. Sitting out a waltz with Andrew would be better than dancing it with anyone else, she thought joyfully.

He bowed to the duchess. "I have Lady Castlereagh's permission to ask Miss Danville for this dance," he said. "May I deprive you of her company, ma'am?"

Her hand on his arm felt the smooth muscles move as he clasped her waist and swung her into the dance. His blue eyes gazing down into hers drove all thought from her mind and she moved in a daze, conscious only of his closeness. Her lips parted in a half smile. His grip on her hand tightened and he drew in his breath sharply, pulling her a little closer, then he forced himself to relax.

"Teresa," he murmured.

She did not answer. Words were unnecessary.

Fortunately, since Teresa's head was still in the clouds, the next dance was one of the simpler country ones. She was not expected to hold a proper conversation with her partner, Mr. Wishart, because the movements separated them often. She managed not to make any obvious mistakes in the steps, and when she faltered, the others in the set—all friends—kindly steered her in the right direction.

After that came the supper dance, which John had reserved, and his lighthearted friendliness brought her back to earth. They chatted merrily as they danced, then went into the supper room with Jenny Kaye and her partner.

At a nearby table Andrew bent solicitously over Muriel, asking her what she wanted from the buffet.

Teresa fell silent, then embarked upon a lively flirtation with her cousin. If he noticed a quality of desperation in her mood, he did not mention it. He responded in kind, and more than one dowager nodded wisely and muttered dire warnings about marriages between cousins.

== 11 ==

TERESA SLEPT TILL past noon, the day after her coming-out ball. She awoke with slight headache, real this time, which she put down to overindulgence in champagne.

She remembered watching Andrew leave with Muriel, placing her cloak carefully, gently, about her slender white shoulders.

She remembered laughing with Cousin John and drinking more champagne and dancing, dancing, dancing till dawn lightened the sky.

She did not dare remember waltzing with Andrew.

She had missed her morning ride with him, but the next day was the one set for the conference with the coffee merchants. She had been indignant when Andrew insisted on going with her. Now, she would be glad to have his support as well as being simply glad of his presence.

With Marco and Annie, they drove down Park Lane and turned into Piccadilly. The Gloster Coffee House was indeed respectable, as coaching inns went. Founded a century and more ago the coffee house had, like many another, become a gathering place for merchants and other men of business. Though it was now the London headquarters of the Portsmouth stage line, it was still frequented by dealers in coffee and tea.

Lord Edward's banker had invited seven of the most prominent importers of coffee to meet there that morning. He had not, however, warned them that a female hoped to do business with them. Enticed by his promise of something out of the ordinary, they were all waiting in a private parlour, set aside for their use, when Teresa arrived at the inn.

The landlord ushered her into the parlour, followed by Annie, Andrew, then Marco carrying the little wooden chest of coffee beans they had brought from Costa Rica.

"Good morning, gentlemen," Teresa said. "I am Miss Danville. I hope to persuade you to buy coffee produced on my father's hacienda in Costa Rica."

A small, skinny man in an old-fashioned long coat and tie wig snorted and marched out with a scowl on his face, muttering something about modern females not knowing their place. The other six remained, their expressions varying from astonishment through scepticism to admiration.

"Delighted, miss, I'm sure," said a corpulent merchant, ogling her. "Out of the ordinary indeed! Always a pleasure to do business with a pretty young woman." He winked.

"I warned you," Andrew whispered, then proceeded to demonstrate his estimable abilities as a diplomat. Without offending anyone, he put the stout cit in his place and convinced the sceptics that it would be worth their while to stay and try Teresa's wares.

She hurried to open the chest and soon they were all sniffing at handfuls of the roasted beans, which she set Marco to grinding in a mill provided by the innkeeper. He had also set out one of the new Biggin coffeepots with a built-in filter. Teresa sent Annie to the kitchens to fetch boiling water and soon the delicious aroma of brewing coffee filled the room.

The merchants sipped her brew, compared it to the best varieties served in the coffee house, tasted again, scribbled notes.

" 'Tis as rich as Jamaica Blue Mountain," observed one, impressed.

"Better," said another.

They besieged Teresa with questions about quantities, shipping routes, agents, and political complications. Oscar had prepared her well during the voyage from Limón to Port Royal and she managed to answer all queries to their satisfaction. She shot a glance of triumph at Andrew, who nodded encouragement, grinning.

Finally, all six merchants promised to send draft contracts for her perusal. She gave them her direction at Stafford House, thanked them, and took her leave. They all bowed low as she swept out followed by her retinue.

Andrew immediately took her to task. "You ought not to have given your uncle's direction," he said. "Your banker could have dealt with the matter without involving your relations."

Teresa was too pleased with herself to take offence at his reprimand.

"I daresay you are right, but never mind," she said gaily. "Boggs already knows I am shockingly involved in trade, so I shall ask him to pass the contracts to me privately. I am too excited to sit tamely in the carriage. Pray let us walk a little."

Marco shook her hand and congratulated her while Andrew told the groom to meet them in Berkeley Square. They strolled down Piccadilly. The street was full of stagecoaches leaving the Bull and Mouth for Shropshire, the Spread Eagle for Liverpool, half a dozen other inns for destinations all over the country. Teresa and Annie studied the shop windows. They were particularly fascinated by the signs at the moneychanger's: "Napoleons sold and bought. Light guineas taken at full value. Old silver taken with rapture. French silver taken with alacrity, quite novel. Napoleons, Louis d'or and gold of every sort and denomination taken with peculiar adroitness."

"They even bought the coins I brought back from North Africa," Andrew told them. "I must bring in my Mexican silver one of these days. Now, how about an ice at Gunter's to celebrate the success of your business?"

At the Sign of the Pot and Pineapple, in Berkeley Square, Andrew insisted on treating Annie, too. The maid's dark face shone with delight as she tasted her cream fruit concoction, made with ice shipped all the way from Greenland. Teresa thanked Andrew with a grateful look for the pleasure he had given her abigail. She herself could not choose between Cedrati and Bergamet Chips, and Naples Divolini, so she had some of each, followed by an ice.

"Engaging in commerce is good for the appetite," she observed. "Now that I have justified my journey to England, I shall not feel guilty abut spending Don Eduardo's money on frivolities. Next stop, Mrs. Bell's on Charlotte Street for a bonnet from Paris."

"I shall walk," chorused Marco and Andrew with identical shudders.

The Parisian bonnet, Teresa's first venture into choosing her own apparel without advice, was deemed charming by the duchess and Miss Carter. More important, it was approved by the duchess's dresser, Howell. With renewed self-confidence, Teresa dashed from rout to ball to Venetian breakfast. It was hard to believe that this was merely the Little Season, with half the ton absent in the country. Every day she had a choice of entertainments and had to refuse many invitations for lack of time.

When the duchess was not available to chaperone her, Teresa was often squired by Lord Danville or Lord John. Since her cousins were both much sought after, she was very soon acquainted with enough people to be able to rely on meeting friends wherever she went.

She even collected her own circle of chattering young ladies and admiring young men, among them Jenny Kaye, Daphne Pringle, Sir Toby, and Mr. Wishart. Whether the attraction was her looks, her stories of Costa Rica, her close connection with the Duke of Stafford, or the rumour that she was an heiress, the gentlemen were as friendly as the ladies.

Andrew was often among the company. If there was dancing, he generally stood up with her for a country dance, but he never again asked her to waltz. Teresa was not sure whether to be glad or sorry. The effect on her of his closeness had been alarming. She made a point of always enquiring after Muriel.

She soon realised that Lady Parr and Muriel moved on the fringes of Society. She met them only once, at a rout accurately described by John as a devilish crush. Muriel seemed quieter and shyer than ever among Teresa's lively friends. Lord Danville was not at that particular rout, where his brother stigmatised Muriel, in an undertone, as dull as ditch water.

"Not that she's not excessively pretty," he added fairly. "Needs a bit of animation."

He turned to flirt with Miss Pringle, who was always willing to oblige.

Teresa did make time to visit the sights of London. After she had travelled thousands of miles to the greatest city in the world, it would have been a pity to see nothing of it but the streets and squares and shops of the fashionable quarter.

Lord Danville, a mine of historical information, escorted her to the Monument, Mansion House, Westminster Abbey, and St. Paul's Cathedral. Lord John took both her and Marco to Astley's Amphitheatre to see the circus, to Mrs. Salmon's Waxwork and Barker's Panorama and a balloon ascension. On a trip to the Tower, John took Marco to the Armoury while Tom paid out some shillings so that Teresa might peek at the Crown Jewels, scarcely visible by lamp-light behind their bars. Then they all went together to the menagerie.

Teresa found the scruffy lions a sad contrast to the magnificent, though terrifying, jaguar of the Costa Rican jungle. As for the rest, she had to agree with Andrew that it would take a lifetime to know London well. Cartago was indeed a village by comparison.

Marco was as busy as his sister. His tutor, Mr. Netherdale, had a scientific bent, so that as well as the classics he was studying mathematics, chemistry, and astronomy. In his free time, Cousin John introduced him to the city's masculine haunts and pastimes.

John advised his young cousin to keep quiet about the cockpits and prizefights and daffy parlours. Females, he pointed out, did not appreciate such things. Marco, who approached these activities with the same intellectual curiosity he brought to his studies, complied. He did, however, go straight to his sister when he returned, shaken, from the slavers' trial.

"Whatever is the matter?" she asked, urging him towards a chair by the fire in her dressing room. "You look as if you have seen a ghost."

"I wish Captain Harrison was a ghost," he replied. "He is a dreadful man, Teresa. I scarcely looked at him before. There was so much else going on aboard the *Destiny* and when we landed in England. But he is truly evil. They had to drag him out, shouting vicious threats. I cannot repeat his words. He vowed revenge on those who had wrecked his business and brought him to gaol."

"I am sure it must have been frightening, but after all, he can do nothing as long as he is in prison. What happened during the trial?"

"He named the man who financed his voyage, the owner of the *Snipe*. Do you remember Captain Fitch was sure the ship was not his own or he would have made more effort to avoid scuttling her? Well, it seems she belonged to someone called Carruthers. Andrew says the law will never touch him because he is a peer, and the papers will not even mention his name for fear of libel suits. There is no proof beyond Harrison's word and he is a convicted criminal."

"Lord Carruthers," Teresa gasped. "I have met him. Both our cousins said he was a . . . rum touch, I believe John called him, though he is received in Society. I suppose he must know that I was instrumental in bringing his enterprise to naught. How shall I ever face him again?"

"Perhaps he does not know. Surely he would not have visited Harrison in Newgate for fear of being taken up, and

I did not see him at the trial. Besides, Harrison did not actually mention any of us by name. He referred to you as 'that hoity-toity female.' "

"Did he, indeed?"

"Andrew says it is best not to tell anyone about Lord Carruthers lest he come to hear of it."

"In any case, he can scarcely blame us for scuttling the *Snipe*. That was Harrison's doing."

"Yes, of course. Andrew was a great gun in the witness box, Teresa. It was on his evidence that Harrison and two others were sentenced to transportation. That was when he started shouting. They could not nab them on the murder charge because there was no proof that they deliberately sank the *Snipe*," he added with regret. "Mr. Netherdale says they will be held in a hulk on the Thames until a convict ship sails for Australia."

"Then I am sure we have no cause to worry. And Andrew is certainly correct that it would be foolish to broadcast our knowledge of the baron's misdeeds. Pray tell no one, not even Cousin John, and warn your tutor to hold his tongue."

"Mum's the word," agreed Marco, looking much more cheerful than on his arrival.

Teresa rode with Andrew in the park the next morning, and he confirmed Marco's report.

"It troubles me that Harrison considers you the chief author of his downfall," he added, frowning. "Of course, even if he should communicate with Lord Carruthers, neither of them can harass you while you are under the protection of one of the premier peers of the realm. All the same, I hope you still carry your pistol, Teresa."

"I never thought to hear you say that," she commented with a laugh. "But yes, I do carry it when I can. It is in my pocket at this moment."

"I am glad to hear it. Though I do not wish to alarm you! I cannot think it likely that you will find the slightest use for it."

Touched by his concern, she remembered these words

when she sat next to John at dinner that night. Her grace-less cousin had not forgotten that he had challenged her to a shooting match.

"I have had a capital notion," he whispered in her ear, a wicked sparkle in his eye. "I shall smuggle you into Manton's Shooting Gallery disguised as a gentleman."

"You shall do no such thing," she replied indignantly. "I hope you are bamming me, for I never heard so outrageous a suggestion in my life."

He sighed mournfully and shook his head. "How tame-spirited, cousin. I had thought better of you. I shall have to borrow a target from them and set it up in the garden. Will the day after tomorrow suit you?"

She murmured acquiescence, preferring not to enquire whether or not he intended to ask Manton's permission for the loan of the target.

The next evening he told her that everything was ar-ranged for the following morning. She felt a sudden qualm about the propriety of the contest, even in a private garden, but the duke would surely have forbidden it if he judged it inadvisable. Her misgivings must be the lingering result of Lady Parr's shabby-genteel instruction. She smiled at John and promised to meet him at eleven o'clock.

When Teresa went out into the garden, she was shocked to find seven or eight of Lord John's fellow Corinthians, most of them occupied in wagering on the outcome of the match. Singularly foolish, she thought, since they had no idea of her ability. Two of them were arguing over a candelabrum. They moved it here and there, lighting the candles only to have them blown out by the slight breeze. Since it was nearly midday and broad daylight, Teresa could not imagine what they were about.

Lord John hurried up to her.

"You will not mind that I brought along a few of the fellows," he said hopefully, meeting her frown with an ingenuous smile.

"This was to be a private affair," she answered, furious.

"But it *is* private. Private garden, wall all round, in my own home, too. Can't possibly be any objection. Now you stand here, I'll give you five feet."

"Certainly not. I shall stand beside you." Challenged, Teresa forgot her concern.

She put a bullet into the bull's eye, to resounding cheers, quickly reloading while her cousin took his turn. He equalled her, so they moved farther away. Again she hit the centre, as did he.

"Equally matched, by Jove," called one of the spectators.

"Here, we've got these devilish candles lit at last," another announced. "They're burning pretty steady. Try for 'em quick, ma'am, before the breeze comes up again."

"You have to shoot out the flame," John explained when Teresa turned to him in puzzlement.

Her hand steady, enjoying herself now, she took aim, fired. A candle went out. It was John's turn. Another flame was extinguished. Teresa put out another—and her cousin missed. She raised her pistol, suddenly aware of the grinning faces of the bucks surrounding them. This shot would be her last, whether she won or lost.

"Good God, cousin, what are you about?" Lord Danville's horrified voice came from behind her.

She turned. The viscount stood on the terrace, Andrew at his side. Boggs, two footmen, and three maids peered from the ballroom. A sound from above made her raise her eyes. At one window of the drawing room she saw the astonished faces of Lady Castlereagh, Lady Kaye, and Miss Carter, at the other Jenny Kaye, Daphne Pringle, and Mr. Wishart.

Somehow Teresa knew that behind them on the sofa the duchess was having a nervous spasm. She wondered why, knowing him as she did, she should have assumed that John's arrangements included notifying the household and receiving the acquiescence of his parents.

Andrew had come to take Teresa for a drive in the park with Muriel. At Lord Danville's grim suggestion, he whisked her away immediately. The viscount then used every ounce of his authority as heir to a dukedom, called in several favours, and issued a couple of threats to exact promises from all his brother's friends that not a word of this morning's doings should pass their lips. Rejecting John's shamefaced assistance, he then went up to the drawing room to face the ladies.

Only Lord Danville's reputation as a serious gentleman of sober tastes enabled him to persuade the Ladies Castlereagh and Kaye that their eyes had deceived them. It was unthinkable, he pointed out, that a young lady of good family should deliberately engage in a shooting contest. His cousin Teresa had heard the shots and gone to investigate. His reprobate brother had then thrust a pistol into her hand and urged her to fire it, which, being an obliging girl, she had done, fortunately without loss of life. She had been very much shocked at the resulting explosion and he had sent her off with her friend, Miss Parr, to recover her composure.

The ladies expressed their hope that Miss Danville's nerves had not suffered irreparable damage from Lord John's thoughtlessness.

Miss Kaye and Miss Pringle, who had been near the window from the first, exchanged a glance.

"We are far too fond of Miss Danville to breathe a word," Jenny Kaye assured his lordship fervently, and basked in his evident gratitude.

Mr. Wishart cast him a cynical look, but he was a good friend and Lord Danville had no fear of his discretion. The visitors left, and the viscount turned his attention to his prostrate mama, who was more than willing to cast the entire blame on the shoulders of her errant younger son.

Meanwhile, belowstairs, Boggs had threatened with instant dismissal all servants who so far forgot themselves as to gossip about their betters. By the time Teresa, chastened by Andrew's tongue-lashing and Muriel's manifest horror, returned to Stafford House, the incident had been thoroughly hushed up.

= 12 =

ANDREW DID NOT call for several days after the shooting match, a much greater punishment for Teresa than her cousin's scold or her aunt's vapours. When he did come to Stafford House it was with a grave face that had nothing to do with her behaviour. He asked to see Marco, and was closeted with him in the library for some time before he sent a footman to ask Teresa to join them.

Entering the room, she was glad to see that his expression had lightened. He greeted her with pleasure and a hint of amusement that intrigued her.

Marco was looking puzzled. "Andrew wants me to explain to you about the gaming hell," he said.

Teresa sank into the nearest chair, feeling pale.

"Gaming hell?" she repeated weakly. "Is that where Cousin John has been taking you? Oh Marco, I hope you are not wasting Don Eduardo's money on gambling."

Andrew sat down beside her and took her hand, patting it soothingly. He was openly grinning now.

"Before you castigate your brother, wait until you know the whole story," he suggested. "I had very much the same idea when I heard rumours that he had been seen playing faro with Lord Carruthers at Seventy-seven, St. James's Street. The place is a notorious hell."

"With Lord Carruthers!"

"A notable gull-groper, among his other faults." Seeing her look of blank incomprehension, he explained, "A Captain Sharp. One who fleeces the unwary at games of chance. I have persuaded Marco to confess to you lest you should hear the rumours and worry about it."

"I really went to watch them playing hazard." Marco patiently ignored the interruptions. "Mr. Netherdale has been illustrating the laws of probability with the use of the dice, you know. However, it was very dull, so I went to see some of the other games. Cousin John stayed behind at the hazard table. He was losing, I think."

"I'll have a word to say to John about this," remarked Teresa, her voice grim. She was less and less able to understand Andrew's amusement.

"Roulette is too dependent on chance, and piquet involves too much skill to be able to predict the outcome. Faro is perfect. I was just watching, honestly, Teresa, until Lord Carruthers invited me to join in. He was sneering so, it was unbearable, so I did. It looked very easy. All you have to do is remember which cards have gone already and work out the odds of the rest appearing at any given moment. Fascinating."

"So you played."

"Yes." Marco's tone was matter-of-fact. "I won five hundred guineas."

Andrew laughed aloud at Teresa's expression. She snatched her hand away from him, glaring.

"You won five hundred guineas," she said incredulously. "I hope this has not given you a taste for gaming."

"It was an interesting mathematical puzzle, but it is more amusing to do complicated calculations, for which one needs pencil and paper. The atmosphere of a hell is not conducive to serious thought."

"I am glad to hear it. Andrew, how could you let me think he was in deep water?"

To her surprise, Andrew frowned.

"To tell the truth," he said slowly, "I am concerned that it was Carruthers who lured Marco into betting. To be sure, it is nothing new in him, but suppose it was an attempt at revenge for the *Snipe*? My informant was very clear that his lordship knew who Marco was and exerted all his wits to involve him in what he must have expected to be heavy losses."

"You think that Carruthers has spoken to Harrison then?"

"I fear it seems likely. I beg you will take care, though I still cannot believe he would try anything dastardly while you are in the duke's household."

She looked at him with anxiety in her dark eyes. "You take care, too, Andrew. You have not the duke's protection."

He smiled reassuringly.

"Men like Carruthers prefer to pick on the weak. I daresay I have worried you for nothing."

He kissed her hand and took his leave, advising her to say nothing to Lord John. At best it would set her cousin's back up, he pointed out. Marco had too much common sense to come to any harm.

The next time she saw Andrew was at a musical evening when her discretion was finally overcome by Lady Mary Hargreave's incessant taunts.

Jenny Kaye had not forgotten Teresa's interest in her brother's guitar. She herself was often asked to sing, and she was eager to add a Spanish song to her repertoire of French, Italian, and German arias. She invited Teresa to join her in the Kaye's music room one morning.

Teresa had not played in several months, but the simple broken chords of the accompaniment soon came back to her. She taught Jenny a folk song, a plaintive tale of unhappy love. Though she had never had voice lessons, her mellow contralto mingled well with Jenny's well-trained, sweet soprano. Jenny was delighted with the exotic sound of the guitar and the simple harmonies of the music.

After that first time, the girls often met to sing together. Soon they had a repertoire of four or five songs. Still, Teresa had no thought of performing before an audience. It was Jenny who grew impatient with Lady Mary's insinuations against her friend and persuaded her mother to hold a musical evening.

Lady Kaye invited some forty guests, mostly matrons with daughters anxious to perform, and such male family members as they could force to come along. Among them were Lady Parr and Muriel. The latter had been polishing her skills upon the harp since her return from Jamaica, and looked angelic playing it. Lady Parr's brother proving adamant, Andrew was cajoled into squiring them.

The duchess was engaged that evening, and Lord Danville decided to go with Teresa. He had kept a close eye on his cousin since the shooting match. Though he could not imagine how she might fall into a scrape at a musicale, he did not consider Miss Carter to be an adequate chaperone.

After two harpists, three pianists—including Lady Mary's superior performance—and three sopranos—all singing Italian arias—the audience was ready for a change. There was a murmur of interest as Miss Kaye and Miss Danville took their places by the piano, the latter bearing a most unusual instrument for a polite drawing room.

Teresa strummed the opening chords, then Jenny's voice joined hers in the first song they had learned together. Andrew, sitting by Lady Parr, could not tear his eyes from Teresa's face as the melancholy air lilted through the room.

The sweet, sorrowful sound died away, and there was a moment's silence before the listeners applauded.

Andrew judged the silence half tribute and half disapproval, the former chiefly from the genuine music lovers, the latter from jealous mamas. The applause ended in an expectant hush, and he clearly heard Lady Parr mutter, "I warned her that ridiculous instrument was not socially acceptable. Sir Archibald would be shocked."

One or two nearby heads turned, nodding assent.

"My dear ma'am," he said with unnecessary loudness, "so very like a Scottish lament, do you not agree, with the Spanish guitar taking the place of the Celtic harp. It brings back memories of many a pleasant evening on my travels."

Since Muriel was about to perform a Scottish ballad, Lady Parr murmured feebly, "So original."

Muriel, overcoming her timidity in her friend's defence, stood up and went to Teresa, saying, "I thought it quite delightful. Do let me see your instrument. Can you play 'Flow Gently, Sweet Afton'?" She hummed the tune and Teresa picked out suitable chords.

As Daphne Pringle and several others joined the group, Lord Danville decided his intervention was unnecessary. Fortunately Lady Castlereagh was not present, and Lady Kaye was stymied by her daughter's complicity in Teresa's latest start. He saw Lady Mary approaching him with a commiserating look, and he quickly made his way over to Andrew.

"Thank you," he said, shaking his hand. "I am glad of an ally in my struggle to keep my cousin within the bounds of respectability."

"She means no harm," said Andrew with a frown. "It's her wretched upbringing."

"I know. Your Miss Parr behaved with estimable loyalty. She is to be commended."

They nodded to each other in mutual admiration of Miss Parr, and both clapped loudly when at last she performed her piece.

Muriel was to have her reward. The very next day Teresa received a note from her: Andrew had agreed to turn down the mission to China in favour of a desk job at the Foreign Office. They were to be married soon after the New Year.

Meanwhile, Teresa grew increasingly discontented with the life of a Society butterfly. The charm of novelty had turned to the tedium of oft-repeated scenes and faces and conversation. Her new friends had few interests beyond the latest *on-dits* and the newest quirks of fashion.

The high point of her days had been the early ride with Andrew, often impossible because of late-night parties or blustery autumn storms. Now he cancelled their outings altogether, saying that approaching winter made the mornings too dark and cold for comfort.

Riding tamely within the confines of Hyde Park had in any case become irksome, Teresa consoled herself, and the leafless skeletons of elms and oaks depressed her spirits.

On fine afternoons, at the hour of the fashionable promenade, she still often drove in the park with Muriel, generally accompanied by Andrew or Lord Danville, or both, on horseback. Despite the November chill, they were usually surrounded by carriages and riders, though few pedestrians dared the muddy walks.

One crisp, sunny afternoon in late November, both gentlemen had joined the ladies' outing. Muriel was engrossed in plans for her approaching wedding and chattered on, apparently unaware that all her companions were exhibiting signs of restless dissatisfaction.

Teresa had guessed that her cousin Tom was increasingly attracted to Muriel. It could not please him to hear her discussing her coming marriage to another. Andrew, she suspected, was regretting the loss of his China mission. How noble he was to give up the life he had planned for the sake of his beloved's happiness. Teresa could only hope that Muriel appreciated his sacrifice, but she showed no signs of being aware of how much it meant to him.

Andrew was looking at Teresa. His face was carefully expressionless but she wondered at the pain in his blue eyes.

They reached the Serpentine, and she turned away to order the groom to drive back to the Grosvenor Gate. Coming towards them, still a hundred yards and several carriages away, was a high-perch phaeton. Teresa recognised John sitting in it, with Marco at the reins. He had been teaching his young cousin to drive, and now it seemed the novice was ready to appear in public.

Marco was managing quite nicely, thought Teresa, watching proudly. Then she saw John lean down to fiddle with something at his feet.

A moment later, Gayo was perched on his shoulder.

Marco glanced at him, startled, and lost control of his team. John grabbed for the reins. Screaming imprecations, Gayo flew up and swooped towards the driver of a nearby curricle.

Horses plunged and reared, the phaeton capsized, shrieks and wails drowned the parrot's scolding.

"How dare he!" Teresa was white-faced with anger and worry. "Oh, I must go to them, quickly!"

She stood up as the groom shrugged.

"No way through, miss."

Andrew pulled his chestnut close to the landaulet, leaned down, and swept her up onto the horse in front of him.

"Hold on," he ordered grimly.

As they galloped towards the tangled mass of carriages, Teresa whistled. Gayo heard her above the commotion and flew to meet them. He landed on Andrew's shoulder and gently pulled on his earlobe.

"Hello, dinner," he said lovingly.

Andrew somehow managed to control his startled mount. He reined in beside the wrecked phaeton and helped Teresa to slide down. John was standing there holding his head, while Marco sat on the ground looking dazed.

"Are you all right?" demanded Teresa urgently.

John looked at his hand. His glove was bloodstained. "Just a scratch," he assured her.

He reached down to Marco and helped him to his feet.

"I'll do," said the youth, blinking. "Honestly, Teresa, don't fuss."

"Game as a pebble," his cousin noted with approval. "Don't worry about us, Teresa. Tom will give us a ride home."

She glanced back and caught a glimpse of Lord Danville leaning consolingly over Muriel, her hand in his, her agitated face turned up to him.

Teresa's immediate impulse was to remove Andrew before he noticed his betrothed's behaviour, and Gayo before he wreaked any more havoc. Raking John over the coals could wait.

"Help me up," she ordered Andrew, and he swung her up onto the chestnut's back again.

"The sooner I get you out of here the better," he said through gritted teeth as they cantered towards the nearest park gates.

Teresa looked back to see that what appeared to be a good five thousand of the Upper Ten Thousand were watching them, gaping and pointing and whispering to each other. She wound her hand in the horse's mane and fought her desire to lean back against Andrew's chest.

Moments later they reached Stafford House. Teresa slid down onto the mounting block, stepped to the pavement, and turned to look up at him. He was scowling.

"Thank you," she said uncertainly, offering her hand. "I cannot say—"

"Why the devil I let your father persuade me to bring you to London, I cannot think," he said, ignoring her hand. "You are no more fit for civilised society than is that Indian witch doctor of yours."

Stunned, she let her hand drop as he rode off. With an indignant squawk Gayo rejoined her. She smoothed his ruffled feathers but her mind was on the bitter injustice of Andrew's blaming her for John's escapade. Shoulders drooping, she went into the house.

Boggs met her at the door with three thick letters.

"These were delivered by hand, not half an hour since," he told her with a conspiratorial wink. "Something to do with *coffee*, I believe, miss, if you take my meaning. I made sure no one else saw them."

Teresa took the packages without interest and thanked him mechanically. He looked offended. She hoped her unintended rebuff would not cause the butler to disclose her secret, but she was too blue-devilled to soothe his ruffled feelings.

Reaching the haven of her dressing room, Teresa leashed Gayo, slumped into a chair, and opened one of her letters.

As Boggs had hinted, it was a coffee contract. She skimmed through it, then a second.

Both bettered the terms Don Eduardo had told her to hold out for. She tossed them all aside, the third unopened, and sat staring blankly at the window until Annie arrived to draw the curtains and build up the fire.

"I came early," the abigail announced, "because His Grace wants to see you in his study before dinner, and the duchess is calling for you to her chamber right now. In the vapours again, Miss Howell said."

"Then I must change very quickly," Teresa said, smiling with an effort.

As she dressed, she wondered whether her aunt would refuse to continue to sponsor her after this latest scandal. Half the ton had witnessed it, and the other half would soon hear about it. Somehow she could not bring herself to care.

Howell admitted her to the duchess's apartments with a grim face. "Her Grace is that upset, miss," she reported in a whisper. "Mr. Boggs just happened to mention to Miss Carter as you'd received papers from some City merchants or other, and Miss Carter let it slip to Her Grace, not meaning any harm, but you know how she does rattle on, miss. Her Grace's nerves is quite overset, thinking you might be engaged in trade."

"Thank you, Howell. I shall go in to my aunt at once."

The pink chamber seemed to Teresa particularly oppressive today. The duchess was reclining on her bed, a vinaigrette clutched in her hand, but she sat bolt upright when she saw the culprit.

"Can this be true?" she demanded in a vigourous voice, then remembered her role, sank back against her pillows, and added faintly, "I cannot believe it of you, Teresa. Engaging in trade!"

Teresa had no thought of dissembling.

"I'm afraid it is true, Aunt," she admitted listlessly. "Papa desired me to arrange for the export of the coffee he grows on the hacienda."

"I understood that Lord Edward sent you to catch a husband. That may well prove excessively difficult if you are seen consorting with cits."

"He sought to kill two birds with one stone, ma'am. Since I doubt I shall ever marry, perhaps it is just as well that my other purpose is successfully accomplished."

The duchess's buoyant spirits rebounded from her horror. "Well, if you must engage in trade, I daresay it is as well to be successful. I am glad to hear it. But what is this about doubting you shall marry? Do not talk such nonsense. You are already much admired, girl, and the Season is yet some months hence."

Teresa felt a momentary urge to fling herself into her aunt's arms and tell her that the gentleman she loved not only was betrothed to another, but held her in aversion. She doubted that the duchess would sympathise, when there were any number of more eligible young men available.

"You are right, Aunt," she said, hoping she sounded convinced. "I am not yet at my last prayers. I am feeling a little mopish this evening, but it will pass. Pray excuse me, now, for my uncle asked to see me."

"Stafford knows about this shocking business?"

"I believe not, ma'am. It is about some other matter, I make no doubt."

"Then do not tell him, if you please. I have spoken sharply to Amelia and Boggs already, and if you will hold your tongue, there is no reason it should become the latest *on-dit*. However, perhaps it will be as well to leave early for Sussex, just in case word spreads. It is not worth more than a nine days' wonder, especially if you are not here to remind people by your presence. By the time we return in March, I do not doubt it will be quite forgot. I shall tell Stafford I wish to go to Five Oaks at once, though I shall be excessively sorry to miss Lady Jersey's rout."

"If you think it wise, ma'am."

Teresa curtseyed and left, wondering whether she ought

to have warned the duchess than any *on-dit* about her business activities was sure to be lost in the furor over her mad gallop across Hyde Park.

She started downstairs just as Marco dashed out of his room, looking none the worse for wear.

"Teresa, you'll never guess what has happened. Harrison has escaped from the prison hulk!"

"Harrison?"

"The slaver. Don't tell me you have forgotten his existence. Honestly, if that isn't like a female, only interested in balls and gowns. Do you think he will come looking for revenge? Ought we to warn Uncle Stafford, in case he has not read about it? And Andrew?"

"Do as you please," said his sister listlessly, and went on her way.

Marco sighed. "Well, if you think it so unimportant, I shall not bother my uncle. All the same, it would be famous if he came after us. Keep your pistol about you."

Teresa knocked on the study door, prepared for her uncle to ring a peal over her, with no intention of trying to defend herself. It was her cousin's fault that it had happened, but as Andrew had implied, no proper young lady would have owned a parrot to tempt him to mischief.

Lord John was in the room with the duke. He looked still more dashing than usual with a court plaster on his forehead. He came towards her with both hands held out, a humble apology on his lips.

"Cousin, I beg your forgiveness. I had no conceivable right to take Gayo without your knowledge. It never crossed my mind that he might distract Marco's attention."

She could not resist the rueful twinkle in his eyes, belying his penitent face and tone.

"It was very wrong of you," she said with what severity she could muster. "It is no thanks to you that neither of them came to harm."

"It is the harm to your reputation that concerns me," said the duke heavily. "You may go, John. Teresa, my dear, I do not mean to ring a peal over you. Once the damage was done, you did what you thought best, though it is unfortunate that involved galloping through the park across a gentleman's saddle-bow. However, Thomas assures me that you had no choice if you were to catch your bird before he caused any more damage, not to mention your very proper concern for your brother's possible injuries. At least Graylin had the wit to remove you rapidly from the scene."

"I am so sorry, Uncle. I truly never meant to disgrace your name."

"It is not so bad as that. It is bound to be the talk of the moment, however. I think it best that we leave for Five Oaks tomorrow, while talk dies down. I had intended to go next week in any case, and we have no important engagements."

"It is not necessary for everyone to put themselves out for me, sir. I can very well go alone."

"That will never do. For one thing, I have no desire to allow the gabblemongers to believe that you are being punished. It was John's fault, after all. For another, your aunt knows nothing of what occurred. If we leave early tomorrow, she need not find out, and by the time we return to town in February the business will be long forgotten."

"Aunt Stafford mentioned to me just now that she desires to go to Five Oaks tomorrow." Teresa was struck by the similarity of the duke's and the duchess's reaction to her misdemeanours.

"I meant to tell her that you have been burning the candle at both ends and are beginning to look sadly pulled." His Grace grinned at his indignant niece. "However, if she wishes to go anyway, we shall let her believe it to be her own notion. Now, we generally get up quite a party for Christmas. I want you to be comfortable, my dear, so I shall invite a number of your particular friends to join us in a week or so. Danville has suggested Miss Parr and Miss Kaye, Mr. Wishart, Graylin, and one or two others."

"Oh Uncle, you are a great deal too good to me! I do try to deserve your kindness, indeed I do."

He patted her cheek.

"Off with you then, child. And keep that parrot of yours safely leashed until we can get him down to the country."

Teresa went slowly up to the drawing room. She could not bring herself to tell him that Sir Andrew Graylin was not at all likely to accept his invitation.

$= 13 =$

Five Oaks was scarce half a day's carriage ride south of London. At first Teresa felt her spirits rise as they left the smoky, bustling city behind them, but her cheerfulness did not last.

The countryside, so pretty on her arrival in England, was now painted grey and dun, and the leafless trees looked depressingly dead to one used to the ever-lush tropical forest.

Andrew blamed her for the turn-up in the park. If she ever saw him again, he would doubtless be already married. Now that she was a subject of scandal, he and Muriel would probably not invite her to the wedding. Just as well, since Teresa did not think she could bear to watch them plight their troth.

Though they had forgiven her, she felt that she was in disgrace with both her uncle and aunt, and for two different *contretemps* since neither knew of both. The duchess, her exuberance at Teresa's commercial success dissipated, was annoyed at missing Lady Jersey's rout. She claimed a megrim and lay back against the brown velvet squabs with an expression of suffering, eyes closed. The duke, sitting opposite, leaned forward and patted Teresa's hand.

"Pray do not look so miserable, child," he whispered, glancing at his wife. "I have assured you that I do not hold you to blame."

She smiled at him tremulously. "I believe you were right, Uncle. I have been drawing the bustle with a vengeance, and am now reaping the effects."

Determined not to let a single tear escape, she closed her eyes tight and leaned back in the corner.

If Teresa had been impressed by Stafford House, her first sight of Five Oaks overwhelmed her. A Palladian mansion, set on a gentle slope overlooking the meandering River Arun, it could have held her jungle home in one wing and scarcely noticed its presence.

Small, fawn Jersey cows wandered about the park, while larger, dusky red Sussex cattle browsed the meadows by the river. The flower beds in the formal gardens were bare, but there was an evergreen shrubbery close to the house which promised shelter for winter walks. Better still, Teresa anticipated long rides across the rolling hills.

Inside, the mansion was less elegant and formal than the London house. Not that anything was shabby; rather it exuded an air of homely comfort. This was the duke's favourite seat, within easy reach of London, where generations of ducal children had grown up and congenial house parties often filled the rooms with lively activity.

Teresa stood in the huge entrance hall and tried to imagine her father as a small boy sliding down the well-polished bannisters.

Her bedchamber had a window seat with a view, framed by a vast cedar, down to the rippling brown waters of the Arun, fringed with bare willows. She saw deer mingling with cows in the park, and a pair of dogs lolloped across the lawn and disappeared into the shrubbery. The setting sun, weak but willing, escaped from the layer of clouds and turned the grey hills to green.

Teresa decided to take Gayo outside before it grew dark. Here, surely, he could not land her in the briars.

Gayo flew wide, joyful circles, shouting "Hello, hello," with never a curse escaping his beak. Calmed by his pleasure and her peaceful surroundings, Teresa blessed her uncle for bringing her to this haven.

The next few days she had little leisure for brooding. She

rode with Marco and their cousins, helped the duchess plan entertainments for the coming party, explored the house, and met several neighbours. Every day she took Gayo out, and they soon had a regular audience of fascinated gardeners, dairy maids, and any other servants who could sneak away from their duties for a few minutes.

One afternoon, she was descending the main stair with the parrot on her shoulder when she saw a gentleman in a greatcoat standing with his back to her in the hall. He was studying a full-length portrait of the first Duke in all his bewigged glory.

Teresa was going to retreat, not wanting to risk Gayo embarrassing a guest, but there was something familiar about the set of his blond head.

She paused, and he turned.

"Andrew!"

She ran down the stairs, her face alight with joy. Then she remembered the terms on which they had parted.

"Teresa!" He took a step towards her, both hands held out, then stopped.

Gayo bridged the gap. "Hello, dinner!"

"I did not think you would come."

"I had to, if only to apologise. If you cannot forgive me, I shall not stay."

"Forgive you?"

"It was all my fault. Well, Lord John was not precisely blameless. But I cannot think what came over me. Had I not swept you onto my horse and galloped off with you like Young Lochinvar in Scott's poem, no one need have connected you with the incident."

"I was afraid Marco was badly hurt, and I had to retrieve Gayo. Given the choice of picking up my skirts and running through the mud, or playing the Bride of Young Lochinvar . . . " Teresa flushed. "Well, you know what I mean." How she would have liked to play bride to this braw gallant.

"You know the poem?"

Somehow they were friends again.

"Papa once bought a whole chest of books from an English captain, without any idea what was in it. That was one of my favourites. I should like to visit Scotland one day. Are you just now arrived?"

"Yes, the butler has gone to announce me to the duke. I am very glad to have seen you first, for I had no notion how to tell him that my staying depended upon you."

She laughed. "But you will stay. I am taking Gayo outside. When you have seen my uncle, if you are not too tired, will you join me?"

"Happily."

He was at her side ten minutes later, and together they strolled about, chatting comfortably, while the parrot enjoyed his freedom.

"It is growing chilly," said Teresa at last, pulling her cloak closer about her. She whistled, and Gayo sped to her. As they turned towards the house, she told Andrew, "The rest of the guests will arrive tomorrow. My aunt has a hundred entertainments planned to keep us all busy."

"Then I am pleased to have arrived early, to enjoy a quiet cose with you." He smiled at her.

"How is it that you did not travel with Muriel?" Teresa asked, her heart aching. She had no desire to talk of his betrothed, but the words escaped her. She fought to keep her voice even.

"I came via my home, to see my family." He seemed no happier to the choice of subject.

"I am surprised she did not go with you, since she will so soon be your wife."

"Muriel and my sister-in-law are . . . I cannot say at daggers drawn, for Muriel is by far too gentle for such a phrase. Nonetheless, they do not deal together."

"You mean, I collect, that your sister-in-law bullies her. I remember that you told me she is an intimidating female. Something like your future mama-in-law, I daresay. Poor Muriel is such a meek creature, you do well to keep them apart, though you cannot separate her from her mother."

"I cannot, but the duchess can. The invitation did not include Lady Parr."

They exchanged grins and went into the house in perfect agreement for once.

That night, in spite of her active day, Teresa lay awake for some time after Annie snuffed out her candle. If only Andrew were not engaged to Muriel. If only Muriel were not her friend. If only Don Eduardo had never invited him to the Hacienda del Inglés.

She realised now that the damage to her heart had been done before ever they left Costa Rica. She had believed Papa that she was attracted to Andrew only because he was a sophisticated stranger. Now she had made the acquaintance of half the eligible gentlemen in England, many of them more elegant, handsomer, richer, and of higher rank. Now she knew for certain that she loved him. And somehow, she must keep both him and Muriel from guessing it.

The next afternoon the rest of the house party arrived. As well as Teresa's particular friends, there were a number of people of the duke and duchess's generation, and their elder daughter.

Lady Pamela Jordan, a pretty matron a year younger than her brother Tom, was accompanied by her husband, Lord Jordan, and four children under the age of ten. She largely ignored the former in favour of the latter, spending most of her time in the nursery. In fact after a friendly greeting that made her hope for a closer relationship, Teresa was disappointed to find that she seldom saw her cousin.

Jenny Kaye and Daphne Pringle, in raptures to be invited to Five Oaks, immediately set about the siege of Lord Danville. Teresa found it impossible to blame him for turning increasingly to the unthreatening, safely betrothed Muriel. Whenever the younger set split up, for instance when they went by carriage to see Arundel Castle, he manoeuvred so that he, Teresa, Muriel, and Andrew were together.

This did not please his brother.

"The devil of it is," he explained to Teresa, "that as soon as Tom's out of view they start after me, though I ain't half such a good catch."

Teresa had mixed feelings on this subject, which she confided to no one. It was a painful joy to be so often with Andrew. The presence of his betrothed increased the pain. Lord Danville's company helped her bear the situation, but at the same time it was a source of confusion. He and Muriel seemed often to have more to say to each other than to Andrew or herself. She knew Andrew noticed it and was hurt.

In spite of the circumstances, she enjoyed the trip to Arundel. She had never seen anything remotely like the ancient medieval castle, rebuilt time and time again over centuries. She listened, fascinated, to Cousin Tom's tales of its history. It belonged to the Duke of Norfolk, and though he was not in residence, his housekeeper made them welcome and provided a magnificent luncheon.

The December days were short, and they left early for the two-hour drive back to Five Oaks. Though the sun was shining, it was bitterly cold. The housekeeper provided hot bricks for their feet, and Andrew and Lord Danville carefully tucked fur rugs about Teresa and Muriel in the smaller of the two carriages. Then they took their seats opposite and tucked themselves in. They set off, followed by the larger coach with the rest of the group.

Some three miles from Five Oaks, they passed through the village of Billingshurst. They were in the middle of the village when their carriage stopped abruptly, with much whoa-ing from the coachman.

"What is it?" called Lord Danville.

The answer was drowned by a confusion of snarling growls and screams. Teresa leaned out of the window, but all she could see was a village girl carrying two pails of water on a yoke, her hand raised to her mouth, an expression of horror on her round face.

"Lord, what's to do?" asked Andrew, peering over Teresa's shoulder.

"I cannot see."

"I shall go and find out," he decided.

He swung open the door and jumped out of the carriage.

"Wait for me," said Teresa.

"Surely you will not go too!" exclaimed Muriel to her departing back.

Behind them the second coach had stopped and several of its occupants descended, calling out questions. The horses were shying and tossing their heads, held with difficulty by the coachman. Teresa and Andrew hurried forward to where they could see past the restless team, and John ran to join them.

A mastiff and a bull terrier were locked in combat in the middle of the street, bloodcurdling sounds issuing from their throats. It was a terrifying sight, but it did not explain the horror on the girl's face.

Then they saw the child. Perhaps two years old, he was toddling towards the dogs with every evidence of fascinated delight, his hand held out as if to pet them.

Somewhere a woman screamed, "Jemmy!"

With one accord, Andrew and John leaped at the dogs. They seized them by the scruffs of their necks and hung on with all their strength.

Teresa dodged around them, picked up the little boy and set him down at the side of the road, well out of the way. He pouted at her.

"Want see doggies," he said indignantly.

A woman in a white apron hurried up, tears pouring down her pale, plump face.

"Oh, Jemmy! Oh, miss!"

Teresa had no time for her. A glance showed her Andrew and John backing away with bloodied hands. The mastiff and the bull terrier, their quarrel forgotten, had both turned on the spoilsports and were advancing with teeth bared. Teresa had not seen so many teeth, so close, since she lay on the ground with the jaguar poised above her.

She dashed to the girl with the yoke, praying that she had already been to the pump. The buckets were full. She seized one of them and threw the icy water at the menacing dogs.

They shook themselves and looked back at her, annoyed at this new interruption of their sport. As she picked up the second bucket and sloshed its contents at them they fled, yelping.

So did John and Andrew.

"Here, I say, cousin," said John indignantly. "That water is damnably cold."

"Your skill with a bucket does not match your skill with a pistol," added Andrew, looking with annoyance at his soaked unmentionables.

"I should have let them go after you." Hurt by their ingratitude, Teresa turned her back on them.

The rest of the party from the second carriage hurried up, laughing at the sodden gentlemen, congratulating Teresa on the rescue.

"Dashed if I've ever seen anything so neat!" exclaimed Mr. Wishart.

"Well done, Teresa," cried Marco.

"How brave you are." Daphne shuddered. "I should never have known what to do."

Then the child's mother approached, shyly pushing through the gentlefolk to thank her baby's saviour. Several other villagers arrived to hear the tale and marvel. Teresa was the centre of attention, and basking in it, until a reproachful voice from the first carriage interrupted.

"We must be on our way," called Lord Danville. "Miss Parr is sadly shocked and must be taken home."

"And we are frozen half to death," grumbled John, with a shiver. "It's a toss-up whether we expire from exposure or bleed to death first."

Teresa took his hand and examined it.

"It is not deep, but it must be thoroughly cleansed, and

soon," she said. "Cousin Tom is right. We must go."

She turned to Andrew, but he had already bound his wound with a handkerchief. He frowned at her.

"It is nothing," he said gruffly. "For pity's sake let us be on our way before dark, if you are done with your admirers."

He and John both climbed into the first carriage with Muriel and Tom, so that only one vehicle would be soaked by their wet garments. Teresa perforce joined the others.

Mr. Wishart took her hand and patted it.

"If they are ungracious," he whispered, "it is because they are mortified at being rescued by a beautiful young lady when they hoped to be heroes themselves. Do not heed their sulks. You were magnificent, Miss Danville."

Unconsoled, Teresa removed her hand from his clasp.

It was dark when they reached Five Oaks at last. Andrew abandoned Muriel, still trembling with shock, to Miss Carter's anxious care and hurried up to his bedchamber. He was shivering violently, frozen to the bone. Rowson arrived on his heels. He took one look at his master and sent for a hot bath.

"And step lively," he called after the footman. Then he turned back to Andrew. "Nice weather for swimming," he said conversationally as he set about pulling off the sodden top boots.

"It was that d-devilish Miss D-Danville," said Andrew, his teeth chattering.

"Shoved you in the river, did she? Daresay you gave her cause. Game as a pebble, our Miss Teresa. Let's get them pantaloons off then."

"She is n-not our Miss T-Teresa and she did not sh-shove me in the river. She threw a bucket of water over a pair of fighting dogs and drenched both Lord John and me."

"What did I say? A right Trojan, she is."

"Dammit, Rowson, will you take her side? She is a perfectly devilish female. Where's my bath?"

"I'll go hurry 'em up."

Rowson was certain that the whole story would by now have passed from coachman to cook and thence to the rest of the staff. Whatever had got his master on his high ropes, it was no mere soaking.

Andrew sat by the fire, wrapped in his dressing gown, gradually thawing. As his shivers ceased, he found himself able to admire Teresa's courage, and still more, her efficiency in an emergency. While he and her cousin had acted like the veriest rattlepates, going for the dogs, she had coolly snatched the child to safety and then turned and rescued them from their folly.

It was all of a piece with everything he knew of her. Before they had exchanged a word, she had saved him from a deadly snake. She had saved herself from the jaguar, with some assistance from Gayo. She had helped him to save four score slaves from the depths of the ocean. When danger threatened, she was not only fearless but practical.

In the same situation, Muriel was more like to swoon. That was how a delicately bred female ought to behave. After all, a man wanted the opportunity to save his beloved from deadly peril. It was just his luck to have fallen in love with an Amazon who stood in no need of a heroic deliverer.

Horrified, Andrew forced a halt in his train of thought. What nonsense! He loved and was engaged to marry a young lady of irreproachable timidity.

The recollection brought him no satisfaction.

Rowson came back, with a footman bearing a copper hip bath followed by half a dozen others with hot water. In no time, Andrew was lounging in a steaming bath and beginning to feel much more the thing.

"Our Miss Teresa gave me a healing wash for your hand, sir," said Rowson, setting out evening clothes.

"It is a mere scratch."

"She said as it's a dog bite it might get infected. I'll do it when you get out. There's a letter, too, came in the morning mail after you left."

"Who's it from, can you tell?"

"The Foreign Office, I reckon. Been forwarded a couple o' times."

"Let me see it. No, I'd best dry off first."

Andrew stepped from the bath and Rowson enveloped him in a huge towel that had warmed by the fire. Feeling at last thoroughly comfortable, he sat in a chair, slit the impressive Foreign Office seal, and opened the letter.

"Damnation! It's back to London for us first thing tomorrow," he said gloomily. "Though in the circumstances, perhaps it's just as well."

"For good, sir?"

"No, just a few days. We'll be back well before Christmas." More's the pity, he added silently.

He was, he thought, in a devil of a coil.

Here he was engaged to Muriel, the prettiest, best behaved, and most docile young lady he had ever known. Yet marriage to her seemed less and less attractive.

On top of that, she was spending all her time in Lord Danville's pocket. He knew, from something Lord John had let drop, that his brother regarded her as a safe object of his admiration, because of her betrothal. The duke's heir had no serious intentions. Since Andrew, as an honourable gentleman, could not cry off, they would inevitably be wed in a few weeks willy-nilly.

And meanwhile, Teresa was mortifying his pride and otherwise cutting up his peace. He had certainly not known a dull moment since first they met. By the end of the coming Season she would be married to one of her many admirers, while he would be stuck in his desk job at the Foreign Office. Their paths would seldom cross.

China began to look more and more inviting.

=== 14 ===

IT WAS STILL bitterly cold when Andrew left Five Oaks, promising to return in a few days. A thin, high haze hid the sun. Teresa, watching from her dressing room as he rode down the drive, thought she had never in her life seen such a dreary scene.

She had no desire whatever for the usual morning ride. For once she would stay behind with Muriel, who did not ride and was generally left with the older guests. She must make a special effort to be kind to Muriel, to assuage her guilt for having fallen in love with her friend's future husband.

As it turned out, only Lord Danville and his brother-in-law ventured out. No one else evinced the slightest wish to risk frostbite for the sake of exercise.

There was no lack of entertainment indoors. Small groups gathered in the billiard room and the music room. Several ladies repaired to the drawing room to sew and gossip. One or two more intellectual souls settled in the library to read.

Teresa had always loved books and there had been little opportunity since her arrival in England to make use of the duke's impressive collection. She went to the library and browsed along the shelves.

History, philosophy, the classics in the original and in translation, books of travel, poetry, biography—they all looked immeasurably dull. She chose a novel and sat down with it. It failed to hold her attention, and her second choice fared no better.

A series of muttered grunts and black looks told her she was disturbing the other readers. She put the books away and went to the music room.

"Teresa,'" cried Jenny Kaye. "I brought my brother's guitar with me. I shall fetch it if you will join us, unless you prefer just to sing with us."

She was seated at the pianoforte with Muriel, Daphne, Marco, and Mr. Wishart gathered round. They seemed to be having a hilarious time—even quiet Marco, who was translating into English for their amusement a Spanish song Teresa knew to be far from proper.

She smiled and shook her head.

"I was looking for Cousin John," she said mendaciously. She had thought music might soothe her. Laughter and merriment were not what she wanted.

"John's playing billiards," Mr. Wishart told her. "I'll come down with you."

"No, no, I should not dream of interrupting your concert, if that is the right word for it."

Teresa wandered listlessly down to the billiard room, for want of anything better to do. Lord John was just finishing a game with one of his father's political colleagues. He greeted her with unabashed relief.

"Cousin Teresa, I'll challenge you to a game."

"Remember the outcome last time you challenged me. Besides, I do not know how to play."

"Nothing could be more innocuous than billiards. I shall teach you. I'd wager, with your eye, you'll soon be a worthy opponent."

Teresa found that learning the rules and techniques occupied just sufficient of her attention, neither requiring intense concentration nor leaving her time to think. Her cousin's casual cheerfulness and good-natured teasing chased her blue devils away for a while.

They played until the gong rang for luncheon. By then he had beaten her hollow in three games, though her score improved each time.

This he announced at table, to his sister Pamela's immediate scorn.

"Indeed you are no gentleman, John, to boast thus. Besides, you ought to have let Teresa win."

"Short of playing with my back turned to the table, that would have been impossible, Pam. And anyway Teresa won last time I challenged her."

"Oh, famous! You beat our top-o'-the-trees Corinthian, cousin? What was the contest?"

Teresa flushed. Lord Danville, Mr. Wishart, Jenny, and Daphne eyed her knowingly but held their tongues.

"Shoo . . . " began Lord John.

"Bless you," said Jenny and Daphne in chorus.

"I hope you are not coming down with a cold," said Lord Danville, frowning at his brother.

"Sneezed myself, this morning," said Mr. Wishart. "It's this dashed weather."

"Spillikins!" said Teresa gratefully. It seemed a pity that she could not boast of her superior talent at target shooting, but she knew the others were right to forestall John's revelation.

"You must come up to the nursery and play with the children," Lady Pamela invited. "Little Tom adores spillikins, and he is very good about not sulking when he loses."

In the event, all the young people decided the nursery was as good a place as any to be on such a day. Even Lord Danville and Lord Jordan forgot their dignity and joined in games of spillikins and teetotum, lotto, and hunt the slipper.

Teresa had never seen Muriel so animated. She and Lord Danville took the lead in romping with the children. When they paused for breath, Teresa heard them expatiating on the joys of family life. Both, it seemed, wanted numerous offspring. She could not help wondering whether Andrew knew that he was expected to father a large family. It made her quite cross to see the two of them so in charity with each other. It was not at all fair to Andrew, the way demure

Muriel turned into a flirt as soon as he absented himself. How would she behave if he was gone for a year or more?

The afternoon seemed endless, the evening worse.

The next morning was still colder, but at least the sun was shining. Teresa could not bear the thought of another day confined to the house. She was the only lady who chose to ride with the gentlemen, and they expressed their surprise at her joining them.

"Are you sure it is wise, cousin?" asked Lord Danville solicitously. "After growing up in a tropical climate, you cannot have the least notion how shockingly cold England in December can be."

"I mean to find out, or I shall never know. Annie has bundled me up in innumerable layers of clothing, and your housekeeper thrust this muffler upon me as I came down the stair. How should I wear it, do you think?"

John offered his assistance. He pulled the hood of her cloak up over her head, then wound the muffler round and round the lower half of her face, tucking the end in securely. Then he stood back to study the result.

He laughed at her.

"Dashed if you don't look like one of those devilish Egyptian mummies in the British Museum."

"When were you ever in the British Museum?" enquired his elder brother sceptically.

"Went for a lark once. Most sobering occasion, I can tell you, seeing all those fellows that died four thousand years ago still standing around."

"I only hope my horse doesn't run a mile when she sees me coming," said Teresa.

Bundled up though she was, Teresa was at first startled by the cold. Until she mounted, the ground seemed to suck the warmth from her feet through the soles of her boots. A vigourous gallop brought tears to her eyes from the rush of frigid air, but it warmed the rest of her and she was enjoying herself when Lord Jordan suggested turning back.

"Not yet," she pleaded. "Do let us go just a little farther."

"Let's go round by the lake," said John. "Another day of this and it may even freeze over hard enough for skating if we are lucky."

Teresa had seen a reference to skating in a book, but had not the least idea of what was involved. As they rode towards the lake, the gentlemen described the mechanics of the sport and told numerous anecdotes about the disastrous and comical efforts of their friends.

"Naturally, none of those present has ever been so disgracefully clumsy as to fall on the ice," Mr. Wishart assured her with a wink.

She had ridden and walked by the lake before and had thought that it must be delightful in the summer. A tributary of the Arun had been dammed to form a sizable pool with paved walks around it. White-painted bridges crossed the stream, and the whole was protected from wind on the north and east by woodland. A pretty summerhouse stood at the edge of the woods, looking rather forlorn at this season.

Already the lake's surface was iced over except where the stream entered and left. Teresa found it an astonishing sight. As they drew near, an unwary mallard flew down to land and went sliding across, quacking indignantly.

Lord John dismounted and went to test the ice with a stick. It held, so he took a cautious step, hurriedly retreating when it creaked under his weight.

"Let me!" cried Teresa.

John helped her down, and despite Lord Danville's objection, she approached the lake's margin. With some trepidation she stepped onto the ice with one foot, holding her cousin's hand tightly. The other foot followed, and she stood very still, not wishing to follow the duck's humiliating example. Suddenly she giggled.

"How my brothers would stare, to see me standing on the water," she said. "I hope it will freeze hard enough for skating. John, I will come back now."

She turned, with the greatest care, and gave him her other hand. As she stepped towards him her foot slipped and she fell forward to land in his arms.

For a moment he held her close, gazing down at her with an arrested look. She flushed at the disturbing light in his eyes.

"You are a cosy armful, cousin," he murmured, setting her steady on her feet. "I believe I'd have stolen a kiss were it not for that muffler."

"Not in the presence of half a dozen other gentlemen, I trust!" Teresa attempted a rallying tone.

"Is that an invitation for the next time we find ourselves alone together?" he enquired with a wicked grin.

"Certainly not. Help me mount, if you please."

They rode back to the house. Teresa was abstracted, wondering whether she had misread her cousin's meaningful gaze. Suppose he did develop a *tendre* for her, suppose he went so far as to offer for her, did she want to be his wife?

Lord John was handsome, plump in the pocket, and of impeccable birth, factors that weighed heavily with all her female acquaintance. It would certainly count as an estimable connexion, though as second son, he did not quite measure up to a splendid match. More important to Teresa, she thoroughly enjoyed his company, and it would be an added tie to her father's family, for whom she had developed a great affection.

Best of all, he was never shocked by her lapses from the highest standards of propriety. On the other hand, he had been responsible for several of those lapses. He had not a serious bone in his body and was more inclined to lead her into mischief than to steer her away. Much as she liked him, she did not hold him in esteem. Nor did she love him.

A wave of desolation swept over her. Andrew had her heart and she would never love another. It would not be fair to wed her cousin when all she could offer was affection.

At that point in her musing she managed to laugh at herself. It was not at all likely that John would come up to scratch. He was only twenty-five, enjoying his freedom, and with no need to provide an heir. Undoubtedly all he wanted was a light flirtation, and she would oblige, while making very sure not to find herself alone with him.

When the duke heard that the lake was in a fair way to being frozen over, he proposed a skating party. If the weather stayed cold, the ice should be thick enough in a couple of days. If not, they must devise some other entertainment for the guests he planned to invite.

Teresa spent the afternoon helping her aunt write invitations to all the neighbours with offspring of an age to enjoy so vigourous a pastime. Recalling the gentlemen's stories, she hoped the ice would set soon enough for her to practise a little. It sounded as if it would be all too easy to make a complete cake of oneself in public.

By the next afternoon, Jenny, Daphne, and Muriel were sufficiently tired of being confined to the house to agree to walk with Teresa to the lake.

"Do pray wrap up warmly," instructed the duchess anxiously. "You will not wish to spend Christmas in bed with a putrid sore throat."

Teresa was soon ready and went to Jenny's chamber. Jenny, wrapped in layer upon layer of wool, was gazing at herself in the mirror.

"I shall die of mortification if any gentleman sees me bundled up like an Esquimau," she announced with a melodramatic air spoiled by a giggle.

"I did not invite any gentlemen to accompany us. I am sure it is perfectly proper to go without. The lake is not far from the house, though it is out of sight, and I shall take my pistol, though I beg you will not mention it to the others. No one will see it under my cloak."

"I scarcely think it will prove necessary. This is England, not Costa Rica."

"I promised my father to carry it when possible. Judging by his stories, there must have been more highwaymen and footpads about in his time."

"In any case, gentlemen are unnecessary for once. We must sneak out down the backstairs."

"Thus providing amusement to the servants instead," agreed Teresa, laughing.

They had a merry outing, all but Muriel venturing onto the edge of the ice, clutching each other and giggling. Jenny proclaimed herself an accomplished skater and slid several feet to demonstrate.

When she turned and picked her way carefully back to them, she was frowning.

"There's a man watching us," she said. "In the wood, over there."

They all looked, but saw no one.

"Either you imagined it, or it was one of my uncle's gamekeepers," Teresa said.

"I did *not* imagine it, and he looked by far too shabby to be one of His Grace's servants. I have noticed that they are all particularly well clad."

"Then it must have been a poacher," Daphne suggested. "Chasing rabbits or pheasants, not young ladies."

They all laughed, and the conversation turned to the more usual subject of the pursuit of beaux.

Walking homeward, Teresa noticed that yellowish clouds were gathering. As she was unfamiliar with the climate she thought only that it was a pity the sun no longer shone. However, when she went up to her chamber, Annie told her that the talk was all of snow.

"It don't make sense to me, miss, but they all say the same thing. The clouds'll make it warmer and it'll likely start snowing tonight."

"Warmer! Do not say so. I hope the ice will not melt before the party."

That evening she asked Lord Danville about the possibility of a thaw.

"Quite likely," he said. "A chance to skate comes but rarely. I hope you will not be excessively disappointed, Miss Parr," he added, turning to Muriel.

"Oh no, I never meant to skate, " she assured him. "I fear Mama would not approve."

"It is a hurly-burly business," he conceded. "Your delicacy of principle is admirable." He smiled at her warmly and pressed her hand.

Teresa immediately decided she must speak to Muriel about her encouragement of his lordship before Andrew returned to observe it. The next morning, she dragged her out to walk down to the lake, ostensibly to test the ice.

No snow had fallen, but the clouds still lowered overhead. It was much warmer and the thaw had turned the paths to mud. There was no difficulty persuading Jenny and Daphne not to go for a stroll with them. Only Teresa's determination prevailed upon Muriel.

They walked in silence for some distance, Muriel attempting in vain to avoid the worst of the mud, Teresa casting about for a way of broaching so delicate a matter. She realised now that she had no real right to intervene. None of those concerned were in any way accountable to her and Muriel would have every reason to resent her interference.

As they reached the lake, in which Teresa had lost interest, Muriel spoke first. "I cannot think why we had to come out here, but I am glad of the chance to speak to you privately. I pray you can advise me, for I do not know what to do."

"What to do?"

"It is all such a dreadful muddle. Everyone will think it is creampot love, but indeed it is not, and they will say I am a horrid jilt. I cannot bear it."

"What cannot you bear? Muriel, pray do not weep, it makes it prodigious difficult to understand you. Here, take my handkerchief. Now, do try to explain this muddle to me, if you want my advice."

Muriel sniffed dolefully. "Oh, Teresa, I am in love with your cousin. He is such a perfect gentleman and would not dream of going off to America or China, and I promise you I do not care that he will be duke."

"Does Tom know this?"

"I have said nothing. It would be most improper even were I not betrothed to Andrew. A lady does not declare her love until she is certain that the gentleman's interest is fixed. And I shall wait forever for him to speak to me, because he is by far too gentlemanly to pay his addresses while I am not free. What am I to do?"

"You are afraid to cry off in case Tom does not come up to scratch," said Teresa scornfully.

"No, it is not like that, I promise it is not. Only I am afraid it will hurt Andrew dreadfully and all for nothing if I do not marry Lord Danville after all."

"I am glad you have some thought for Andrew's feelings! How can you treat him so? It is the outside of enough, when he has loved you all these years and you have at last set the date for your wedding. And he is prepared to give up China for your sake, though travel is the joy of his life. I had not thought you so hard-hearted."

Muriel was silent, abashed, and in the quiet Teresa heard a twig break. She glanced around.

Three scruffy men were bearing down upon them.

She could not see their faces, wrapped in mufflers, but the middle one, the one with the gun, looked vaguely familiar. The other two, one brawny, the second slight, waved fearsome cudgels.

"Run, Muriel!" she cried, struggling to draw her pistol from the entangling folds of her cloak.

Terrified, Muriel froze.

Teresa grasped the gunstock. It was too late to draw. The ruffians were upon them. Better that they should not realise that she was armed. She turned to flee, though she knew the attempt to be in vain.

The big man wrapped his arms about her. She kicked

backwards at his shin, missing as he swung her round. Muriel was squirming in the scrawny man's grasp, her face so white she looked about to swoon.

They both faced the third man now.

"What do you want with us?" cried Teresa. "The Duke of Stafford is my uncle, you will never get away with this."

"Oh, I know who you are, right enough, Miss Danville. I have been waiting a long time for this moment." He pulled down his muffler. "Captain Harrison, late of the good ship *Snipe*, at your service, ma'am."

= 15 =

TERESA LAY FACEDOWN in mouldy straw in the bottom of a rickety farm cart. Her wrists were tied behind her, her ankles roped together, and her heavy cloak wound stiflingly about her head.

In spite of the cloak, she could smell the manure the cart must once have carried. The empty sacks strewn on top of her did little to shield her from the glacial draughts that penetrated every chink in the ancient vehicle.

She could not stop shivering, though she tried to persuade herself it was just the cold. Still, the memory of Captain Harrison's mocking sneer crowded all other images from her mind. He blamed her for his imprisonment. He had sworn vengeance, and yet when she learned of his escape, she had done nothing. Every aching bruise told her she had been a fool.

Muriel moaned.

"Are you all right?" Teresa whispered.

There was no answer. She risked a louder voice.

"Muriel, are you all right?"

"Stow yer whid," growled Brawny incomprehensibly, "or I'll bash yer 'ead in."

"I don't 'old wiv bashing gentry coves," whined Scrawny. "We'll 'ave the Robin Redbreasts arter us, mark my words. If I'da knowed wot you wuz . . . "

"That will do," commanded Harrison. "The Bow Street Runners have been after me since I escaped that damnable hulk, and they've not caught a whiff of my traces yet. After this we'll be off to America, free and clear, and live like lords the rest of our lives. Hush now, someone's coming. Bert, climb over in the back and keep our little birds quiet."

To judge by the way the cart swayed and creaked, Bert was the man Teresa had labelled Brawny. She felt his huge hand press down on the back of her head. Suddenly it was impossible to breathe. Blackness closed in.

When she regained her senses, nothing had changed except that, if possible, she was colder. Though she still wore gloves and half-boots, her hands and feet were numb, both from cold and from the ropes cutting off the circulation.

The painful journey seemed to have been going on forever, but she had caught a glimpse of the wretched nag pulling the cart and suspected that they were moving very slowly. The closer they were to Five Oaks, the better the chance of rescue. Yet that chance seemed slim, and what might not their vengeful captors do to them in the meantime? It was up to her to save herself and Muriel.

With a jerk that rattled her bones, the cart stopped.

"Bring 'em in, boys," Harrison ordered.

Again the cart shook as the men climbed from the front bench into the back. Teresa was swung up onto Brawny's massive shoulder, her head hanging down his back, his arm about her thighs. Helpless, she dangled there, feeling dizzy and sick as he jumped down to the ground.

The cloak round her head slipped a little and she saw Scrawny pulling Muriel's limp form by the feet across the bed of the cart to the tailgate.

"She's too 'eavy," the little man complained. "No way I can carry 'er."

"I'll come back for 'er," offered Brawny. "You leave 'er there, Sid, and go put the prancer in the shed."

"Prancer? You lost yer marbles? This nag's fit fer the knacker. Still, yer always wuz bright as a rusty nail." He went off muttering disapprovingly.

Teresa stifled a hysterical giggle. Brawny Bert and Scrawny Sid made a charming pair.

Despite her whirling head, she noted that they were in a clearing in a wood. The sticky mud that squelched beneath Brawny's scuffed boots smelled of leaf mould. That and his torn coat were all she could see until they entered a ramshackle building.

The floorboards were split and warped. The lower part of the whitewashed walls was grimy, and heaps of blown leaves lay in the corners. The rickety stairs protested loudly as Brawny thudded up them.

At the top he turned to the right. Teresa's head hit the wall and she fainted again.

She woke to find herself lying on a straw-filled palliasse in a tiny room. Her cloak had been unwrapped from her head and pulled roughly around her, so she was able to examine her surroundings. The room was open to the rafters, in fact open to the sky in one corner, but the floorboards, though rough, looked solid enough. The tiny window, high under the eaves, had no glass. On the floor nearby lay a battered valise with a ragged shirt cuff hanging out. A dented pewter mug lay beside it.

This was probably where Harrison slept, with his henchmen sharing another room. It could hardly be described as a bedchamber, but Teresa quailed at the realisation that she was lying helpless on her abductor's bed. Though she knew it would make not the slightest difference if he chose to ravish her, she rolled off the thin mattress, becoming thoroughly entangled in her cloak.

Wriggling in an effort to find a more comfortable position, an impossible task with her hands and feet bound, she felt the hardness of her pistol jabbing her ribs. At least they had not discovered it, though she could not reach it.

Then she heard the stairs protesting again. She hoped it was Brawny bringing Muriel to join her.

On the other hand, if she had been unconscious for some time, it might be Harrison. She swallowed convulsively as a spark of terror shot through her. Forcing her tense body to lie limp, she closed her eyes. Surely he would leave her alone if he thought her in a swoon.

Heavy footsteps entered the room, followed by a thump and a grunt. She opened her eyes the merest slit. Brawny had dumped Muriel on the floor and was standing hands on hips looking down at her as she lay motionless, insensible. Her face was white, with a bruise on her chin and a trickle of blood running down from the corner of her mouth.

"What have you done to her?" cried Teresa, struggling to sit up.

Brawny turned to look at her and grinned nastily.

"The guv'nor don't care tuppence if this 'un sticks 'er spoon in the wall. It's you' e's int'risted in. The guv'nor don't take too kindly to them as queers 'is pitch." He nudged her with his foot. "Us is gonna 'ave a bit o' slap an' tickle wi' you once we gets our fambles on the rhino."

"Rhino?" Teresa did her best to ignore the rest of his speech, which in any case she found incomprehensible for the most part.

"The ready. Ransom. 'Is lordship reckons the dook'll come down 'andsome if 'e thinks 'e's gonna get 'is pretty niece back in one piece."

"Lord Carruthers? Is he behind this?"

"Guv'nor never told us 'is name," said the villain indifferently. "Reckon it don't matter if you guessed, for you'll not be squeaking beef when we'm done wi' yer. Sid's off wi' the ransom note already. This time termorrer, us'll be swimming in mint sauce, and you ain't gonna be worrying about it." Grinning again, he bent down and squeezed her breast with his huge, filthy paw. "There, just to keep yer going," he added with a wink.

Teresa felt her gorge rising and prayed she would not vomit. Her only defence was to pretend to faint. She heard his footsteps going towards the door.

"Feeble creeturs, them gentry morts," he muttered. "Ain't gonna be much fun if she keeps passing out."

Thud of wood on wood as he barred the door, again the

stairs creaked, then there was silence but for the distant rumble of voices.

Andrew found the falling snow soothing. It drifted gently down, too slow and light to impede his progress. The miles between London and Five Oaks disappeared beneath his chestnut's hooves, and Rowson kept pace on a sturdy cob a few strides behind him.

The calming influence was welcome. He was feeling distinctly unsettled. In London he had reached a decision which was bound to change his life, but how and to what degree depended on others.

They rode through Dorking, then took the right-hand branch in the road at Kingsfold. Ten miles to go. It stopped snowing and Andrew gazed round in wonder at the white landscape. He had spent the last two winters in hot climates and had forgotten the beauty of snow-clad hills and trees. Teresa would be astonished and, knowing her enjoyment of new experiences, delighted.

Reaching Five Oaks, they rode directly to the stables. The groom who took his horse seemed to be in the throes of strong excitement.

"Aye, sir, I'll see 'im rubbed down proper an' all. 'Tis a terrible business, sir!"

"What is? What has happened? I have been away for several days."

"Why, the young ladies, sir! Miss Danville and Miss . . . the one wi' golden curls. Disappeared, clean as a whistle. They say His Grace is in a fair pucker, not rightly knowing what to do, and young Lord John ready to ride out in all directions. I'm just off now meself, searching."

He spoke to Andrew's rapidly departing back, but Rowson paused to demand further details before following his master through the side door into the house.

A dreadful hollow filled Andrew's chest as he strode towards the entrance hall. If this was more of Teresa's mischief, he would strangle her, he swore. And this time she had managed to tangle Muriel in her coils. He had a feeling it was Muriel, though Miss Kaye also had golden curls.

But no. Though she was sometimes heedless, Teresa would never deliberately set out to worry her relations, nor to involve her gently nurtured friend in her escapades. If they were missing, they were in trouble. Perhaps even in danger.

Several servants were gathered in the hall. The butler stepped from the agitated group as Andrew appeared.

"His Grace is in the library," the butler said, without a word of greeting. His usual poker face was creased with concern. "It's a shocking business, sir."

Andrew nodded his thanks and hurried to the library. He found there all the gentlemen and several ladies of the party. The duke was standing by the fireplace, studying a torn scrap of paper with an air of desperation.

"There is no clue here," he said, his voice weary. "Ah, Graylin, I am glad to see you. Perhaps you can see something we have missed."

"Tell me what has happened. Just a minute, Marco, let me hear the whole thing."

Marco had rushed to his side and was twitching at his sleeve. "I must talk to you," he hissed.

"In a minute. Hush."

Lord Danville took it upon himself to explain the situation in his long-winded way.

"It seems Teresa and Mur . . . Miss Parr went walking this morning. They mentioned that they were going to the lake to test the ice. When they did not appear at luncheon, we sent out a couple of men, who found no sign of them."

"The ice?"

"Unbroken. Our first thought, naturally, was that they might have fallen through. We then sent out gardeners, footmen, and grooms, all the menservants, in all directions, in case they had lost their way. It had started snowing by that time, and there was little hope of seeing them, but what else could we do? Then, just ten minutes ago, this ransom note arrived. It seems that they have been abducted, and the villains want ten thousand pounds for their return."

"I shall pay, of course," said the duke heavily.

"Who brought the note?"

"An ostler from the Six Bells in Billingshurst. He did not know who sent it. We shall send the search in that direction, of course."

"Likely they expect that and used that inn to draw us off the trail," said Lord John. "They could be anywhere. Remember the note says to take the ransom in the opposite direction."

Marco plucked at Andrew's sleeve again. "I *must* talk to you," he insisted, his eyes pleading.

Andrew looked at him. The boy was frantic, his face dead white.

"Excuse us for a moment."

"Use my study," the duke offered. "I hope you have something useful to say, young man, for otherwise we must confess ourselves at a standstill."

"Muriel!"

The blue eyes opened.

"Thank God you are alive," Teresa said on a sob.

"I did not want him to know I was conscious. What a dreadful man! What are we going to do?"

"Do?"

"You always know what to do, and then do it. Andrew told me he had rather be in a tight place with you than with any gentleman of his acquaintance."

Teresa flushed. "He said that? Well, your faith in me is touching, but I have never before been abducted by three villains and tied hand and foot in a ruined cottage in the wilds of Sussex."

Muriel looked frightened but said bravely, "I know you will think of something."

"As a matter of fact I do have an idea, only it depends so

much on chance, I cannot like it. At least I still have my pistol."

"Your pistol! What a complete hand you are, Teresa. Not that I am not profoundly thankful, since I am in this fix, that you are with me."

"I am astonished that you are not in hysterics," said Teresa frankly. "Your nerves were overset when I stopped that dogfight, and you did not even see it."

"Mama taught me that gentlemen prefer delicate sensibilities in a young lady. There are no gentlemen here."

"Unfortunately."

"Do you think they will search for us?"

"Of course, but I cannot think they will find us except by the merest luck. Listen, let me tell you my plan, if it can be called a plan, so that we are prepared just in case we have a chance to try it."

She explained what Muriel would need to do if the opportunity arose.

"I will do my best. It does seem excessively unlikely that everything will work out right. I hope you will try to think up an alternative."

"Believe me, I do not intent to wait like a lamb for the slaughter," Teresa assured her grimly.

They fell silent, recalling the big man's words. Teresa tried to put her mind to devising another plan of escape, but it kept returning to his face as he bent over her, the feel of his hand on her.

"It's snowing," said Muriel. "A few flakes are coming in through the hole in the roof. I am so cold. I have not been able to feel my hands and feet this age."

"Perhaps we can roll over next to each other." A flash of memory brought Teresa the comfort of Andrew's touch that day in the jungle. If only he were here, she would be perfectly happy to let him rescue her to his heart's content. But he was in London and did not even know she was in danger. It was all up to her. "At least the exercise will warm us," she said, beginning to squirm towards Muriel.

"You look like a caterpillar."

If their giggles were subdued, still it was better than weeping.

They managed to reach each other, but their tied hands made it impossible to get close enough to be useful. In the end they lay back to back, their shoulders pressed together, trying to pretend that the minimal warmth of that contact was spreading throughout their bodies.

"I'm terrified," confessed Muriel suddenly in a shaking voice. "I shall never again pretend to be frightened when there is nothing to be frightened of. I do not know how you can be so brave."

Teresa was terrified, too, but admitting it could only distress her friend further.

"Taking into consideration the atrocious situation in which we find ourselves, your composure is admirable," she said with deliberate pomposity. "I am confident that Andrew would be prodigious proud of you."

"And . . . Tom?"

"And Tom." She sighed. "You really love him?"

Her only answer was an unhappy sniff. The silence that followed was broken by the complaint of the dilapidated stairs.

Marco started talking as soon as the connecting door between library and study closed behind them.

"Andrew, I'm certain it is Harrison. I read in the paper an age ago that he escaped, but Teresa told me not to bother you with the news."

"Why have you not told your uncle? At least it is some sort of clue." Hope mixed with dread as Andrew remembered the slaver's threats.

"He would not listen to me privately, and you know how determined Teresa was to keep that business secret. If you had not come just then, I must have blurted it out before everyone, regardless."

"The duke already knows abut the *Snipe*. Anyone else? What of your cousins?"

"John knows. I think Cousin Tom does not."

"Well, he is not like to spread the news, and the more heads put together the better." Andrew opened the library door. "Your Grace, Danville, Lord John, a word with you, if you please."

The duke and his sons hurried to join them.

"Uncle, I'm sure it's Harrison, the slave captain. He escaped before he was transported."

Lord Danville looked at Marco blankly, then turned to his father. "What is this, sir?" he demanded, frowning in puzzlement.

John, Marco, and Andrew all started talking at once. Andrew won. He told a brief version of the rescue of the slaves from the *Snipe*, and then Marco went on to describe the trial and to explain how he had read about Harrison's escape in the *Times* before they left London.

"I was going to tell you, Uncle, but Teresa thought it unimportant. I wish I had told you, all the same. So you see, it must be Harrison, and I daresay Lord Carruthers has a hand in it, too."

"Carruthers? What the devil has he to do with this?" asked John, surprised. "I know he's a dirty dish, but kidnapping is going a bit far."

"Harrison named him as the owner of the *Snipe*," said Andrew. "You know him?"

"He is a neighbour, unfortunately," John told him.

Andrew frowned in thought. "Carruthers cannot blame Teresa for the loss of his investment, but he might hope to recoup something from the ransom and then leave Harrison to wreak vengeance."

"Vengeance?" The duke paled.

"Yes," Andrew said grimly. "Whether you pay the ransom or not, sir, I doubt very much that Teresa will be released unharmed."

The horrified silence was ended by Lord Danville, who had been preoccupied since Marco named Carruthers.

"I'll wager I know where they are," he said. "Let me see

the ransom note, sir." He took it from his father. "Yes, the meeting place named to hand over the money is behind Clock Cottage, by the Blue Ship Inn at The Haven."

"The Haven?" asked Marco.

"A tiny hamlet scarce three miles from here," John answered him. "In the opposite direction from Billingshurst. How does that help us, Tom?"

Lord Danville had all their attention.

"Carruthers's place is near Loxwood. I saw a map once that showed the estate. It is an odd shape, long and narrow, and one end reaches nearly to The Haven. There's a wood there, used to be good pheasant shooting. You know how Carruthers has let the place go to rack and ruin. The house is in fair shape but he has no interest in farming or sport. He has made no effort to keep up the coverts and he dismissed the unfortunate gamekeeper long since."

"What of it?" demanded Andrew impatiently. He cared not a groat for the baron's coverts.

"The gamekeeper's cottage was in that wood near The Haven. No one has lived there for years."

"Let's go," cried Andrew, striding from the room.

His heart leapt within him. Here at last was his chance for a heroic rescue. He was determined to be the first through the door of the abandoned cottage. He imagined Teresa looking up as he entered, her dark eyes widening with the glow of gratitude and admiration.

Somehow her face, her eyes, were all that he could picture. Had she been tied up? A pang of terror shot through him as he realised she might even be unconscious.

Then fury rose. If Harrison had harmed her, he should not live to see his next trial.

Ten minutes later Andrew rode out of the stable yard followed by Marco, Lord Danville, Lord John, Mr. Wishart, and Lord Jordan. All were armed to the teeth.

= 16 =

DESPERATELY TERESA INCHED away from Muriel. In her need for warmth she had forgotten Brawny must not know that they were strong enough to move. Her plan depended on his belief that they were weak, feeble creatures; but it was too late to put more than a couple of feet between them.

He came in, a dirty bottle in his hand. If he noticed anything amiss, he did not comment, and Teresa was encouraged to hope that he was as stupid as Scrawny Sid thought him. Taking no notice of Muriel, who had again pretended to swoon, he pulled the cork from the bottle with his teeth and ordered Teresa to open her mouth.

"Guv'nor says to give yer a drop o' gin so's yer don't freeze to death afore he's ready. Bloody waste, if yer ast me." He kicked her. "Open up."

She gave in and parted her lips, but she closed her throat, determined not to swallow. The vile stuff set her mouth on fire. She managed not to gasp in shock, and it ran out again, down her cheek to the floor.

"I cannot possibly swallow lying down," she protested in a tremulous voice.

He put the bottle down and hauled her to a sitting position. As soon as he let go of her to reach for the gin, she slumped over sideways. Again he raised her up, and again she fell to the floor.

"Untie me so that I can sit," she moaned feebly. "It is quite impossible to balance without the use of my hands and feet."

Incredibly, it did not dawn on him to prop her in a corner. He looked at her in doubt.

"You cannot be afraid of two defenceless girls," she said with scorn, careful to speak shakily. "If we expire from the cold, how much fun will you have with us?"

He glanced suspiciously at Muriel, who looked half-dead already. Reaching out, he wound one fair ringlet about a finger like a sausage. The girl did not stir.

"Always did like 'em wiv golden 'air," murmured the big man. "I'll untie you so's you can get 'er moving. Never fancied cold meat."

He fumbled at the knots without success, then drew a knife with a rust-spotted blade and sawed at the ropes around Teresa's wrists. Fibre by fibre they parted, and he turned to her ankles while she flexed her numb hands. Feeling returned fast and painfully.

"Now sit up and swaller some o' this gin."

She pushed herself halfway up and then collapsed.

"I cannot. Let me warm my hands a little while you untie my friend."

Muriel's bonds parted with still more difficulty. If the knife had ever had an edge, it was long gone. By the time Brawny had finished the job, Teresa was almost sure that her hands would do her bidding.

When he turned back to her, he found himself gaping down the barrel of a gun. "Drop the knife," she demanded.

Blinking in confusion, he obeyed. Muriel, miraculously recovered from her swoon, grabbed the knife and backed away, holding the blade in front of her with nervous awkwardness.

He shook his head stupidly, then brightened. "If yer shoots me, the guv'nor's bound to 'ear it and come running."

"I can reload before he arrives," Teresa pointed out coldly, "and you may ask any of a dozen London bucks whether I am a crack shot. I was brought up in the jungle, you know, surrounded by fearsome beasts. I have never shot a person before but you are more like a poisonous snake than a man, as far as I'm concerned, and I shall not hesitate." The pistol pointed unwavering at his heart. "Lie down on the floor, on your front."

Grunting sullenly, he sank to his knees, his beefy face unhappy.

"Yer won't get past the guv'nor," he said. "He's in the room at the bottom of the apples."

"Apples?" asked Muriel, bewildered.

"Stairs," Teresa explained with a grin. "Apples and pears—stairs. It's Cockney rhyming slang. Cousin John was talking about it one day and fortunately that is one of the words he mentioned." Her eyes never left her target. "Go on, get down on the floor."

Brawny stretched full length.

"Teresa, he cut the ropes instead of untying them," wailed Muriel in sudden realisation. "How am I to tie him up?"

A moment of panic was sternly suppressed and Teresa glanced quickly around the room.

"That bag, see what is in it. The shirt will do to tie his legs, and perhaps there is something else that you can use for his hands. Hurry."

Muriel pulled the shirt from the shabby valise, followed by a pair of trousers, which made her blush. The garments were ragged, but most of the cloth was still good. She wound the shirt round the man's legs and knotted the sleeves as tight as she could.

"I hope that will do," she said doubtfully.

"It will have to. You, put your hands behind your back. Can you tear those . . . inexpressibles, Muriel? They are too bulky to make a good knot."

A few moments of effort proved the task beyond her strength. She rummaged in the valise and triumphantly withdrew a grubby neckcloth. Soon Brawny lay trussed like a turkey cock and at last Teresa dared put aside her pistol to test the bonds.

"Oh dear, I hope they will hold. If he wins free, we shall be in trouble."

The man had lain passive and silent all this time. She guessed that having surrendered, he had not the wit to resist. However, if they left him here for any considerable period, he would inevitably attempt escape, and she doubted the cloth with Muriel's inexpert knots would hold him.

Still, Teresa could not bring herself to shoot him in cold blood, even just to disable him.

Her eye fell on the gin bottle. Enough of that poured down his throat would immobilise him. She found the bottle nearly full. The trouble was that they must turn him over to administer it, and when they tried to move him, he would likely rouse from his lethargy and struggle.

She felt Muriel's worried gaze upon her as she sought desperately for an answer. There was nothing else in the little room that might help them—or was there? The thought sickened Teresa but a well-placed blow with a pewter pint pot ought to knock out even the undoubtedly thick-skulled Bert.

"Don't look," she ordered Muriel, and brought the pot down on the back of his head as hard as she could.

Since he did not voice any objection, she assumed the blow had worked.

Gingerly she felt for his pulse, with a prayer that she had not killed him. Failing to discover any sign of life, she bit her lip, then stripped off her glove and tried again. It disgusted her to touch him with her bare skin, but this time she found the pulse and breathed a sigh of relief.

"Help me turn him over."

Lying on his back, he was an unlovely sight. His mouth hung slackly open. She did not want to drown him, so they rolled up the straw pallet and managed to stuff it beneath his head and shoulders. Then she cautiously poured a little gin between his yellowed teeth.

He swallowed automatically. Judging by his breath, he had already been imbibing that day. Little by little she emptied the bottle into him.

He emitted an enormous belch and started to snore.

Teresa and Muriel looked at each other and giggled. Teresa sat back wearily on her heels. "Well, that is all we can do. We had best go down at once before Harrison grows suspicious."

Muriel helped her to stand. They went out onto the tiny landing and lowered the bar across the door with as little noise as they could manage. Teresa eyed the dark, rickety stair with foreboding.

"If we march down together, perhaps he will think it is his henchman," whispered Muriel.

"A nice idea, but the two of us together must weigh less than he, and I doubt we could stay in step. We had best creep down the side as close to the wall as possible and hope that the wood is less rotted there. At least there is a wall between the stair and the room. I shall go first. When I reach the bottom step, come after me."

Muriel nodded and Teresa started down the stairs.

Step by cautious step, holding her breath, she made her way down. Under her slight weight the cracked boards scarcely moved, their token protest no louder than the scurry of mice within the walls.

On the bottom step she paused. It would be best if Muriel did not follow until Teresa knew the situation. Her friend might alert Harrison by making too much noise, and she would very likely get in the way if sudden action proved necessary.

Teresa twisted round and made shooing gestures, mouthing a silent "Wait!"

Muriel nodded understanding. She looked pale and fearful, and Teresa was filled with gratitude for her steadfast help. Their situation was a far cry from the drawing rooms and ballrooms Miss Parr had been bred up to grace with her decorous presence.

Now Teresa must count on the darkness of the stair enclosure to protect her. Moving by inches, she peered round the edge of the wall.

Harrison faced her at an angle. He was sitting on a

broken-backed chair at a sloping table with his horse pistol in his hand. On the table lay the remains of a meal and, right beside him, an oily rag, a ramrod, a small glass vial, and two leather pouches.

Teresa guessed that the vial contained oil, the little bags powder and ball. He had been cleaning and reloading his gun. At any moment he might decide to go upstairs to see what Bert was doing.

She moved back behind the shelter of the wall. He was holding his gun, so she could not hold him up as she had Brawny. She had to disable him before he could shoot her. She closed her eyes and bit her lip. Pretend he's a snake, she told herself fiercely, a deadly snake.

In one swift, fluid motion she stepped round the corner into the room, raised her pistol in both hands, and squeezed the trigger. Harrison's gun clattered to the floor. He gaped at her, then stared down in horror at the river of blood flowing from his wrist.

"My God, I shall bleed to death," he moaned.

"Grasp it tight with your other hand and raise it above your head," ordered Teresa crisply. "Muriel, come on down. We must make a tourniquet."

With the victim's grubby neckcloth wound round his upper arm, and the long barrel of his pistol to twist it tight, they managed to staunch the bleeding. The bullet had barely nicked his vein and they used their own handkerchiefs and strips of petticoat to bind the wound.

By the time they were done with their ministrations, their patient had fainted from loss of blood. It was an easy matter to tie his ankles together with the red-stained neckcloth.

"It does not seem quite right to tie his wrists together," said Muriel, frowning. "I know he is a dastardly villain and he intended to kill us, but I cannot like it."

"I know what you mean," Teresa agreed. "His hand ought to be kept in the air, too. I have the answer! Help me pull him over here by the end of the table. Suppose we tie the injured arm up against the table leg, like this. Then we can stretch his other arm over here and tie his wrist to the other leg of the table."

"The very thing. The table is somewhat wobbly, but he is in no case to exert his strength upon it."

"And if he did, the top would fall on his face."

"I should like to see his face when he wakes," said Muriel, "but I daresay we shall be far away by then."

"I'm afraid not. Have you any idea where we are?" Teresa finished the knot binding Harrison's wounded arm to the table, then went to the window and looked out. "Oh, Muriel, come and see!"

Muriel hurried to join her and peered through the small, smeared panes. "It has stopped snowing. Quite a lot has fallen already, but at least it is not drifting."

"That is snow? It is beautiful. I never imagined anything like that."

"Wait till you see it on a sunny day. You will think yourself transported to another world. Walking in it is quite. a different matter, though, even if we knew which direction to take. Oh Teresa, what shall we do? We are as much captive here as ever."

"But now we have the upper hand." Teresa moved back to the table, where she sat down and began to clean her pistol. "Just in case Brawny Bert wakes up and breaks out," she explained. "At least we will hear him coming. I think we must wait till Scrawny Sid returns with the horse."

"Scrawny Sid?"

"The third man. Did you not hear? He went with the ransom note to my uncle."

"Then they will follow him back and find us."

"I fear not. Bert may be a knock-in-the-cradle but Harrison has his wits about him. I imagine Sid found someone else to send with the message, someone who is not involved in their plot. Anyway, fit for the knacker or no, that unfortunate animal will have to carry us away from here."

Muriel looked dubious but she said, "Luckily this is a well-populated part of the country. Whichever direction we go, we are sure soon to cross a road which will lead us to a village."

"And in the meantime, all we can do is wait. Tie his other arm now before he wakes. I shall feel better once I have reloaded my gun."

Andrew realised abruptly that much as he desired to lead the rescue party, he had no idea which way to go.

"Danville," he called reluctantly, looking back, "you had best go first to show us the road."

"I know where it is," said Lord John, riding up beside him. "Follow me."

Andrew stayed with him neck and neck. The viscount was not the sort to try to seize the glory of rushing first into the cottage, whatever his feelings for Muriel, but his dashing brother was another kettle of fish.

They started down a hedged lane, then Lord John led them through a gate to ride cross-country. All six gentlemen were mounted on the duke's hunters, which took hedge and ditch and stream in their stride. Marco gasped when he faced the first jump, but though he had never hunted, he had spent much of his life on horseback. He let his mount carry him over after the others, and thereafter enjoyed the exhilarating sensation of flying through the air. Andrew glanced back at his grinning face and envied the resilience of youth. The lad seemed to have forgotten his sister's peril.

And Muriel's, Andrew reminded himself sternly.

They soon reached the wood. Their way was barred by a tangled mass of brambles and fallen trees; neither had been cleared for years. It reminded Andrew of the un-touched jungle of Costa Rica, except that this undergrowth was bare and grey. They rode along the edge, looking for a way in, till at last they came to a narrow track.

"Hoofprints in the snow!" cried Lord John triumphantly, drawing rein. "A single file leading inward. I'll wager it's the man who took the note to Billingshurst."

Mr. Wishart leaned down in the saddle and studied the

prints. "On a sorry nag, or an excessively tired one," he commented. "Look how short its stride is."

Marco had stopped beside Andrew. His face was white and pinched, the thrill gone. Andrew leaned over and squeezed his shoulder.

"We'll find her," he reassured the lad, trying to ignore the tight knot in his own chest. "Come on," he urged impatiently, and started forward.

There was only one way to go now, so he rode ahead. A short distance into the wood the track curved to the right. Then it straightened and a hundred feet ahead he saw a clearing with a tumbledown shack in the centre. There was no light in the windows, no smoke rising from the chimney, but the hoofprints led directly towards the hovel.

Andrew held up his hand and everyone stopped. "Back around the corner," he mouthed silently, gesturing at them to retreat.

Out of sight of the cottage they dismounted and tied their horses to nearby trees, then gathered to discuss the next move. They had left Five Oaks without pausing to plan.

Quickly they decided to move through the edge of the wood to surround the clearing, then one of them would creep up to the window and try to see what was going on. Unless he saw good reason against it, he would signal and they would all converge on the shack and break in with guns drawn.

"I shall go to the window," said Marco. "I am smallest and fastest and it is my sister."

"It's my—," chorused Andrew and Lord Danville, then stopped, glanced at each other, and flushed. The rest looked at them with interest, somehow divining that the missing words were not "betrothed" and "cousin."

Marco was already slipping through the trees towards the clearing, so the others hurried to take their places. Andrew moved to a position opposite the door with such a determined air that no one disputed his right to it.

Darting from tree to bush to rotting fence to ancient farm

cart, Marco reached the window and crouched below it. Then he cautiously raised himself to peer in at one corner, shading his eyes against the reflected glare of the snow. Andrew saw his mouth open, then stretch into a broad grin.

The poor boy had lost his wits with horror, Andrew thought, aghast.

Marco, still grinning, stood up and waved. Andrew burst through the rickety door bare seconds before Lord Danville.

Teresa stood there with her pistol trained on a small man who lay on his front on the floor. Over him bent Muriel, tying his hands with a filthy cloth. Behind them Harrison sprawled on his back, unconscious and bloodstained, a gun lying nearby on the floor.

The girls looked up as the door crashed back against the wall, shaking the wretched hut to its probably nonexistent foundations. Then, Muriel rose with a wordless cry and flung herself into Lord Danville's arms.

Teresa smiled a wavering smile. "Thank heaven you are come in time," she said. "Now we shall not have to force that unfortunate horse to carry us."

Her face was sallow with exhaustion, bruised, dirty. Her hair was tangled, her clothes torn and filthy. Yet Andrew saw only a gallant woman strained to the breaking point. To him she looked unbelievably beautiful, simply because she was alive. Their eyes met and held for a long moment.

And Muriel had run to Thomas Danville.

Andrew was turning to make sure that his eyes had not deceived him when he caught sight of a movement on the floor. The scrawny villain had escaped his half-tied bonds and seized Harrison's pistol. The barrel that pointed at Teresa wavered, but she was too close to escape even the most uncertain shot.

The man's dirty finger tightened on the trigger, and Andrew threw himself across the room. A red-hot flash exploded in his side.

The flood of darkness that overwhelmed him was suffused with joy. He had saved his Teresa, and Muriel had run to Lord Danville. Through dimming eyes Andrew saw Teresa kneeling beside him. He must explain to her that all was well.

"Muriel . . . ," he murmured, and passed out.

$=17=$

TERESA GAZED DOWN blankly at Andrew's limp form. Her mind refused to work. The look they had exchanged had warmed and supported her weary spirits. Then, a single whispered word shattered her hopes. She had rushed to succour him and he had called for Muriel.

Blood was seeping through his torn, charred coat. With clumsy, trembling fingers she tugged at his neckcloth. How convenient that the essential article of male apparel made a perfect bandage, she thought with a giggle that was half a sob.

John lifted her to her feet. "We'll take care of that," he said gently. "Sit down, Teresa. You are burnt to the socket."

She glanced around. Andrew's weight had winded Scrawny Sid, and Mr. Wishart was now efficiently binding his wrists. Muriel was still in Cousin Tom's arms, her wide, horrified eyes fixed upon her betrothed. Lord Jordan had taken off his own cravat and was staunching the flow of blood from Andrew's side.

Suddenly Teresa could bear no more. "Marco, take me home," she said.

Her brother put his arm round her shoulders and they went out into the snow.

John followed them out of the cottage. "The sooner you get on home and into bed the better," he said sympathetically, walking with them through the snow to the horses. "You were devilish brave and devilish clever, cousin, but we shall take care of things now. I'll set you on your way, then I'll get back to lend a hand with the villains."

Marco mounted his horse and John lifted Teresa up behind him. She clung to him, her cheek pressed against the rough cloth of his greatcoat. She had not said a word since asking him to take her home.

John led the horse back to the clearing and pointed out another track going off to one side.

"You'll come to a lane," he said. "Turn left, then take the right fork and you'll be in Bucks Green in no time. You know the way from there? We've ridden it often enough. Right then, off you go and don't worry your head about a thing, Teresa."

The pampered Thoroughbred hunter bore both of them with ease, and in spite of the snow the hedged lanes were easy to follow. They made good speed, but, even so, dusk was falling when they reached Five Oaks.

Only one ancient groom remained in the stables, the rest being out still scouring the countryside. He took their mounts with the incuriosity of the aged and merely nodded when Teresa asked him to saddle her mare and have her ready in half an hour.

Marco gaped at her, stupefied. "What maggot's got into your head now?" he demanded. "You're in no fit state to go out again."

She bit her lip, fighting back tears. "I cannot bear it, Marco. If he lives, he will go on loving Muriel. If he dies . . . if he dies, I do not want to know it. I am going to pack up a few things and fetch Gayo, and I'm going home."

"Home? You mean to the hacienda?" Her brother was understandably confused.

"Yes. I have completed Papa's business and I have an excellent contract to take him. There is nothing to keep me here now."

"Then I shall come with you," he assured her stoutly. "Shall we go to Portsmouth?"

"Yes . . . No . . . I mean, yes I go to Portsmouth, but you must stay and complete your education. That is what Papa sent you for, it is your duty."

"He sent you to find a husband."

"I never shall," she said wearily, sorry to have exposed her feelings for Andrew, though Marco did not seem to grasp that she had done so. "The gentlemen of the haut ton are different indeed from our Costa Ricans, but I find them no more interesting. You must stay at least until you have spent a term at the university, or you cannot know whether it is to your taste."

Unconvinced, Marco protested, "I cannot let you go without a male escort. You cannot ride to Portsmouth tonight."

"I mean to spend the night at the Six Bells in Billingshurst. I shall be long gone before anyone asks to see me in the morning. Then you may tell my uncle where I am gone and I shall leave a letter for him at the inn. I cannot stand here brangling any longer. It is growing dark already. You must tell everyone that Muriel and I are safe, and to send help for Andrew. Say that I have retired to bed and Annie will do what is needful for me. I am by far too tired to see anyone tonight. Oh Marco, I shall miss you. You have been the greatest comfort to me."

"I shall go with you at least to Portsmouth. Do not argue, Teresa. I'll do as you say and tell everyone you have retired, then I'll come to join you. We can decide later whether I shall return here or go home with you."

"Bless you," she whispered.

They hugged each other hard, then slipped quietly into the house.

"Wait till morning," begged Marco in a whisper as she started up the backstairs. "You are too tired to think straight."

She shook her head, her look despairing, and went on. The only thing she knew for certain was that never again could she face Andrew.

She found Annie in her dressing room, huddled in a chair, weeping. The maid raised a tearstained black face, then leapt to her feet.

Gayo flapped his wings with a bright "Hello."

"Miss Teresa! I was sure you was dead. Gracious heavens, you're worn to the bone. Let me undress you and it's straight into your bed you go."

Teresa shook her head. "I'm leaving, Annie. Please pack a few of my simplest dresses and some linen in a couple of small pormanteaux. Hurry, I must go at once."

"You're never going out at this time of night!"

"It is not five yet, it grows dark early these days. Please, Annie, I am by far too tired to argue."

The abigail pulled the bags out of a cupboard and began to pack, but she said firmly, "You're not going anywhere without me, miss, that I can tell you."

"I am going home to Costa Rica." Teresa took two small leather sacks of sovereigns from a drawer, emptied them onto the bed, and sat down to count them.

When Marco came in a few minutes later, Annie was philosophically unpacking again and Teresa was fast asleep. "Good," he said, grinning at the maid. "I daresay she will have more sense in the morning."

Andrew recovered consciousness to find himself the target of four pairs of worried eyes. Every breath felt like a dagger in his side.

"Where is Teresa?" he demanded, ignoring the pain.

"She is on her way back to Five Oaks," said Lord Danville soothingly. "She is quite exhausted."

The look of hurt and reproach in Andrew's eyes was meant for the woman he loved, who had deserted him in his hour of need, but Muriel intercepted it.

"I . . . I must explain," she stammered.

Lord Danville realised he still had his arms about the injured man's betrothed. Hurriedly he let her go.

Lord Jordan and Mr. Wishart, sensing deep waters, glanced at each other, shrugged, and went to check the captives' bonds.

Muriel knelt beside Andrew and touched his shoulder.

"I'm sorry, Andrew. I ought not to have run to Tom—Lord Danville—like that."

Andrew shook his head, wordless, then moaned as the unconsidered action lit a fire beneath his ribs. Mr. Wishart caught Lord Jordan's eye and they hurried upstairs to explore the rest of the cottage.

"It is difficult to explain," Muriel went on bravely, dismayed at Andrew's silence. "I have behaved very wickedly, I know. Somehow I could not help myself."

Painfully he reached for her hand. "Little goose," he said affectionately, "I believe some of Teresa's courage has rubbed off on you. I must tell you that I have accepted that assignment in China. I know you cannot like it and I shall quite understand if you feel you do not wish to marry me after all."

Lord Danville moved forward to stand with his hands on Muriel's shoulders. "I, too, must apologise, Graylin, and thank you for releasing Miss Parr so graciously. Believe me, it was never my intention to fall in love with another man's promised wife."

"If you love each other, what more can I have to say?"

The way they smiled at each other assured him of their mutual regard. A spasm of envy shot through him. He closed his eyes to shut out the sight.

"Why did Teresa leave?"

"She was exhausted," repeated Lord Danville. "You saved her life, Graylin, and I know she will express her gratitude when she is a little recovered from her ordeal." He went on to express his own gratitude in somewhat flowery periods.

"It is not her gratitude I want," muttered Andrew fretfully under cover of the viscount's words.

"How are you doing, Graylin?" asked Lord John, coming in. "I must say I've lost my faith in the Diplomatic Corps, seeing you resort to physical measures like that. Dashed heroic thing to do, all the same."

Andrew shook his head in dismissal, eliciting a groan.

"Don't move, man," said John in alarm. "Just how badly did you come off?"

"Wishart thinks the bullet glanced off his ribs," his brother told him. "Probably broke one or two, but it is not serious. He has lost considerable blood, though. We will need a litter to carry him home."

With newfound self-confidence, Muriel turned the subject. She had been pondering Andrew's muttered words and had come to a conclusion as welcome as it was unflattering.

"Does she know you love her?" she asked, bending over Andrew. "You are so often at odds that I never guessed till now, and I know you are too much a gentleman to have spoken to her while you were engaged to me. You do love her, do you not?"

"Who?" asked Lord Danville, bewildered.

"Teresa," said his brother and his beloved together.

The former went on, "Never say, Tom, that you had not noticed the pair of them smelling of April and May. Too busy doing the same yourself, I daresay."

"I love her to distraction," confessed Andrew.

"A deuced appropriate word," said John with a grin. "What the devil is going on up there?"

The stairs were shrieking a protest as Lord Jordan and Mr. Wishart descended with a heavy burden between them. They dumped the third kidnapper on the floor, where he continued to snore stertorously.

Muriel, back in Lord Danville's arms, looked down at him in distaste. "That's Brawny Bert," she announced.

"Brawny Bert?"

"His name is Bert, and the little man is Sid. Teresa called them Brawny Bert and Scrawny Sid."

"If that ain't like my cousin," said Lord John with a crack of laughter. "Joking in the midst of deadly peril. How the devil—begging your pardon, Miss Parr—did the two of you overcome this great oaf?"

Muriel told the story, her listeners all agog. Lord Jordan was the only one startled to hear that Teresa had been carrying a pistol and had used it to such good effect. The others were admiring but unsurprised by her ingenuity, bravery, and capability.

"Poured a bottle of gin down his throat," said John, grinning hugely. "Dashed if she ain't just what you need with you in China, Graylin. Better tell her you love her soon as may be, if you ask me. Tom, you take Miss Parr home and send us a couple of carriages. We'll manage here, between us."

He looked to his brother-in-law and Mr. Wishart for confirmation and they nodded. Muriel glanced anxiously at Andrew. He anticipated her thought.

"Go on," he said wryly. "I'll do. I daresay these fellows will not let me bleed to death."

"Teresa would know what to do to make you more comfortable, but I confess I do not," she responded. "I shall make sure there are plenty of cushions and rugs and hot bricks in the carriage that comes for you."

"I'll send for the sawbones," promised Lord Danville. "He will doubtless reach Five Oaks before you. Again, my thanks, Graylin."

Andrew smiled feebly as he watched the duke's heir pick up Muriel and carry her out. It was good to have matters settled between them, but the long conversation had tired Andrew and the ache in his side spread throughout his body. He closed his eyes and tried to breathe shallowly.

As the pain eased, he tormented himself with wondering why Teresa had left him so abruptly when he had risked his life to save her. Had she really not guessed that he adored her? Even if she had not, it was most unlike her not to have stayed to nurse him, however tired she was.

So perhaps she had guessed his love. Seeing Muriel's understanding with Danville, she had fled lest Andrew turn to her and demand more than she was able to give. In either case, it seemed that she did not return his love. Yet John had spoken of the two of them as smelling of April and May.

Despite the evidence, Andrew could not quite crush a seed of hope.

The carriage ride back to Five Oaks severely tested his

endurance and made him doubt Wishart's diagnosis of his injury as not serious. However, the doctor from Billingshurst concurred. So cheerful was his report that the duchess recovered from her hysterics and the duke ventured to repair to Andrew's chamber. Marco followed his uncle.

"My dear fellow!" cried His Grace, approaching the invalid's bed. "I shall never be able to thank you enough for saving my niece's life."

"It was nothing," mumbled Andrew, embarrassed. "I beg you will not refine upon it." He sent a beseeching look at Marco, hovering by the door.

Always considerate, the duke stayed only a few moments more, to assure himself of his guest's comfort. When he left, Marco remained at Andrew's bedside, his face troubled.

"I must see your sister. Has she retired already?"

"She don't want to see you. Or anyone else," Marco added fairly.

"I *must* see her. I shall go to her chamber." Andrew winced as he tired to throw off the bedcovers.

Marco gripped his shoulder and held him down. Though he did not understand what was going on between Teresa and Andrew, he could see that his friend's anguish was mental as much as physical.

"She's fast asleep," he said gruffly. "I cannot let you wake her. Besides, the doctor said you are not to move for at least three days lest your ribs pierce your lungs."

Andrew subsided. "To the devil with my ribs! I cannot wait so long. Marco, tell her in the morning that I must see her. I love her."

"Love her? Then why is she carrying on as if the world is coming to an end? No, it's all right, don't try to explain." He grinned. "I ain't likely to join the petticoat line for a few years yet. You really love her? What about Miss Parr?"

"Miss Parr is going to be the next Duchess of Stafford," Andrew exploded. Unfortunately, the laudanum the doctor had given him had not yet taken effect. "Ouch! Will you ask her to come and see me?" he added in a more moderate tone.

"Yes, but I ought to warn you that she is planning on going home to Costa Rica."

"To Costa Rica! Does your uncle know?"

"No, not yet. She was going to leave tonight, to stay in Billingshurst. She meant to write to Uncle Stafford from the inn before going on to Portsmouth."

"But she has not left?"

"She fell asleep, and I was not about to wake her, I promise you." Marco eyed Andrew thoughtfully. "You really love her?" he asked again.

"I adore her. I want to marry her, but if she cannot bear the sight of me, I shall leave in the morning and she need never set eyes on me again. I will not let her flee the country because of me."

"Good. Then I will not let her flee the country before you have spoken to her."

Andrew relaxed with a sigh of relief. Suddenly drowsy, he smiled sleepily at the thought of Teresa dashing off to Portsmouth, a naval dockyard, when what she really wanted was Bristol. The courageous woman was also a green girl, in need of someone to guide and protect her. Who better than himself?

Marco tiptoed out of the room.

= 18 =

TERESA DREAMT SHE was back at home on the hacienda. It was one of those nights when, even up in the mountains, the air was still and hot and oppressive. Restlessly she threw back the covers.

The sudden chill on her skin woke her. She sat up and looked around, dazed by the sudden transition from her simple whitewashed room to the luxurious furnishings of an English mansion. It was winter, she remembered, yet still she was unbearably hot.

A fire glowed on the hearth, and a strange white light outlined the window. It was morning then. She slipped down from the bed and went to draw back the curtains. That cold light would cool her. Feathers of frost on the glass melted at her breath; she looked out and gasped.

The strange light was sun reflecting off snow. The world sparkled and gleamed. Every branch of the great cedar was outlined in white. Entranced, Teresa leaned her burning forehead against the windowpane.

Two dogs gambolled across the lawn, oblivious of cold feet. Teresa realised that her own feet were icy. She began to shiver uncontrollably, though she was perspiring and her cheeks felt on fire. It dawned on her that she was feverish. As if the knowledge had somehow intensified the symptoms, her head began to ache and her limbs grew leaden. Overcome by lethargy, she forced herself to stumble into her dressing room to find her medicine chest.

"Hello, hello, hello!" Gayo greeted her. When he received

no response, he grumbled irritably, "Misbegotten son of a sea snake."

Teresa was not amused. The catch on the chest was inexplicably recalcitrant to her fumbling fingers. She had just decided to give up and go back to bed when Annie came in.

"You're never up already, miss!" she exclaimed in surprise. "After all those goings-on yesterday I made sure you'd sleep late."

Teresa's memory flooded back. Yesterday she had been kidnapped. She had shot Harrison. Muriel had thrown herself into Cousin Tom's arms.

Yesterday Andrew had been shot, and in his agony he had called for Muriel.

Teresa astonished herself and her abigail by bursting into tears.

Annie ran to her and hugged her. "Heavens above, miss, you're frozen to the bone," she scolded, dismayed. "Back to bed with you this instant. And your forehead's hot as coals of fire. Lawks, you've taken a chill, and no wonder. Come now, miss, let me tuck you in and I'll bring you your herbs. You just tell me what you need and I'll see it's made proper. You'll be right as rain in no time at all. There, let me fluff up your pillows. Here's the medicines now. This one, is it? Cinchona? Made into tea, isn't that right? I'll take it down to Cook right away."

Soothed by the little maid's comforting chatter, Teresa reached out to her. "Annie, Sir Andrew . . . how is he?"

"He'll be up and about in a day or two, I hear. He's a real hero, Sir Andrew. Everyone says he risked his life to save yours."

"He did," said Teresa, her voice nearly inaudible. "But perhaps when Muriel deserted him, he thought his life not worth living."

With the cinchona tea, Annie brought enquiries and best wishes galore. Teresa refused to see anyone, even her brother, but her maid was unequal to keeping out the duchess, who swept in just before noon, her round face distressed.

"My dear child, what a horrid business. I am not in the least surprised that you are fallen ill. Your girl says you do not care to see the doctor, but I shall send him to you when he comes to see Graylin, and I shall be excessively displeased if you do not let him examine you. He is an excellent man. I fear you must be thinking that England is quite as dangerous as your wild jungles."

"Oh no, ma'am. I am sure there are villains and rogues everywhere."

"Well, do not bother your head about them, my dear. Stafford and John are gone to speak to that dreadful Carruthers and you may be sure he will not try anything again. I daresay he will not dare show his nose in public for years." She kissed Teresa's forehead. "I will leave you to rest now, for I wager that is what you need most, and you must be sure your abigail asks for anything you fancy."

"Thank you, Aunt." Teresa blinked away tears. She was turning into a regular watering pot, she who prided herself on her self-control.

The bitter infusion of cinchona bark had cooled her fever, leaving her weak, depressed, and aching all over. It would be days, at least, before she could put into action her plan to depart for Costa Rica. Confined to her bed, she would be spared seeing Andrew, but there was nothing to distract her from her unhappy thoughts.

She had been a fool to hope that he might come to care for her as more than a friend. Now she knew that hope was what had buoyed her throughout yesterday's ordeal. Muriel's confession that she loved Tom had opened the door; Andrew's final word had slammed it shut.

Teresa knew she had been a fool, too, to think of running off at night without a word to her relatives. As soon as she was well enough, she would discuss her departure calmly with her uncle, ask him to find her an escort. She prayed it would not take him long.

Don Eduardo would be sorry that she had not found a husband she could love and respect, but if she could not have Andrew, she had just as soon dwindle into an old maid.

Andrew, though still feeling somewhat battered about the middle, was by then fretting and fuming at his enforced idleness. Lying flat on his back was a poor perspective from which to view the world. Besides, it made eating very difficult and he had missed his dinner the night before.

Along with his breakfast, Rowson had brought the news of Miss Danville's indisposition. While his manservant ineptly spoon-fed him, with frequent pauses to wipe egg yolk off his chin, Andrew silently cursed Harrison and his plots. With both himself and Teresa confined to their respective beds, how was he to persuade her of his love?

He had just irritably ordered Rowson to take away the rest of the ham and muffins when there was a knock at his door. Rowson admitted Lord Danville. Andrew was glad to see that his lordship looked distinctly sheepish. After an exchange of the usual amenities, the duke's heir enquired after his guest's health.

"I am happy to hear it," said Lord Danville on being assured that Andrew was much improved. "We are all deeply in your debt for your prompt and brave action in saving my cousin's life." He hesitated, and when Andrew looked at him expectantly, he flushed. "I fear it is a poor recompense that I should . . . er, appropriate your betrothed."

"Think nothing of it," said Andrew cordially. "I am fond of Muriel, but you are more than fond, I think?"

"I loved her. She is everything I most admire in a woman." Tom's voice was fervent. "We are going up to town today to obtain her mother's blessing on our union. I can only hope the lady will not be quite overset by this sudden change of *dramatis personae*."

"I can think of few things capable of oversetting Lady Parr. Nor can I suppose that the exchange of the impecunious second son of a viscount for the wealthy heir to a dukedom will be unwelcome."

Tom frowned. "You are cynical, Graylin."

"I do not mean to imply that any such consideration influenced Muriel. But a word of warning, Danville. You may find it expedient to keep her mother at arm's length once you are wed. I take it you have His Grace's permission?"

"My father has been most tolerant. I believe he feared I should never find a woman I wished to wed, though of course I must have married eventually to secure the succession. Muriel's lack of fortune is unimportant. Her family is not impressive, but her breeding is irreproachable. He concurs with me that she will be an excellent duchess. I had wondered whether her timidity might be a drawback, but she has admitted to me that she has not always been as shocked and frightened as she appeared. It seems her mother taught her to behave so."

"If she has indeed made such a confession, she must truly love you. As I said yesterday, some of Teresa's courage has rubbed off on her."

"And you truly love Teresa?"

"I do."

"Well, she's a taking little thing, my cousin, if a trifle unconventional." He shook his head indulgently. "But then, you are unconventional, too, are you not. I daresay you will suit. I must be off now."

Andrew stared after Lord Danville with a bemused look. Unconventional? Him? He had always thought of himself as the most staid and proper of men. After all, a diplomat must above all be courteous, composed, and sober.

On the other hand, how many gentlemen of his acquaintance had the least desire to travel to the less civilised portions of the globe? How many would have gone aboard the *Snipe* to rescue a shipload of slaves? He could not imagine Thomas Danville involved in that expedition. Lord John would have joined in, had he been present. Yet only the most unlikely circumstances could have led to John's presence on board the *Destiny*, whereas he, Andrew, sought out and enjoyed the unexpected exigencies of foreign travel.

Like Teresa he flung himself into new experiences with zest. What had ever made him suppose he wanted a conformable wife? Not only did he love Teresa, she was precisely the kind of wife he needed. Not for one moment had he considered leaving her behind when he went to China. Guidance and protection had nothing to do with the matter. He wanted to share his life with her.

Marco, dashing into Andrew's chamber, found him grinning with pleasure at the thought of travelling with Teresa again.

"You look happy," he observed. "Just as well, because I came to tell you that Teresa won't receive anyone, not even me, so I can't ask her to come and see you."

"I understand she is ill."

"Oh, yes," said her brother without sympathy, "but she's not at death's door, it's only a chill. It is my belief she's sulking."

"Teresa does not sulk." Andrew was outraged. "Something happened yesterday that distressed her."

"Well, she was kidnapped and tied up and shot at. Enough to distress even my sister, I should think."

Andrew groped for something to throw at Marco. "I mean, you young mooncalf, that something made her miffed at me. It's the only reason I can think of that she should have run off leaving me bleeding on the floor."

"Perhaps, but I cannot imagine what," said Marco dubiously. "Anyway, the other thing I came to tell you was that Uncle Stafford and Cousin John and I are going to Loxwood to deal with Lord Carruthers. Pity you can't come. I must run or they will leave without me."

Whether or not Teresa was indulging in a fit of the sulks, Andrew's frame of mind for the next half hour might certainly have been described thus.

A luncheon as unsatisfactory as his breakfast had come and gone before Marco returned to his chamber, accompanied by the duke and Lord John.

"We've put paid to all this nonsense," announced His Grace with a satisfied air. "How are you doing, my boy?"

"Very well, sir. May I hope you refer to Lord Carruthers?"

"You may, and I do. We have just returned from a visit to Loxwood."

"Cousin John wanted to shoot him or run him through with a sword," Marco said, "but Uncle Stafford said that the signed confession from Harrison was an equally potent weapon."

"Pity," said John, "but I daresay it was more satisfying to draw his cork and blacken his daylights."

"And send him to grass," added Marco with enthusiasm. "You never saw such a neat bit of work, Andrew."

"Bloodthirsty cawker," Andrew teased him. "I wish I had seen it."

"I fancy the bad baron is not well acquainted with the noble science of fisticuffs," said the duke dryly. "It seemed fairer, however, than taking a horsewhip to him, the alternative proposed by my impetuous son. After all, the man is a gentleman by birth if not by nature."

"I seems insufficient punishment, though, sir," Andrew frowned, "and an inadequate deterrent."

"Ah, there the confession came in handy. When I pointed out to Carruthers that his choice lay between a voluntary exile in the Americas or an involuntary sojourn in Australia, he wisely opted for the former. I have left two of my larger grooms to escort him to Bristol and ensure his embarkation."

"Bravo!" An incautious movement made Andrew wince. "And what of Harrison and his henchmen?"

"Harrison will hang," said the duke with unwonted harshness, "and the other two will be transported. My influence is sufficient to ensure it. I admit that I find it difficult to credit that such a man should dare raise his hand to the granddaughter of a duke. He shall learn that it is not an act without consequences."

Andrew shivered at his haughty tone. He wondered whether that unexpected arrogance of rank might cause the duke to deny him Teresa's hand. It would take forever to obtain permission from Lord Edward in Costa Rica.

"Might I have a word with you in private, sir?" he requested diffidently.

Marco and John departed with grins and nods of encouragement, guessing his purpose.

"Well, Graylin?" queried His Grace of Stafford. The habitual affability had returned to his manner.

Andrew found it was a great deal easier to approach the subject of marriage with the duke than it had been with Lady Parr.

"I want to wed Miss Danville," he said baldly. "Since her father is too far distant to consult, I believe I must approach you for permission to pay my addresses."

"So that's what is in the wind. When Thomas told me he hoped to make your betrothed his bride, he hummed and hawed so that I knew something was afoot. Never seen him at a loss for words before. I take it you are not turning to my niece out of pique at losing Miss Parr to my son."

"I love her, sir. I cannot imagine life without her."

"That sounds adequate. I am somewhat acquainted with your father, and my friend Castlereagh speaks highly of you. I may say that I have put in a word for you myself in that quarter, since you escorted Teresa and Marco from Costa Rica. I know your prospects in the Foreign Office are excellent. However, I understand you are leaving shortly for China."

"I have no doubt that Teresa will be eager to go with me, sir. If she will have me."

"Then I can see no objection, my boy. You have my blessing and Edward's also, I make no doubt, since he saw fit to entrust her to your care. If she will have you, of course."

* * *

Three days went by before Andrew was allowed to leave his bed—three days which he spent alternately buoyed by hope and cast into the dismals. Marco reported that Teresa was much improved, though still, in Annie's words, very languid and low. She refused to see anyone other than her maid.

"At least," he pointed out, "she has not yet discussed with my uncle her wish to return home."

Andrew passed yet another impatient day recovering his strength, strolling about his chamber, and sitting by the fire, playing chess and backgammon with his constant stream of visitors.

On the fifth day he could wait no longer. Marco, suborned into spying for him, reported that Annie had been sent to fetch tea. Andrew lay in wait for the maid in the corridor outside Teresa's rooms, and she gave up the tray with a minimal protest and a saucy wink.

"It'll do her good," she opined, opening the dressing-room door for him.

Andrew wondered whether she meant the tea or his visit.

He stepped into the room. Teresa was reclining on a chaise longue by the window, her back to him, well wrapped in an azure velvet peignoir. Her unbound hair was a dark cloud about her head.

"Annie, have you brought the tea?" she asked, her gaze still on the snowy landscape beyond the window.

"Hello, hello, hello, dinner, hello, hello!" cried Gayo in a paroxysm of joy.

"Andrew!" Teresa turned to look at him, jumping to her feet.

"Your tea, madam," he said. He carried it over and set it on a small table by the chaise.

She moved away from him and stood looking out of the window again. He went to stand behind her.

"I knew you would appreciate the beauty of the snow," he murmured.

She started and began to turn, then realised how close he was and changed her mind. "Why are you here?" she said in an expressionless voice.

"I brought your tea. I am glad, by the way, that you have developed a taste for it. I collect coffee is near unobtainable in China."

"Why have you come?" she repeated crossly.

"Because I love you, Teresa."

Now she did turn, a questioning look on her worn face.

"Love me? But you are betrothed to Muriel."

"Muriel is betrothed to your cousin."

"Oh!" She paused. "It is very noble of you to give her up to him."

"It is not in the least noble. I have been wishing myself free of that entanglement this age. You are the only one I love."

"Then why did you call out to Muriel when Scrawny Sid shot you?"

"I did?" he asked, startled. He thought back to that moment. "What exactly did I say?"

"Just 'Muriel.'"

A grin of delight and relief spread across his face.

"Is that why you ran away? Of course it must be. You could not guess that I was just trying to tell you that Muriel and your cousin Tom were obviously in love and I was free at last."

Teresa's resistance was at an end. She threw herself into his welcoming arms.

Manfully ignoring the pain in his ribs, he pulled her to him and buried his face in the black waves of her hair. "I do love you, Teresa. Do you think you can ever come to care for me?"

She looked up at him and the warmth in her dark eyes made him tighten his clasp.

"I have loved you a long time, Andrew. Even when I thought it was quite hopeless."

Despite his rapture, the ache in his side warned him to

209

sit down. Fortunately the chaise was nearby. He pulled Teresa down at his side, his arm about her shoulders, her hands in his. She snuggled against him.

"My darling, will you come adventuring to China with me?"

A glimmer of a smile turned up her lips. "As your *chère amie?*"

"You promised six months since not to talk to me of lightskirts, my incorrigible sweetheart. No, as my wife."

"Can Annie and Gayo go with us?"

"Of course, if you promise not to teach Gayo to swear in Chinese."

"I promise. I will go anywhere with you, Andrew."

He bent his head to kiss her.

Gayo took exception to this. "*Cochon!*" he shouted. "*Cannaille! Sacré nom d'un chien!*"

Distracted from his purpose, Andrew glanced at the parrot reproachfully. "Chef Jacques, I suppose," he murmured. He looked down at his beloved to share his amusement.

At last their lips met.

"What a pity," sighed Gayo.

If you would like to receive details of other Walker Regency Romances, send for your free subscription to our Walker Regency Newsletter, "The Season."

Regency Editor
Walker and Company
720 Fifth Avenue
New York NY 10019